Cris Freddi was born in Reading and now lives in London with his wife, the actress and editor Francine Brody. His previous works of fiction include *Pork*, an acclaimed collection of short stories.

# PELICAN BLOOD

*Cris Freddi*

FOURTH ESTATE • *London* and *New York*

First published in Great Britain in 2005 by
Fourth Estate
A Division of HarperCollins*Publishers*
77–85 Fulham Palace Road
London W6 8JB
www.4thestate.co.uk

A catalogue record for this book is available from the British Library

ISBN 0 00 718518 9

Typeset by Palimpsest Book Production Limited,
Polmont, Stirlingshire

Printed in Great Britain by
Clays Ltd, St Ives plc

# PELICAN BLOOD

IT'S NOT EVEN five in the morning, but the light's already good and Owen Whittle's up and about, like he is every day of the week, coming up the same hill, looking around like he always does. There's some cloud cover for a change and more wind than yesterday, otherwise much the same as usual. But things are going to be different today and it's not the sky he ought to be watching. Today I'm going to try and kill him.

Fucking hell. Listen to me. Not exactly the most confident statement of intent you ever heard. Still, it's hardly surprising, considering it's my first time at anything like this. I haven't even flung a punch since I left school.

Even just looking at him scares me rigid. The moment his black donkey jacket appeared down the bottom of the hill my pulse started up and now it's going fuck-fuck-fuck even though I've done all the right breathing. I keep telling myself not to be so piss, I can pull out any time I want, but it doesn't help much.

He's left his car down by the road as usual and come up the back of the hill, where there's a dirt track through the stubblefields, walking quite quick, binocular case bouncing on his hip. See him hitch the strap higher up his shoulder.

Top of the hill there's a small conifer plantation cordoned off with barbed wire. He stops by one of the fence posts and gets his binoculars out, not from out the case but inside his jacket where they're hanging round his neck. Down in the valley there's a mature deciduous wood, the beech trunks looking like elephants' legs.

Two people suddenly appear out of nowhere in front of this wood, moving across the face of it, and they're a real surprise, it never occurred to me somebody else might be up and about this early. Owen Whittle checks them with his binoculars and I have a look through mine. Just an old couple out for their early morning walk, one pair of bins between them, probably up for the dawn chorus. Well they'll hear it alright, though I doubt they'll see very much the way they're blundering into the wood, crunching through the undergrowth. Yellow anoraks too: any self respecting bird's going to spot them halfway across the county. Owen Whittle sticks his bins away. Pair of amateurs. No interference there.

When I look at him again, he's got his back to me, climbing over the barbed wire before walking off into the plantation. It's not forestry commission, so the trees aren't laid out in straight rows close together. Sometimes there's as much as thirty yards of cleared ground between them, most of it taken over by the ferns they've allowed to grow to provide cover for the pheasants they release for shooting. Some of the pheasants breed in here, so you've got the risk of disturbing a sitting hen, with all the noise it entails – but Owen Whittle knows he can steer clear of the ferns, there's narrow rides through the plantation, which he knows like his own backyard. Halfway across, he disappears from view behind one of the big fallen trees covered with ivy, the last thing I want. The longer he's out of sight, the more nervous I'll be.

If he follows the same path I did, he'll get to a small wooden gate with half an acre of clearing on the other side. From the gate, he'll look across and see the same things I saw. Straight ahead, a mass of dark green conifers with flat tops, one or two leaning over to break up the curtain effect, some with what look like mini christmas trees sprouting out their sides. In the clearing itself, two uprooted trees with sawn-off trunks, looking like giant clumps of mud with root beards. The path looks like it's made of burnt wood shavings.

He'll take most of this in with a glance, but the one thing he won't see, I've been telling myself, is me. Too much foliage, surely. And meanwhile I'll be able to keep him in sight once he reappears. If he reappears. What's he doing, having his morning shit in the woods? Get on with it, you evil old cunt.

He hasn't reached the gate yet and I'm listening out for him, but it's so quiet you can hear the ticking of an electric fence and the weird sound of a sheep clearing its throat, like a tractor miles away. It's cold up here this early, but I thought of that in advance, putting on two extra layers and wearing gloves so's my hands won't shake. I'm still shivering more than I'd like.

I knew there'd be gaps like this, when I'd feel unsafe anytime I wasn't sure exactly where he was. Knowing that, it ought to be easier to sit it out, but I can't help the creeping suspicion he's found his way in behind me somehow. I almost turn round and look.

This sort of loony paranoia probably comes from hanging round in a wood in the dark, even for the couple of hours I've been here. Dark and wet. It didn't rain last night, but I swear these places make their own moisture, and there's mud everywhere. And I wish I hadn't worn these fucking boots. They're thick leather and I've slapped plenty of wax all over them, but the sides of the tongues are thinner, to make them more flexible, so they let the rain and mud in like they're pleased to see them.

So now I've got freezing cold wet feet, which does surprisingly serious things to your confidence in the small hours. There was an owl too, spooky as a soundtrack. And things sound bigger when they're rustling through the undergrowth. You start imagining somebody else is already in there, as if they'd be lying in wait at that time of night on the off chance somebody might come in. Get a fucking grip. By the time Owen Whittle showed up, I was almost glad to see him.

Then when I clock him next, he puts the wind up me again, specially as he hasn't appeared by the gate as you'd expect. He's in the corner of the clearing instead. Without a fucking sound. When I walked through here I set the woodpigeons off, exploding out the trees – but he's got the knack of moving quiet as well as quick, and he seems to have just materialized without so much as a blackbird clucking. And he's turned up in just about the only spot I didn't check to make sure I'd be hidden.

It can't make any difference. There's no way he can see me, of course not. He can't know if I'm flat on my front in the ferns or up in the trees. But this is hard to believe when I can see *him* so easy through a tiny gap in the leaves. I'm supposed to be the predator here, his struwwelpeter scissorman, the monster in the medieval wood. Instead I'm like a flight animal suddenly, pump and sprinkler system on overload. I can't even blink because he'll see it in his headlights. Madness. What is he, some kind of fucking wood sprite? Come *on*.

His eyes never keep still when he's walking, living up to his reputation. I knew he'd be frighteningly thorough. If it moves, he sees it, names it, sexes and ages it in a glance. Hears it all too, though right now there's just the usual small fry – blackbird, wren, great tit – and he's after something much bigger than that.

Owen Whittle's one of the leading egg collectors in the country. Taking the eggs of any wild bird has been illegal here since the sixties, but that didn't stop him building up a collection of fifteen hundred from two hundred british species. Eventually he got caught and fined a couple of grand and they confiscated the collection, but in six years he rebuilt it almost completely. He got caught again, given another fine and three months suspended. That was a year ago and I reckon his third collection stands at about a hundred and twenty, with all the common birds accounted for. He probably knows every yellowhammer's nest in the area.

The eggs he's after today are real rarities. He's stopped next to the tallest group of pines, growing quite close together near the middle of the plantation. It was too dark last night for me to guess where the nest might be, but even in broad daylight I wouldn't have had much chance even though it's enormous. I'm not that good, for a start – and all raptors are secretive nesters.

I've been wondering how Owen Whittle discovered it. The usual way probably, a quick flight view. These birds are unbelievably shy for their size, so you don't see them very often, and then it's normally just a glimpse before they disappear over the tops of the trees. The first one I ever saw, though, was better than that, and it was all my own work, in that nobody told me where to look and I was by myself when I found it.

I was walking through another conifer wood like this one but much bigger, a real forest, squares of pine packed tight with cleared patches between them. Above one of these patches, I see a crow on its own in the air, tumbling about like a raven, and I put my bins on it because you're taught to. It wasn't behaving like a crow normally does, so you're supposed to have a look because it might be mobbing a raptor, the original air rage. So you always have a look, and you never see a thing.

Even this time, nothing flying except the crow, which soon flaps off. I'm about to walk on when something catches my eye, what looks like a small sheepskin rug high up on the face of the next rank of conifers. I've no idea what it can be, maybe just a gap in the trees, so I put the bins up again – and I know soon as I see it. Jesus christ goshawk, giving me the eye. The size, the buff-coloured front of a young male, above all the ferocious expression you get from that gleaming white eyebrow.

Suddenly all the times you spent checking every sparrowhawk you saw, it was immediately all bollocks, they look nothing like this boss of the woods. Owen Whittle would've understood me punching the air when I saw it.

Maybe that's how he caught sight of this one. Or he was just looking up like the good birder he is, and he saw it coming out the sky like a small cargo plane, with its sheer bulk and the obvious power in those shortish broad wings. And to think it, she, was right here on his local patch, thousand-to-one-shot. Eggs he just had to have.

He'd have made up some excuse for hisself like he always does, how he might as well take them because they wouldn't survive long in any case. Raptors are protected by law, but when a pair set up nest right above a rearing ground for pheasants and when a day's shooting can be worth ninety quid a head to the landowner, a thousand pound fine begins to look an acceptable risk. I wouldn't have given much for this female's chances of rearing a brood even if Owen Whittle hadn't discovered her.

So what's wrong with him taking them? They're the biggest and rarest hawk in northern Europe, that's what's wrong. They were wiped out by egg collectors and gamekeepers thirty years back, and every egg they take or crush increases the chance of it happening again. Better for a single Owen Whittle to become extinct.

He's standing looking up at the tops of these tallest trees, head right back so his mouth's wide open. Is this the place then? He's come prepared, I know that. The binocular case isn't for binoculars, no proper birder carries one. It's stuffed with cottonwool in a polystyrene case, to put birds' eggs in.

Hard to believe he's really going to climb this tree. Corsican pines have these practically smooth trunks. But some of the stumps look strong enough to form a ladder of sorts, and anyway Owen Whittle climbs like a pine marten. He's twice my age but he scaled a sheer cliff in Pembrokeshire last year to get to a peregrine's nest. For a second or two, he's stock still under one of the trees, having a quick look round. Then he starts climbing.

Even now you're going wait wait wait. Maybe he won't do it today. Say he's only going up to check the nest? That was the deal, remember. Only if he's really going to take the eggs. Otherwise you give him the benefit and leave it. Anyway, listen out. The landowner might be around for once. The gamekeeper. Wait.

Yeh right. As if you've got time for this whites-of-his-eyes bollocks. Next time he moves round the other side of the trunk, you'll bottle it and pack everything away. Do it now so's you can get back for beans on toast like a good little psycho.

Patience for fucksake. He's nearly under the canopy itself. Wait till he plants his feet for the final push. Alright *now* you can shift the binoculars in your rucksack and take the handgun out, and all you have to do now is point and wait, which is just as well because your hands are wobbling as much as you expected, though you still think when the moment comes it'll be easier than they say.

So let's hear it. How does a first-timer like me get hold of a gun, complete with silencer and full magazine of bullets?

Well for a start nobody asks questions like that any more, not in London, not when forty quid buys you an airgun and another forty gets it adapted for bullets. But this isn't even one of those. It's an ancient old luger my dad's uncle brought back from the war. Belonged to a german general, according to him. Lugers were obsolete even then, so they only let the top brass carry them. The magazine's broke on this one and there's no takedown tool for reloading, so you have to push the bullets up one by one like suppositories.

Why the old boy came back with bullets, I've never known. What was he going to do with them, shoot rabbits? Settle disputes with neighbours? Scary. I thought it was just an old family legend they could frighten us kids with, but when my dad died I found the sinister thing in the attic. I had to clean all the dust off or it wouldn't fire, but that's alright I'm good at cleaning. I fired it in Larkeyvalley Wood to make sure they were live rounds, digging the bullet out of a beech tree. Dangerous things, guns. The spent cartridge hit me on the ear when it jumped out.

There weren't enough of them to practice with, so I'm closer to Owen Whittle than I'd like to be. I can see the grey in his beard. He grew it to break up the pale oval of his face so's the birds wouldn't see him so well from a distance. Wish I had his dedication.

He's quite close to the top by now, gripping with his legs, testing the next stump with a big tug before reaching down with the other hand to move the binocular case sideways, fixing one boot on the trunk with his toes bent at right angles.

Better touch the trigger now. You'd think the gloves would get in the way, but actually they make your finger feel nice and strong. On the other hand, your heartbeat's making your teeth knock together so loud you're sure he can hear it, the blood pumping into your eyes. Deep fucking breath.

He's in full view now, right under the canopy. Remind yourself how he'll be killing three unborn chicks by taking these eggs, maybe just a few days short of hatching, so he'll have to inject them with embryo solvent and dissolve them alive. This is going on all over the country, and you think of the goshawk disappearing again, this time maybe for good, and honey buzzards and all the rest –

9

This is me trying to summon up a red mist, you understand. So's I can tell myself I didn't really shoot him in cold blood. Because in cold blood I'd just laugh at what I'm thinking of doing. Me with no background in anything like this. The ordinariest little life imaginable. About to put a bullet in somebody, as seen on TV. Don't be so silly.

But you took the biggest step just by coming here, so it's pretty much inevitable by now. Even if the hen hawk flies off the nest now, or a green woodpecker yells across the clearing, it's too late.

He's stretching up for the top branches. I'm aiming as best I can for somewhere near the top of his spine. I've got nothing to rest the gun on, so my hand's shaking so much it's making the barrel waggle all over the place – and maybe it's that, or my elbow knocking a twig, or nothing at all, that makes him turn round and look in my direction.

No, shit, what's this. I've been really careful and surely he can't have spotted me through all this foliage, he can't. But it's like he's staring straight at me, and I'm actually holding my breath in case he sees it, like smoke signals to an indian scout. Fuckfuckfuckfuckfuck.

Then it dawns on me he's not looking at anything at all. He's listening, with his head on one side (yeh, like a bird), a last check for the farmer or those two out for their walk. Like a prat, I listen too. Fuck-all except thrushes. Then he snaps out his tableau and reaches up again, almost hanging from a branch.

This is where the consequences crowd in. The life you'll be giving up when you do this. And the fear's making you blind and giving you neckache. Anybody would understand if you pulled out at the last minute.

But there again. I planned for this. This life, I said. It's something I've had enough of for years. Why not just leave it? And why not take Owen Whittle with you when you go? You'd be doing some good, I said.

Anyway, look at him. He's got his back to me, which helps. No flesh and blood, just his black jacket filling the frame. So that's alright, so that's alright.

Squeeze it, they say. It's a cliché by now. Don't pull it. The way I do it, it's not one thing or the other, but the result's alright. There's the famous sound like a spit, not too loud even on an empty morning like this. Then I'm unscrewing the silencer and putting it all back in the bag. The cartridge didn't hit me this time.

Owen Whittle knows what size a female goshawk can grow to, and maybe in the back of his mind he was half expecting this massive slam between the shoulders. Or maybe he's felt the thump of an eagle's claws when he climbed up its rock, and he knows it's nothing like this. Whatever, when I look he's gone, but I heard him and I know the fall was heavy and incontinent. Sure enough, he's lying twenty feet away from the trunk, his donkey jacket lumped up in the bluebells and his legs bent back under him at this terrible angle and everything so bloodless.

Then I come out and leave as quick as I can, giving him a wide berth. The safety catch is fucked on this gun, so I take the clip out as I walk out the wood. I zip the rucksack shut and put my arms through the straps on the way down the hill and over the road. I can't see the old couple or anybody else so I assume nobody sees me all the way down the disused railway cutting, over a stile, and back to the hire car.

Notice how steady your hands are when you drive, which means nothing one way or the other I suppose, and your pulse is back to normal more or less. In fact I'd be pretty unscathed if I hadn't tried to put my bins on a dark shape flying over the wood and spiked myself on the barbed wire fence. England's green and pleasant land. Dig the fucker up.

THE DAY MY mum died, I started twitching.

And I don't mean I was out birding when I heard the news. The other way round. I got the phone call but I went anyway.

Sod's law. The first time you're offered a lift to see a rare bird, somebody goes and dies. What can you do – turn it down and they might not ask you again. Anyway she was dead, what difference could it make to her. The only reason you rush back at a time like that is so's you don't look a complete heartless cunt, and there was no surviving relatives to do that for.

You tell yourself it's what she would've wanted, but that's always a lie. When you die, you want people there don't you, round your bedside sobbing their hearts out, not carrying on like nothing happened.

Instead I went on the twitch regardless. I saw the bird – dark-eyed junco overwintering near Fleet – and got other lifts after that. They'd have done it even if I turned them down the first time (your mother dying is an acceptable excuse) but you're not necessarily sure at the time. That's my story anyway.

Anyway I say it was all my mum's fault in the first place. She bought me my first pair of bins, which means she must've run out of ideas for birthday presents. I don't know what parents think you're going to use binoculars for when you're thirteen. I tried looking in people's bedrooms across the street at night, but I couldn't see very much so I put them away and forgot about them. She never said anything, not then or six years later when I started birding and bought a proper pair instead of using the ones she got me.

She died five years ago (long enough for the junco to have a name change) and in that time I've done thousands of miles up and down the country chasing birds, spending the money and putting in the hours in all weathers. I've seen two other juncos, crawled on my stomach in the mud for something as common as a stock dove, and waited ten hours in the rain for a terek sandpiper I knew was already gone. I drove five hours to Penzance once, slept three hours sitting upright in a car, spent a fortune on a plane ticket to Scilly and back, all in twenty-four hours – for what turned out to be a common starling somebody misidentified. You turn work down, lose your latest lover, start hallucinating because you forget to eat for three days, and don't wash for so long your body regulates itself and other people stop noticing. Apart from that, mrs lincoln.

You can see how this might add up to the identikit of a nutter. Obsessive nature, values birds more than humans, shoots egg collector. Except I think I'm quite normal really. My own boss, my own place, an A level, alright with dogs and kids. I play five-a-side once a week, get my leg over on a regular basis and get pissed with my mates. I do have mates, and not just from birding, and I'm not the quiet one in the group, or the oddball, the one when it comes out you shot somebody people say oh yeh now you come to think of it. Of all the people I know, I'm probably the last one you'd expect. If I can do it, anybody can.

I think it's important you keep to your normal routine after. Otherwise it's like Owen Whittle won in a way, which defeats the object. So here I am, the night before my twenty-fifth birthday, cleaning my bins with lighter fluid. Unscrewing the lens on my telescope, checking I've packed the waterproofs. And all for a quiet day at the local patch. I got on the phone, but nothing rare's come up on the birdlines, Stevie Red Bus Oxford is working, and Bish Novak's got a gig out of town. So it's an hour round the reservoir then a lunchtime drink on my own. Sad, I agree.

I never need an alarm. I just fix a time in my head and set the body clock. It's half-ten now and there's already a police helicopter overhead and somebody's kicking a can outside the window, terrorizing the empty street. Sad tosser mark two.

I'M ASLEEP ABOUT an hour and a half.

I suppose I'll be shitting myself every time the phone goes from now on, and it's the worst sound in the world when it wakes you up. Then I'm being hammerdrilled by the voice at the other end. 'Gently does it Bus, for fucksake. I'm still asleep.'

'No you're fucking not. Listen, I'm at Kew Bridge. I'll be there in ten minutes. The ivory gull's back. Ten minutes. Don't forget you owe me the petrol from last time.'

Fucking hell. I put some clothes on and clean my teeth on autopilot, pupils too big to switch any lights on. Maybe I'm delirious and it's all a dream, that'd be nice. No, sorry, ivory gull alright. One of the great bogey birds, a real fucking nemesis, and even further away than last time. Today of all days.

When I open the front door, Stevie Red Bus barges past me like a scrum half. 'Not using your bog are you? I need to have a puke.'

Nothing surprises me about the Bus any more, even when an arm appears round the bathroom door five minutes later. 'Another towel, quick. I've got it in my hair.'

16

'Fucking hell Steve, I don't need this. What sort of state are you in? You'll kill us both.'

'Don't worry, you're driving till we pick Bish up. Anyway I'm not in a state, I've only had three drinks. Went out with some people from the publishers.'

That's not enough to make her puke, she can drink like a fish, and she says yeh she knows, but she's just put two fingers down her throat.

'Hang on, this is too much for me. You made yourself sick on purpose? You've lost it Bus, I swear to god.'

'Fuck off and listen. I'm going to be sick sometime, right? So I might as well get it over and done with, then I won't feel so bad on the trip. It's called preparation.'

'It's called certifiable. I thought the ivory gull had pissed off.'

'No,' she says, 'just moved further down the coast. They didn't phone the news in all day. If they had, we'd have seen it by now.'

'Groan. It's a fucking jinx Steve, it's not meant to be.'

'Oh ye of little faith as usual.' She finishes drying her hair, which looks like dried blood in the light from the bathroom, and asks me where I was the other day. She had the day off, we could've gone out someplace. I tell her Barn Elms. Then doing a job in Hammersmith Grove.

'Get a move on,' she says. 'We're picking Bish up at Leicester Forest.'

'I don't know why we're bringing him. He'll be two hours late as usual.'

'I keep forgetting what a miserable toss you are sometimes. Fill a bottle of water, I don't want to get dehydrated.'

Soon as we hit the North Circular, I get flashed. Keep to the fucking speed limit, she tells me, but it's easier said than done when it's only forty and the roads are clear for once. There's so many cars nowadays, birders are travelling this time of night more and more. And we've all got away with being flashed on the North Circ, there's never any film in the boxes.

I put my foot down once we're on the M1 at Hendon. With nobody about, you can average ninety all the way and reach north Scotland in seven hours. Ideally we'd want to be there before dawn, to catch the gull before it leaves the roost, but there's no chance of that now they've put the message out so late. Too busy enjoying the bird theirselves no doubt. Fuckers, but you can't blame them, it really is a stunning animal, fully deserves a name like ivory.

But it's always been a cunt of a bird for us. Out of the other four ivories since I started birding, three only stayed a day, and though the last one was there nearly a week we couldn't get time off till the end, so by the time we got to Inverness harbour it was gone. Worse still, I thought I saw it soon as we got there, getting my bins on an all-white pigeon-like bird on the shoreline, little black eye and everything. Ivory gulls look like white doves at a distance.

And that's what it was. A white dove, total fucking heartbreak. Then, because that particular ivory gull had a habit of disappearing mid-afternoon but coming back next morning, we spent the night in the car, in our summer gear while the scots were starting their winter. Then we stood around freezing to death till lunchtime before driving all the way home, the usual retreat from Moscow.

This time it's turned up even further away, at Fraserburgh on the corner of the same coast, with me hundreds of miles away and doing a ton while I'm still groggy, the sound of the Bus sucking mints booming through my head. The god of birds is in one of those moods, even adding some drizzle as part of the entertainment.

By the time we get to Leicester services it's turned into full-blown rain, thundering on the car roof and hitting the tarmac so hard the rebounds look like colourless snowdrops.

At the services there's people running all over the forecourt. We're working our way towards the petrol pumps, all windscreen wipers and headlights and people dodging the car, when somebody runs straight at us, brick shithouse with a hooded parka over his head. Before I can get to the handle, he's pulled the door open on my side. 'Get out the fucking car.'

He's shouting through the rain, face like an unfinished mugging, and the only thing I'm worried about is the water that's dripping off his clothes onto my legs. You don't want damp thighs all the way up north.

'What are you doing, you big cunt. Break that door and you'll fucking pay for it.'

'Get out or I'll pull you out.'

'Fuck off my arm.'

'Get in the back,' he says. 'Hurry up, there's a car behind us.'

'You're tearing my jacket, you polish prick. Get in the back yourself.'

'You always drive like a cunt at night,' he says. 'Risk my fucking life. Out you get.'

He won't let go. We're doing a tug of war with my sleeve and I'm shouting at him if I get out the car I'll get fucking drenched and he's telling me not to be a tart all my life and takes his parka off in the rain and puts it over me as he drags me out and stuffs me in the back. He's seventeen stone of pigheadedness, so there's a limit to how much of a fight you can put up, specially when you're starting to giggle under your breath. 'You twat Bish.'

'Fucking stubborn yourself. Have a sleep back there, you're doing all the driving on the way back.'

'And paying all the petrol apparently. Fuck me, this has mega dip written all over it.'

Then Stevie Red Bus says stop the car she needs to retch and Bish wants to know what the matter with her is. I tell him she made herself sick on purpose. Very sensible, he says, being on the same wavelength as her. I take his parka off and curl up on the back seat under it with its ten years of grunge. I'd wash it for him except it'd fall apart.

'There's fucking gratitude for you,' he says. 'After we arranged an ivory gull as a birthday present.'

'You arsehole. You forgot didn't you.'

'No,' says Stevie, 'we had a surprise drink planned. Pretzels and everything.'

'You forgot, the pair of you. With friends like these.'

'Nod off you po-faced cunt,' says Bish. He squeals the car onto the slip-road, the speed and noise levels go up a notch, and the twitch is properly under way. His ponytail's glossy like an eel. He undoes it with one hand and rubs his hair a bit drier. In the rearview his face is shiny with sweat from the night's gig and the car suddenly smells of puff.

The two of them start talking soon as he gets in. I fall asleep to discussions on wind farms and green party courses in direct action. He probably only put me in the back so's they could yak the night away as usual.

Fine by me. The side windows are completely covered in raindrops and soon there's just the sound of the windscreen wipers, leaving me to doze, the best part of these trips, travelling better than arriving, the constant sound like a plane or a hovercraft in the dark, a good noisy womb, when you don't have to face things yet: the shit weather, every chance the bird might be gone, this whole mad succubus of a pastime.

Time to time, with half an eye open, you see road signs lit up, and just about every place name is somewhere you've been, but always to see birds, some weird and wonderful locations among them, rubbish tips in Loughborough and Bolsover, a sainsbury's car park with two pied wheatears perching on the shopping trolleys. Try explaining to the local plod why there's three hundred of you with telescopes watching a school playground in Dewsbury. You only know your own country because of the birds you've seen in it.

Halfway through Lancashire there's a sign saying The North. Look at that, says Bish. Where do this lot think they live? We don't have signs back home saying The South, do we. Fucking natives. Every road sign's a rugby league score.

A few more hours go by, I fall asleep twice, and I've just seen the sign for Perth when Bish lets out a groan and stops the car. The petrol's on empty, all we fucking need.

'Shit,' says Stevie. 'Anyone know if there's a petrol station open?'

I tell her I don't think so. Nothing before Inverness at this time of night.

'Right,' says Bish, and he turns the car round and starts driving back to Perth.

We're seething of course, mostly because there's nobody to blame except ourselves. We all got distracted at Leicester services, we all forgot to fill up. We drive back slow as a hearse, find the nearest garage in Perth, and hope this isn't going to cost us the bird. We've lost an hour, so there's no chance of being there by first light. Getting back on the A9, there's a strip of light on the horizon, like the slit when an ivory gull opens its eye.

Twitchers don't think of petrol as one of the world's great evils, our lives run by multinationals. You only think about it when you're running low. We don't really care about conservation in general, not if it gets in the way of birding. What we want is to be serviced, same as everybody else. Motorway with no other cars on it, somewhere to have a piss and a bite to eat, regular updates on the pager. Everything laid on.

And the people who say it's too easy, not really birding at all, they're just jealous, the low listers. When a twitch goes like clockwork, you don't think how artificial it all is, you take it with both hands, because there's enough days when it goes horribly fucking wrong. The bird god giveth but gets more kicks from taking away.

For the moment, this is that part of a twitch when you pretend to be philosophical. You've done this exact same journey before, for the same species, miles and miles and hours in the car, now you're doing it again only more so. If you miss the bird a second time, at least you'll have a story to tell. Gives you a certain cachet. To dip on one ivory gull is unfortunate, to dip on two is showing off a bit.

It's too early for anything to come up on the pager, might as well try and get a bit more kip, specially as they've both shut up in the front. I hate the way Bish bites his fingernails while he's doing ninety-five.

Next time I wake up we've stopped, but I know we're not there yet. He's shaking me but there's none of the right urgency. Piss stop, he says.

'I don't need one.'

'No, the Bus.'

'Christ, she's not still puking.'

'No,' he says, 'definitely a slash. Come on, let's have a look.'

'At what? Oh you sick cunt.'

'Come on, don't tell me you've never thought about it. You wouldn't mind catching it off her.'

'Stevie? She's one of the boys. Your words not mine.'

'Yeh but tell the truth,' he says. 'You must want to see what it looks like. See if it's got freckles same as her face.'

'Not with a night's piss coming out of it.'

He ruffles my hair, making a really disgusting noise with his tongue, then gets out the car.

I roll over and try and will myself back to sleep. Except my knees are aching by now, might as well stretch the legs.

The rain's stopped, though it's still prickling the air, and it's turned colder, you can see your breath. We're parked on the grass verge next to a ditch running the length of the road. No sign of Stevie, so she's probably behind the hawthorn hedge at the bottom of the ditch. Miles of rough pasture everywhere, hills in the background, the kind of countryside that somehow only looks right in this kind of weather, with the clouds so low and full they make everything dark. Bish is standing on the edge of the ditch with his back to me, having his first joint of the day.

You sometimes forget what a man-mountain he is, even without his parka. He always was. I knew him when we were kids, living in the same street, going to the same infants. We lost touch after that and I didn't see him again for ten years, then I heard there was a band on at one of the pubs and the frontman was somebody I used to know. So I went along, and there was the Bishop, twice the size by now but playing blues harp like an angel. It amazed me how a sound like that could come out of such a huge great slob, which is a shit way of thinking, but we all do it.

We met after the gig, but it wasn't exactly like a house on fire – we were never close at school – till it came out we both did a bit of birding, which I called a coincidence and he said was fucking kismet. It turned out our local patches were within a couple of miles of each other, but mine was better than his so he transferred. Since then we've been knocking about together, on and off, seeing our four hundredth tick in tandem, finishing each other's sentences with the same swearwords.

In that time he's had almost as many jobs as he's seen birds. When I met up with him again he was a screever, doing those chalk drawings on the pavements, then a drainer, which I didn't even know existed, making a tenner a day picking coins out of drains and cracks in the pavement. Sundays were the best, with all the saturday nighters dropping their loose change or their wedding rings which he pawned. He used a two-pound coin he found to pay a road toll on the way to a grey-cheeked thrush.

He sold the Big Issue for a month outside one of the Hammersmith tubes, you could hear him the other side of the Broadway, bishoosuh, bishoomadam, sound of the times. Then he graduated to putting up tartcards in phoneboxes, making a fortune for a while, and even worked for me once, till I had to sack him for chronic oversleeping (mutual consent, he calls it).

But this was all just a way of filling his time. You don't need to do that kind of work when you can play a blues harp the way he does, one of the great sounds of west London. I keep telling him to give up the day jobs.

His name's not his real one. His parents came here from Poland and they christened him Zbigniew, for which the diminutive is Zbishek which nobody could pronounce at school so he let us call him Bishop. He's tying his hair back, like a sumo wrestler doing his topknot. When they come and get me for Owen Whittle, this is one of the sights I won't be seeing again. I didn't realize it was one I'd miss.

I ask him if anything's come up on the pager yet.

'No, probably still too early. Or maybe the reception's shit up here.'

'Doubt if anybody's looking any more. Every other fucker's seen it.'

'Well,' he says, 'at least it might think twice about flying off in this weather. Be even better if it was still pissing down.' I hand him his parka and he puts it round his shoulders.

I tell him I like this part of the world. Wish they'd found the bird here. Fraserburgh's a right dump.

'Yeh but this is worse,' he says. 'Private land as far as the eye can see. Cunts. How much damage do they think we could we do, walking on it. And you can never find out who the fucking landowners are. Hey, what about Owen Whittle.'

'Yeh, it worked at last. All those years sticking pins in his effigy. Scary.'

'Except I got a buzz out of it, didn't you? No, well, you didn't care so much. Jesus, Owen Whittle. A bullet in the back.'

'And they used a silencer. There were dog walkers around, but nobody heard a shot.'

'Yeh,' he says. 'Fucking hell. One minute he must've been jumping for joy at finding a gos nest on his own patch. The next: splat. I thought he was going to live for ever. Remember that time he was on the box, saying how they should let him keep his egg collection, then he wouldn't have to go out and start another one, the usual bollocks. Real caricature of a birder he looked, beard and knitted hat. A silencer, for fucksake. Imagine a birder doing something like that.'

'Yeh but nobody's saying it was a birder are they. Be real.'

'Alright,' he says, 'but it's got to be something like that, read the papers. He was near the top of the trunk when they shot him. They found a branch he broke off when he fell. So somebody waited till they were sure he was going for the nest.'

'One of the big egg dealers, you mean? How much do you get for goshawk eggs now?'

But Bish says this is pure red herring. It's true Owen Whittle got up the egg dealers' noses, finding nests before they could. But you can't believe it was ever going to come to this. Most of the eggs he took were common stuff the big exporters aren't interested in. Anyway, these particular gos eggs were still in the nest, they weren't taken by any egg dealers.

Besides, he says, he doesn't go along with the idea that *anybody* paid to have him shot. It's true silencers are generally used by people who kill other people for a living, and since you can presumably discount the army in this case, it should point to Owen Whittle being shot by somebody who was paid to do it.

'But if that's what happened,' he says, 'they hired a pretty crap assassin. The bullet hit him in the side of the body apparently, not much higher than the hip, glancing in off one of the ribs. Then the fall knocked him out and he died of internal bleeding while he was unconscious. If you're a pro you'd go for the head or heart wouldn't you, and at that range you couldn't miss if you tried. Plus you'd put an insurance bullet in him when he was on the ground.'

I tell him it's got to be better than his alternative. Some birder taking him out. With a fucking silencer.

'Remember him saying he was going to do his community service and start his collection all over again? That trouble-at-mill accent that gets on your tits.'

'We said we'd dance on his grave.'

'Yeh,' he says, 'but when it came to it, it was the last thing I wanted to do. Does this make sense to you: I almost wanted to pay my respects.'

'Yeh I know.'

'Don't get me wrong,' he says. 'I'm glad he's not around any more. So I suppose I'm glad he's dead, because it's the only way he was ever going to stop. But he was the other side of the same coin as us. He loved the birds as much as we do and his fieldcraft was on another planet. I'm almost glad it happened like it did, him walking through his local wood with rare eggs for the taking.'

He puffs his cheeks out and says it's all bollocks though isn't it, you still had to hate him. 'He put more threatened species at risk than anybody else we knew – when he could've been doing some good with all that knowledge. RIP, the cunt.'

'Jesus,' he says. 'It's weird. Remember me saying I'd shoot him myself, given the chance?'

'No.'

'Come on, I was always saying it.'

'I don't remember.'

'You're having a laugh aren't you? All the different ways I suggested doing it. What do you mean you don't remember?'

'You're always on about shooting somebody, I can't keep track of every potential target. Who was it last time: master of the local hunt. Then you wonder why I stop listening.'

'Alright,' he says, 'but Owen Whittle was top of the list. How can you forget me mentioning him?'

'I must've thought he was another one of your fantasies. I don't fucking remember. Alright?'

'Easy. Somebody might think you cared for once. Fuck me. Anyway, fact remains. I mention Owen Whittle once or twice and now look. It's like somebody read my mind. Has the Bus talked to you about it?'

'No.'

'It's agitated her big time,' he says. 'Hark, I hear her dulcet tones.'

'Don't throw that butt in the grass,' says Stevie coming out the hawthorn hedge. 'Polluting the landscape you love so much.'

'Let the fucking landowners pick it up,' says Bish. 'They get enough of our money.'

'Come on,' she says, bustling past. 'Get back in the car, we're wasting time.'

'We'd better not miss this bird because you've been wetting your whiskers.'

'Get it right, fatso. I was having a shit. Big enough to bring in a whole flock of pipits.'

'You're a foulmouth cunt Bus, honest to god.'

By the time we get to Fraserburgh there's a bird on her pager, a little egret in Staffs which has Bish muttering about common shit like that being put out on a pager. Fucking inland egrets. 'Look at this place,' he says. 'You're right, it's a tip.'

It is, too. I've got a lot of time for Scotland, but there's a lot of grey buildings up here and none of them are really ancient. Fraserburgh in the rain, probably the best weather for it.

And of course we haven't got directions to the old lighthouse where the bird was seen, and there's no signs anywhere. 'Wind the window down,' says Bish. 'Ask a jock. Fucking one-ways.'

We've moved on to the next stage, twitchy now we're so close, which is supposedly where the word twitcher came from. After eight hours keeping a lid on it, you're all fingers and thumbs and weak jokes when you get out the car and start fitting telescopes on tripods. Because we *really* want this one. All the shit about what a laugh it'd be, coming all this way to dip out twice on the same bird – fuck that, you'd sell your house for a five-second view. Then they can come and arrest me.

I've only had one birthday tick, which is a bit unlucky considering I was born on the cusp of migration time. Still, at least I found it for myself, a willow tit on my twentieth, when I was still a beginner. To miss this one now, jesus what a fucking horror story, your whole sense of well-being depending on a single bird's trick of the blood. If it's gone, part of you's going to be scarred for ever, no exaggeration.

They've turned the lighthouse into a museum, stuck on top of what looks like a fortress, though none of us is paying much attention to surroundings. And lo and behold: the rain's back. Well naturally. We're doing the stations of the cross for this one.

Bish asks what the exact directions on the pager are.

'Follow the coastal path,' says Stevie. 'Anywhere between here and the point. Could be fucking miles.'

We're still doing up our waterproofs and slamming car doors when a young kid appears round the side of the wall, the only other human being in sight. About ten years old, zipping up his top. 'Here for the ivory gull, are you?'

'Yeh,' we say, trying to sound offhand, like we see them every day back home. 'Still here, is it?' If it left an hour ago, he'd better not smile when he tells us.

He saves his life by saying yeh it's been on the rocks all morning, and you almost want to toss him a coin for his trouble. We set off without getting any more details from him, thinking he means just round the corner. It's just a thin headland.

Big mistake. The headland's thin alright, but it's full of indentations, you're always turning a corner expecting it to open out, and above all there's nobody about, which is a real disaster. Normally if you're trying to locate a rare bird you just look for where the birders are, but ivory gull falls in that category where the really heavy birders have all seen one, the dudes aren't going to come all this way, and those in between like us have already come and gone. What's worse is there's not even many gulls, so you know immediately the little fucker isn't here.

Then and only then, the real world rushes in. Owen Whittle, the consequences thereof, what these two are going to think of me when they find out. I feel actually, physically, sick – not because I killed a man, you understand, and I'm going to be arrested soon, but because one single bird isn't showing. Maybe even the kid lied, telling us it was still around, winding the english up. The god of birds twisting the knife to the end.

You can see it on their faces. Stevie and Bish. Nobody can hide the despair of dipping out. No pretending to scan with the bins, no oh-well jokes. It's a beautiful part of the world here, wild and windswept, the sea breaking on chocolate-brown rocks. And you hate it like the fucking plague. You'll remember it for ever as a place that beat you, sent you homeward tae think again.

Then suddenly it's there.

Fuck knows where it came from, none of us saw it fly in. The bird god's hands probably, releasing it like a white dove because we've suffered enough for it. Flying towards us, no less. You'd swear it's coming to welcome us.

Your brain automatically clicks into birder mode, instantly ticking off the identification features. Yeh its wings do look bent back in flight, yeh they're noticeably broad-based – but it's the famous speckles that stand out a mile on those white wings, like rows of dark stitching.

This all takes about three or four seconds, then you're doing what all experienced birders should do when faced with a new bird. Go absolutely fucking mental ape demented. I've got one knee on the ground, punching the air over and over and not even looking at the gull any more. Stevie's waving her scope and tripod over her head like she's slain a giant, and Bish is just jumping up and down on the spot, nothing else, piledriving the grass, the clifftop fearing for its life. And that's only the tip of what you feel like doing. You want to *really* let loose. Slash yourself with a stanley knife or piss on somebody's face.

Because we can hold our heads up now, oh jesus yeh. When the bird talk turns to ivory gulls and we laugh at ourselves for dipping out first time, we won't be hiding our purgatory behind gallows humour any more. Because we've seen it. We've fucking won. And everybody else who gripped us off by seeing the last one, they can all go shag theirselves. Hence the three of us whooping and laughing like inmates while the bird in question drifts past, ivory white and oblivious, on its way back to roost on the rocks. Come on down, I'll be holding court for a while.

Stevie runs on ahead. She'd run even if the bird had a broken wing and was tied to a post, she can never believe they're going to stay. Bish is floating meanwhile. He gets me in a headlock and takes me all the way down the path like that, the drizzle dripping through my hair onto my legs, and I never felt more comfortable in my life.

Most rarities are more colourful than ivory gull. It's only a gull, let's face it. Rock thrush is about as good as it gets: powder blue head and orangey underparts. Or a parula, like a mini-rainbow. But there's something about this single white bird, with that backdrop of dark rocks and foam, so white it shows up how shit my scope is, throwing a yellowish cast round the edge of the bird's body. And we're seeing it at its best in my opinion. Later on in the spring it'll turn pure white, which should be wonderful but really it needs this immature stitching to frame its outline. And it's lost that dirty face mask it would've had a month ago. We walk right down to the rocks and watch it with our backs against the cliff face, pipe and slippers.

What the fuck's it doing here. This time of year, when it ought to be north of the arctic circle looking for a mate. Mad fuckers, birds. You can study the weather maps all you want, know your migration patterns – then they turn up out of season, wind in the wrong direction, miles from where they should be. On your birthday.

And performing for you like this. Preening at close range, so you get perfect views of the wing formation. Then feeding only twenty feet away, toe-tapping the surface of a rockpool to nab scraps of fish and shellfish. Having a crap as white as itself.

And even while you're enjoying it to bits, you can't help making the field notes. Bill quite thick, with a pronounced gonydal angle, vaguely dodo-like, the dots on the primaries in the shape of down-turned arrowheads, others forming a subterminal band on the tail.

It's while you're fixing its exact leg colour in your memory that you realize your cheeks are aching because you haven't stopped grinning all over your face, partly because you've had one of Bish's happy pills for once, without which no twitch would be complete. He's staring at the gull, so close he doesn't need bins, and whispering fucking hell to hisself.

Meanwhile the Bus is doing her drawings, page after page of lightning sketches in case it decides to fly off. This is what I like about birding with Stevie, you're guaranteed some time with the bird. Not like the tick-and-run merchants who only hang around for ten minutes after driving five hours to get there. With the Bus you can relax in the knowledge you'll be there as long as you want. Make your notes on tricky plumage details or just watch it feed, because she can't leave till she's sketched it from every conceivable angle.

It's her job by now. Professional bird illustrator. We got here a bit late, so hers won't be the first sketches of this gull, but the bird mags and websites will wait for them. She does the best bird drawings in the country.

She's rabbiting on about the shape of the dots on the primary edge, how they're black as opposed to the dark grey elsewhere. Look at the shape of them: you'd swear they've been applied with a paintbrush. She tears up half her drawings nowadays, not good enough according to her, though of course they look alright to me.

It's odd how quick you move on to the next stage of any

twitch. Sheer boredom. A bird's only really good when you haven't seen it.

So your eyes start wandering. Anything else around? I start scanning the sea for longtailed ducks, and eventually even Bish starts asking her how her drawings are coming along, then suggesting we might go for a coffee someplace and come back later, then outright moaning, till she snaps, go on without me then, it's only up the road. Fairweather twats.

After two hours she's drawn every feather tract on the fucking thing and we've all paid it due homage and can slope off back up the path to the museum caf. I get through two pots of tea while Stevie has dry toast for her iffy stomach and Bish eats everything that isn't nailed down. When there's a break in the rain we nip back out and the ivory gull's gone.

That makes it all the better somehow. The fact we only got here with a couple of hours to spare, phew christ, our luck well and truly in. Nobody's in a great hurry to start driving all the way back, so we stand around and scan for incidental birds, and you can enjoy the common ones now you've got the one you came for. The landscape's great, the sea's majestic, even herring gulls are smart. Stevie's hair is dark red and sticking to her face and she's got freckles in all the right places.

There's oystercatchers on the rocks. Black-and-white waders with pink legs and red bills. Smart birds, shit name, catching oysters not being specially difficult. Suggestions for a more appropriate moniker on a postcard. Cocklecracker's nearer the truth.

'Can't remember the last time I saw you cry.'

'What? Fuck off.'

'What's this then?' She fingertips my cheeks. I tell her it's the wind. We all look like we're crying.

'Sure.' She dries my face with her glove – then starts telling me off. 'Sign the logbook next time you're at Barn Elms. You didn't do it the other day.'

'I never sign it unless I see something good.'

'Angelo signed it,' she says. 'He had a pair of turnstones in the afternoon.'

'Yeh but he's a nutter. Turnstones, for fucksake.'

'Notifiable species,' she says. 'Sign the logbook or they'll think nobody goes there. They'll take our fucking keys away.'

'Yes, mum.'

'Diver,' says Bish, using those great eyes of his. You ask him where, which is always pointless when you're seawatching, there's never anything to help you get your bearings. 'I've got it,' says the Bus. 'Redthroated.'

Me, I'm not so sure. Actually I *am* sure, I've got it in my scope down to a hundred yards and it's blackthroated, supposedly hard to tell apart in winter plumage but not at all really. Bish wants confirmation and I point out the whitish patch at the rear of its flank, almost on the waterline. 'Can't see it,' he says and Steve can't either.

'Well the waves hide it sometimes, but it's there. Anyway look at the shape of the thing, the oily look to it. How long have we been doing this? It's a fucking blackthroat. Come on.'

'It's got an upturned bill,' says Bish.

'Fuck off.'

'Upturned and thin,' he says. 'And the upperparts are scaly not oily. That's redthroated in the field guides I've got.'

'Change the fucking prescription. Scaly? Does it look scaly to you, Bus?'

'Even at this range, more scaly than oily,' she says. 'I would-n't say oily.'

'I'm going mad here. You really can't see the white side patch?'

'Stop being a stubborn cunt,' says Bish. 'You've just had a fucking ivory gull, be content with a redthroat for afters.'

'Fucking hell, the pair of you. It's oily, not scaly. Look through my scope.'

'Oily *and* scaly,' says the Bus. 'There's two different birds.'

Fuck. She's right, there is. One close to the shore, the other miles out. Typical cross purposes, but nice to get both species.

Look at me. Two days after Owen Whittle's funeral, debating the subtleties of diver ID. But what do people expect? I'll spend all day indoors beating my breast? They'll get their pound of flesh soon enough.

'Check them again,' says Bish. 'One of them might be a banana bill.'

He means white-billed diver, a real giant rarity. We're never likely to find one for ourselves, but that's never stopped him. He's always been the optimist out of the three of us, the fantasist, he honestly believes he's going to find a new species for Britain. It's the attitude that makes him a better birder than us. He double-checks every bird he sees or hears, so his identification skills are sharper. When Bish sees a bird, it stays seen. But right now he's not being serious, and he gets me in another headlock to emphasize it. There's nobody else about by now and we've got the whole coast to ourselves, just me and my brother and sister geeks here.

'Shit,' says Bish, 'I forgot my camera. I'll have to buy some shots of this gull from a photographer. Give the Bus something to draw from.'

This is his little joke. Stevie's a vegan, she stopped buying photos when she found out photo film's got gelatine in it, and she can't afford a digital camera on her pay.

We get in the car and the Bus settles down for a kip, she's short enough to stretch out on the back seat. They make me drive all the way back like they said, but that's usually the deal anyway. Stevie's invariably knackered from work, I'm more relaxed once I've seen the bird, and Bish is so relaxed when he's had his tablets the police once stopped him because he was doing seven miles an hour. He leans back in the passenger seat, says ivory gull tee hee, waits till he hears me chuckling, then gets some sleep.

I wait till we're out of Scotland before stopping for a break, an old-fashioned motorway caf we've known for years, then I go to the bog on my own. We've stopped at exactly the right time, bladder so full I can have a good long slash. Then I wash my hands for the first time in hours, getting all the dirt out from round the nails, and put them under the dryer till they're bone dry. They're almost dry first time, dry as makes no difference, but I switch it on again. I'm itching to get back out to where the other two are sitting, I can hear them from here, ordering my birthday drinks – but I dry my hands one more time, savouring the wait. Food and a drink waiting for you, knowing your being away has made a difference – for the moment, I've got it all.

Yeh, Bish would say, but it helps we saw the bird.

I drive too fast on the way back sometimes. If it wasn't for the fact the other two might object, and I might end up paralyzed and not deceased, I'd be tempted to put my foot down and drive off Bempton Cliffs or someplace. But all in good time. For now, there's ivory gull in your veins, Stevie Red Bus quiet asleep, and Bish's purring farts. It doesn't get much better than this.

PART OF ME thought even getting out of bed would be a task from now on. I'd be under the duvet waiting for the knock on the door. I imagined when I went out I'd feel like I had a sign round my neck saying here I am, it was me, I did it. There's a police station at the top of my road and I'd be wanting to go in and say come on stop fucking about you must know by now.

Instead I get up for work same as ever, same person in the mirror. When I write the ivory gull up in the diary, I'm not teary-eyed because it's the last lifer I'll ever see. I suppose if you're capable of doing what I did, it's likely you'll be able to deal with the aftermath.

But I say that like I'm a total iceberg. Or at least I've done some serious mental preparation. Truth is, anybody can deal with the aftermath if they know the aftermath's not going to last too long.

I had a go at covering my tracks about Owen Whittle. Wearing boots two sizes too big, binning my clothes, false name for the hire car. But only basic and half-hearted. You can't expect to get away with it for ever. I don't know how long these things take, it seems to vary. Couple of weeks maybe before the police come round. Months if they find it tricky. But sometime. And that's alright, I've already had a bellyful. When I told Bish I was going to get to five hundred ticks then top myself, I knew he wouldn't take the piss. He was jealous, if anything. It's the nearest either of us had to a goal in life.

We both used to say everything was a total drag, hardly worth going on with. Except I'm not sure how much he meant it. Whereas me, I've been meaning it since I can remember. One of my first memories is me having dinner and my mum and dad sitting either side of me like judges and one of them saying maybe it was time I started school. Crash. The moment I knew my life was over. At four and three-quarters.

After that, it's there in pictures of me as a kid, if that means anything. No long faces exactly, no carrying the world on my shoulders. Just neutral, null. Just another kid a bit low on the joy juice.

Fuck knows where I got it from. People are always trying to work out how they became what they are. I wasn't abused, for example. I wasn't neglected. My mum read me bedtime stories and I kicked a ball with my dad. I wasn't bullied or specially shy, or bothered about attention. Exclude the Bish from a conversation for five minutes and he'd do his party piece, head-butting road signs till he started bleeding. Or slash the back of his hand with a ringpull.

And they'd be jealous of it, imagine that. You got others copying him, except they didn't have the bottle to really go for it. Never scratch a vein like Bish did, get that tell-tale spurt. He's still got the scars. The best you can say for him is it was his idea, he wasn't copying anybody else.

Naturally I was too smart for all that. Standing out from a crowd, that's for mad people. Can't use your hand for days because you've sliced it. Except I was so smart I never did anything at all. Shoplifting you got caught, mountain biking you fell off. There's a whole list.

Ambition too, what was all that about. They get you both ways. If you're ambitious you're a cunt, if you're not you're scared to compete. Careers officer asks you and you'd invent something, any fucking job that came into your head. Acrobat. Chicken sexer. Because how could you tell them you didn't want to be anything at all.

I mean, why would you. Whatever you ended up doing, it was going to stretch into fucking infinity. You'd look at people who were middle age and think no way you were going to end up like that. Ugly with misery. Your own mum and dad. Mouths drooping at the corners, ugh terrifying. As for pensioners: oh no.

Just getting there was going to take for ever. A week's an eternity when you're a kid, so imagine how many you had to get through if you lived a long time. Just so DULL.

And there's nothing you can take for that. I couldn't anyway. You follow the football team that's top of the league, get laid soon as somebody lets you, take speed with the rest of them. But whereas Bish went on from there, i.e. the entire medicine cabinet, I got bored with it quick as anything else.

Music too, another example. Bish got into ancient R & B

because it had more blues harp in it. I hated it. Liking something your parents liked. Your parents' heroes. Obscene. I never had heroes. And recent music was just kids' stuff and wanky. So a simple solution: don't listen to music at all. One thing less to concern yourself with. Why play the same song over and over. I even used to stop eating halfway through a meal sometimes, and I wasn't usually full. Once you've had a good taste, and you know the rest's all going to be the same, why go on and on.

So when I was about fifteen I started investigating ways you could put an end to it. And it turned out there was no shortage of advice. Get this: there's a hundred thousand websites on suicide, I kid you not. Not just samaritan sites, there's tips on how to do it. But I never tried any. I mean, how hard can it be.

Anyway I'd've felt a fraud. I knew I wasn't that far gone – and some of these people really mean it. Four thousand kill theirselves every year in this country. And it's not spur of the moment mostly. They actually practise it, can you believe that. I used to read about them like they were experts in the field, like you might look up to birders with bigger lists than you.

So then it got complicated. If you don't particularly want to carry on living, and you're not cool enough to die, some serious inertia sets in. You don't learn to skate, say, or ride a motorbike, or wolf whistle. I couldn't swim or play computer games till secondary school, and if you don't vote they can't blame you afterwards. Fuck any skills training, never mind a career. I only learned to drive when Stevie Red Bus said she wouldn't take me twitching any more.

Getting to five hundred then topping yourself – goes without saying that was me playing for time. It takes years to see that many birds, and I thought I'd be grown up by then. I mean, you can't be serious can you. Kill yourself if you're terminally ill, by all means. Or clinically depressed, or money troubles. But not because you're a bit bored by it all: they'll giggle at the funeral. Never mind five hundred, you'll grow out of it by four-twenty, four-twenty-five.

But then I go and do what I've done – and now I'm stuck in this no-man's land in my head, somewhere between suicide and a murderer who doesn't want to get caught. Still, it's something I won't need to resolve. They'll come and collect me and that'll be an end to it. So if you're expecting a study of how somebody deals with the one extreme act in their life: too late, I've already done it.

What time I've got left, I always knew how I was going to spend it. Doing nothing very different. I'm not going to sell my place and go on a mad birding trip round the country or buy a ferrari. I'm not going to live every day like I'm on death row. How red a London bus is, or smelling the fucking flowers. I'll carry on as normal for as long as possible, the biggest luxury of all.

Hence the admirable equanimity I'm displaying. Hands steady as a rock, look. It's true I find it a bit hard looking them in the eye in the asian shop and so on, but then I always did. And I don't even have to see the people I'm working for today, they've left me their key.

Ah yeh, work. I talk about being my own boss and having a turnover and I say I've got clients, but everybody's a client nowadays, even when you sign on. I clean my clients' houses. I'm a cleaner. A char. I clean their sinks and bogs and hoover and dust. I do their gutters and down the backs of their sofas and the corners of the kitchen floor where everything's congealed because their previous cleaners were shit. All for seven quid an hour, which is more than the minimum wage, as people are quick to tell you. Except I do twice as much in that hour as the old dear you get from the ad in the newsagent's window. Plus it's only what it costs to clean up a kilo of farmers' pesticide, paid for by our water bills. Anyway fuck them, anybody who can afford a cleaner, the salaries they're allowed to earn.

Here I am, then. All I've got to show for twenty-five years and that A level is a ganglion on the back of my hand and the beginnings of housemaid's knee. It's not the birding that makes me a sad sod, it's getting excited by an electrolux with a thirteen hundred motor. Too smart to work for anybody else, so I clean their places instead.

There's still some daylight left after work, so I take a seventy-two bus and get off after Hammersmith Bridge and take the Thames towpath. There's a gravel car park, and a car drives in just as I get there. I take a key from the old fishing box by the lodge, go in through the side gate they're letting us use, and I'm in mecca, a.k.a. the old reservoir that's been turned into a bird reserve.

This is my local patch since I started. Barn Elms, spiritual home of West London birders. In the early days I used to climb in over the chainlink fence, dodging the Thames Water staff on the way round. After three weeks of watching me do that, they took pity on me and told me I was allowed in anyway, showed me where the front gate was. Duh.

It's all changed now, even the name. A proper wetland reserve, waldorf salads and toilets. The standard of birds went up too, but then it stopped, so my list of species for the place isn't likely to increase in the time I've got left.

The fact this depresses me so much, it all adds to the lunacy, you might think. Somebody who can't enjoy birds without making lists of them. But it's how everybody starts out. Soon as you start looking at birds in your garden, you want to know what they are. Then how many different kinds you've seen. You start a list whether you mean to or not.

Plus context is everything. What's the prettiest british bird? Say blue tit. But even the RSPB grannies don't sit and watch blue tits all day. It's the unusual birds that count, not the most colourful. So you don't even look at jackdaws in Richmond Park where they're two a penny, but one flying over Barn Elms a couple of miles away is a real rarity. That's what keeps your interest going in all the birdless days and shit weather. That's what the lists are for.

All birders keep lists. British list, i.e. the different species you've seen in this country, which is sometimes also your life list. County lists. Local patch lists. Garden lists. Year lists. Day lists. Trip abroad lists. TV lists. Birds fed from the hand list (my party piece was a coot and the end of a mars bar).

Most people keep a county list, but just for the county they live in. Only the real addicts keep lists for every county. Bish for instance. In his really mad days he drove overnight from London for a ringbilled gull so's he could reach a hundred for Powys. If it wasn't for birding, he wouldn't know where Powys was.

You need the lists, they're like putting a finger on your wrist and counting. Two hundred you lose your beginner status. Three hundred there's a few rarities in there, so you can hold your end up in conversations. Four hundred you're a junior member. Four-fifty, and people might defer to you sometimes.

Me, I keep a british list, a Barn Elms list and sometimes a year list, and I'm always looking to add to them. Like when Owen Whittle fell off the tree. He must've disturbed the sitting hen, because something big smashed through the treetops on its way out the wood. I only saw a dark shape but enough to put goshawk in my bird diary. So it wasn't all doom and gloom.

Nothing new today, but you expect that. Law of diminishing returns. Lists are best when they're just beginning.

Take this place for instance. Can't tell you what it used to mean to me. Every time you came here, you half expected to see something new. Not a lifer necessarily, but a place tick at least. So you went there with optimism, and you didn't lose it if you didn't see anything. You went back with optimism next time. You'd go home believing your life had a point to it.

And when you did see a new bird, there was a serious sense of achievement. Birders go through the motions, saying what we do is barking, but we apologise too much, in my opinion. Wanting people to think we're self-aware really, self-deprecating. But fuck them, to be honest. Seeing your first slav grebe after walking round the site twice, that *was* an achievement. And fuck any god of birds. You got it yourself, with your perseverance and experience and optimism. Walk tall, kid. You're a cleaner by choice.

But that was then. There's nothing to add to the list here, so it's just more of the same like everything else. Every time you come here now, you'll be looking back, not feeling optimistic about tomorrow.

There was a sort of pioneering spirit when I first started coming here. None of the double-storey hides they've got now. Your outline was always above the horizon, so you had to show some field-craft to get close to the birds. And it was the right place for beginners or second years. I saw my first wheatear and sedge warbler here. Lesser whitethroat, whimbrel, you name it. Doing your Knowledge.

With that sort of background, I can see a bird shoot across the far side of the reserve and tell it's just a feral pigeon by its flight silhouette. This means it takes you less time to realize there's not a single decent bird today, so you haven't even got the suspense. Alright a kingfisher, which is probably the very best british bird, all round – but I don't need it for any lists, so it's shit. No offence.

That's it in a sentence. Once a bird goes on a list, it disappears in a way. Bird by bird, so does the place you see them. So it doesn't matter what they've done to it, you were losing it anyway. There's a collection of captive species with their flight feathers pulled out, and the patron's one of the royals who shoots birds for fun. I won't miss it when I go. There's a certificate inside saying they've got a licence to keep a zoo, which says it all.

At the staff houses, there's a bird log in a wooden box. They leave you an exercise book and some old biros for filling in the date, the time you came in and out, the notifiable species you saw. I never usually have anything to put in it, but today I write down the number of lapwings so's Stevie won't get on my case next time.

On the way out, I go back past the car park. There's still only the one car in it. I can't see anybody inside, but when I walk past it the headlights come on and hit me full beam. I stand there not blinking till the engine starts up and the car drifts round, passes close by like a shark, and drives off almost silent down the road.

Back on the towpath, the willows are out in catkins with a chiffchaff singing in there somewhere. There's swifts fizzing low overhead, missing you by inches just because they can. Five hundred birds then top yourself. Those were the days. You're not going to make four-fifty now.

You'd think, wouldn't you. Having killed a man. You'd want to bay the moon. Burn the pavement with tears of blood. Something. But it's hard to rip your heart out like a black root when boats are futfutting down the river and there's a dusty pink sunset like a woodpigeon's chest. All nothing and normal. Like somebody up there wants to turn a blind eye.

I'M DOING A job top of Fulham Palace Road, so I go down early on the off chance I'll find the Bish. Stevie left me her pager, and a bluewinged teal's landed on the lake at Lonsdale Road. In shit female plumage, but a good bird for where we live. He's left his mobile off as usual.

I'll try the Posk first, the polish centre on King Street. Whenever there's enough poles in an area, according to Bish they always build someplace to congregate. Churches, etcetera. And there's a lot of poles on the Hammersmith-Chiswick border. I'm making it sound like a war zone. The Hammersmith-Chiswick frontier. Near me it's mostly kosovo and a serb caf.

The Posk's all grey concrete with steps. I try the youth centre inside and the canteen where you sometimes see him, best meatballs in London allegedly. Not much chance of finding him in the bookshop or the art gallery. Outside, past the polish import-export shop and the polish travel agent's, there's a newsagent's on the corner, the whole front window covered in cards: accommodation and part-time jobs. Bish holds court out here sometimes, there's always a dozen people looking in. Try the polish caf then leave it.

It says deli on the front, and there's shelves inside and a food counter, but they've put in some tables and a newspaper rack and a small TV showing a polish quiz show. It's cool inside and quite dark, takes you a second to get accustomed. I've been here with Bish, so the owner knows me by sight, but he's not in. There's two customers but they're both leaving. I sit down at one of the tables, next to one that's piled with boxes of kleenex. Probably better not to ask.

There's nobody behind the counter, then a girl comes out from the plastic strip curtain at the back, drying her hands on a cloth. It's not really her hands I'm looking at. This is the most stunning woman in the world, hair so blonde it's paper white, classic polish face. Alright she could be former Yugoslavia for all I know, but that part of Europe anyway. Big cheekbones and narrow eyes. Just my luck to be in my work clothes.

I was going to go straight back out but I think I'll stay a bit now. I'm trying not to stare at her when she brings me a menu. I put my workbag under the table and ask her if Bish has been in. Zbigniew. Big guy with a ponytail. 'Yes,' she says. 'He is in the toilet.'

I look through the menu like I'm actually going to order something. There's a lot of meat, mostly pork. We came here with Stevie once and she ended up with a plate of sauerkraut and a doughnut.

The girl starts clearing the next table. A bottle of beer and some leftovers, presumably Bish's. I ask her what they are, which is hardly the greatest chat-up line she ever heard but I'm a bit short of options.

'*Pierogi*,' she says.

'Oh yeh, dumplings.'

'*Pierogi leniwe*. Dumplings with cottage cheese and the polonaise, also sugar and cream.'

'Ouch yeh I remember.' I try a rueful smile in the hope it's vaguely endearing, but it probably looks like something a sheep would do. She takes the plate away and disappears back behind the curtain.

There's photos of polish VIPs on the wall. I'm watching the game show on the box when Bish bursts out the strip curtain after the longest crap in history, drying his hands on his shirt. 'Shit, you've finished my beer.' I ask him how many dumplings he's had.

'What are you, the fucking food police? I was thinking of having the *golonka* next, the pork knuckle.'

'You cannibal.'

'Oh thanks a lot,' he says. 'What sort of comment is that? I suppose you're having your usual nothing, are you? I don't know how you manage to stand upright, the amount you eat. Do you want another beer?'

The girl's come out again, a smile like the moon cracking the ice at night. What am I saying. 'Um, filter coffee please.' Surreptitious sniff, in case I've worked up a sweat walking here.

Bish asks me if I want any plum brandy in the coffee. I say alright and he tells her, I recognize the word *slivovitz*. She comes back with a glass and Bish asks me if I can taste the plums.

'No.'

'No, me neither. Just fucking firewater.' He drizzles some in my coffee then has twice as much in his. 'At least it's plums,' he says. 'You should see some of the things we make booze out of. My granny used to use red cabbage and brussels back home. What are you doing here?'

'You left your mobile off. There's a bluewinged teal at Lonsdale.'

'Yeh, Stevie told me. Have you seen it?'

'I was thinking of going there after work. What are *you* doing here?'

'Came to see the owner,' he says. 'Greg. Grzegorz. Get this: he's from my home town.'

'What, Bedford?'

'Very droll. My dad's town. Szczecinek. Try writing that when you've had a few. It's weird meeting somebody else from there, it's a really midget place.'

I have a sip of my coffee then put a bit more slivovitz in it. I ask him where Greg is. I didn't see him when I came in.

'He's gone home,' says Bish. 'He thinks his wife's been seeing somebody else. My old man always said he was paranoid. Talking of extra-maritals, have you heard the latest? Owen Whittle was playing away too.'

'Yeh, I know.'

'Oh, you do?'

'I read it somewhere. The police are interviewing husbands in his village apparently.'

'Imagine that,' he says. 'Not husband, husbands. The dirty old sod. Of course, if the police are talking to local husbands, they can't think he was shot to protect those goshawk eggs.'

'I guess.'

'If they're wrong and it *was* a birder, whoever did it must be laughing.'

'You sound like you're happy about it.'

'I don't sound like anything,' he says. 'This country can start a civil war for all I care.'

'And Owen Whittle was a start, was he?'

'How would I know? I never think about him.'

'Oh yeh? Then how do you know he was playing away?'

'It was in the paper,' he says. 'I saw it when I was looking for something else.'

'No, that doesn't compute. You couldn't stop talking about him on the way to the ivory gull.'

'That was then. Things change.'

'Shit, Bish, I never know with you. You used to talk about him all the time. Your words, not mine. And now you don't give a toss? Bollocks.'

'What did you expect? I'd be pleased because somebody did a murder?'

'When did I say that –?'

'Or the opposite? I always wanted him dead – and now he is, I'd be full of remorse? It's only Owen Whittle. We've all got other things on our minds.'

'And therefore what? You've lost interest, just like that?'

'Well you haven't, obviously. Careful, people might think you give a shit about something.'

The girl's back again, asking if I want any more coffee. I don't, so she takes the cup away. Bish says thanks, *dzięki*, which I recognize, then jabbers at her in a mixture of polish and english, which I don't. Nor does she, if her expression's anything to go by. 'She's just stunned how good my accent is,' says Bish.

I look at my watch and he says yeh it's time he went too. He leaves a twenty on the table. When he does that, there's no point offering to pay your share, he'd rather fight you first.

A group of people come in when we're leaving. They start talking to the white-haired girl in polish and one of them kisses her on both cheeks. This fucks my chance of getting her phone number, so I'll have to get Bish to introduce me. When he's not in such a hurry.

Once we're outside, he switches his mobile on. 'Call me if you see the teal,' he says.

'Listen. You said the police are interviewing husbands apparently.'

'And?'

'You said apparently. Are they interviewing them or not?'

'What do you care?'

'I'm mildly interested, alright? If that's allowed. I knew him too, remember.'

'I remember,' he says. 'I remember you never used to mention him. What's brought this on?'

'He was shot dead. That focuses your mind a bit.'

He gets some chewing gum out and offers me one but I shake my head.

'So are the police interviewing husbands or not?'

He looks around, glances at me, and says he can't remember, it was just a line in a paper. 'Anyway, fuck the husbands. If I'd done Owen Whittle, I wouldn't be thinking about husbands. You know he owed people money? Some serious sums apparently.'

'What? Who told you that?'

'Well think about it,' he says. 'How did he afford those bird trips abroad, on a cab driver's pay? He borrowed from people you shouldn't borrow from. Frostbite told me.'

'And how would Frostbite know?'

'You don't need to ask that. He's like fucking interpol, the number of people he knows. He got this from a reporter on the local paper. Owen Whittle owed money in the wrong places.'

'And what, they topped him because he didn't pay it back? Come on.'

'Oh no. He *was* paying it back. Worked seventeen hours a day and never missed a payment.'

'And this is gospel according to Frostbite, is it?'

He shrugs. 'Take the piss if you like. I'm just repeating what I heard. These people Owen Whittle owed, they won't be happy their golden goose was shot. All that interest he was paying them.'

I look around, as you do. There's some people gathering outside the polish newsagent's. Two of them walk past and give us a quick look. 'Why didn't you tell me this in there?'

'Didn't want to worry you,' he says.

'Why would it worry me?'

He comes a step closer and drops his voice, conspiratorial and irritating. 'The people he owed money to, if they think Owen

Whittle was shot to protect those eggs, I'd expect them to be
enquiring about birders, wouldn't you?'

'What, gangsters chasing twitchers? What comic did this come
out of?'

'Suit yourself.'

'Have you told Stevie about this?

'I haven't told anybody,' he says. 'Angelo, Jace, Terry Chai. I
don't know why I told *you*.'

'I see.'

'And don't spread it around. You know Frostbite, he doesn't
always filter what he hears. There's no need to worry anybody
else. I've got to go.'

'So have I.'

'Got any change for the tube? I left my last twenty in there.'

'You prat, Bish.'

We split up at Hammersmith station. I can walk to work from
here. Under the flyover and down to the rec on the corner of Lillie
Road, one of the terrace houses opposite. I get the key from next
door and put on the indoor trainers I brought in my bag. I cleaned
the soles with washing-up liquid this morning.

Being a cleaner, you're like a call-girl in some ways. There's
clients who like to abuse you by leaving the place as filthy as
possible, getting their money's worth and making some distinc-
tions clear. Then there's those who apologize for having a cleaner
at all, doing the washing up and hoovering before you get there.
Some of them just want to talk, you don't have to do much actual
cleaning. These are skills you pick up.

This lot today, they're the most extreme I've got. I only do a day a week, and I know they won't touch it theirselves – so they must have a whole army of cleaners, because there's not a speck of dust in the eight rooms. And you get strict instructions: every scrap of dirt, in every crack, however long it takes. I'm booked for two hours, and if I only manage half the bathroom in that time, they'd rather have that spotless than the whole place slightly less so. Mind you, they use me because they know I'll get it done in the time to their specifications.

They've left me a pair of rubber gloves, not to protect my hands but to safeguard their bathroom from my germs. I start by feeling with my fingers for hairs down the plugholes in the sink, bath and bidet. They never leave any, but it's best to check. I put the bathmats outside then take the bottles of shampoo and bath oil out the bathroom cabinet and wipe them with an old hand towel I brought with me, washed yesterday and aired last night. Then I open the window and dust every surface in the room. The window sill and the shelves, the top and the inside of the cabinet, the top of the cistern and the door, the back of the radiator and the underside of the toilet bowl.

I squirt some toilet duck under the rim and put a few soda crystals down plugholes in the bath and the sink and the bidet. I spray antibacterial glass cleaner on the window and mould remover on the tiles round the bath. I dab descaler round the bottom of all the taps and plugholes. I get down on my hands and knees and use an old hard-texture toothbrush to clean where the skirting boards meet the floor. I get their hoover out and do the floor with the soft brush attachment, then put it away again. I use a dust-pan and brush for what the hoover left behind, followed by the towel all over, then hoover the mats both sides and leave them in another room for now.

I get a screwdriver and an old bottlebrush out my bag and unscrew the toilet seat and take out the plastic screws that fix the bowl to the floor and the metal screws that fix the pedestal to the floor. I drop the rubber attachments in a weak bleach solution and use the bottlebrush to clean the plastic screws and the holes on the back of the bowl.

I put the toilet seat in the bath and clean it, using the toothbrush on the maker's name on the inside of the cover. I throw the metal screws in the bin in the kitchen and replace them with the two new ones they've left out for me. They filled a box with a hundred and four screws, two for every week of the year, because the worst kind of dirt is the dirt they can't see. I screw the seat back on, then scrub the inside of the bowl with their bog brush, put in the new rim block they left out for me, flush the bowl and rinse the bidet. I put the bottles back in the cabinet.

The screws are a bit over the top, and I could leave them I suppose, I can't believe they'd unscrew them to make sure. But I wouldn't put it past them to have a hidden surveillance camera, like people checking up on their kid's nanny. And anyway it's not my way. My mum and dad were the sort who brought you up to do every job to the best of your ability. Even if you're only cleaning a floor, your floor should be cleaner than next door's. Smacks of keeping the workers in their place, but it's too late now it's in the blood.

I kneel down by the side of the bath and use the toothbrush to scrub the shower attachment and scrape round the base of the taps, same with the bidet. There's still some limescale left, and I don't want to use a scraper in case it scratches the bath. I told them I'd do it bit by bit and they'll also need to get somebody in to peel off all the sealant round the edge of the bath if they don't want any mould showing, the mould remover won't shift it. There's only a couple of spots, and they're so small you almost need binoculars, but that's probably enough to bring them out in a cold sweat. I didn't offer to sort it myself because I couldn't do it to their standards.

I sponge off what I've done and use the shower attachment to wash the tiles down. I open a new packet of j-cloths and dry the window off so there's no water spots. Bog paper would do but they don't use it.

People imagine a job like this, where they reckon you don't use your brain, it leaves you more time to think, and more than I want right now. But whatever job you do fills your head while you're doing it. You concentrate where you trail the flex on a hoover so's you don't run over it and slice it through. Based on your professional experience, you make decisions about how much longer you can keep using the same scouring pad. Just because I'm only wiping a surface down doesn't mean I'm going to see Owen Whittle's face reflected in it.

You could eat your lunch out the bath, so I don't bother with a creme cleanser. Some washing-up liquid on a sponge. Melon not lemon because it hasn't got so much of a smell. I bring my own, a present from Stevie, not tested on animals. I have a slash in the bog then go round with the dettol in case some poor germ still thinks it can loiter with intent. I sponge the floor with the bleach solution and let it air with the window open while I go out and collect my pay packet.

I don't know why they've left me three fivers in an envelope, they know I don't charge seven-fifty an hour. Are they expecting me to do an extra quid's worth, a seventh of an hour? It could be a tip I suppose, but I leave a pound coin in the envelope, go back in the bathroom, dry the floor with the towel, shut the window, put everything back in my workbag, and give the key back to the neighbour. A two-twenty turns up the moment I get to the bus stop.

You've got to envy them, these people. They've got things I haven't got. They were lucky to find each other, and now they'll have their tea in their sterilized cups and saucers and go to bed together in their freshly boiled sheets and sleep like logs with all their tomorrows in front of them. Bacteria permitting, there's some serious peace of mind here. Mad as frogs, but they've never done me any harm. Anyway, from my point of view it's a good gig. The two hours go by past faster than most, and you almost feel like you've achieved something getting down to those little details of dirt, like restoring the sistine chapel. Well, maybe not.

I get off the bus and walk back over Hammersmith Bridge, warm down with a look at that bluewinged teal at Lonsdale. I'm half expecting to find Bish here, but there's only somebody jogging on the far bank and a car pulling away on the other side of the fence next to me. I follow the jogger through my bins then use them to scan the water, but there's nothing except mallards and swans.

All that stuff Bish takes is making him paranoid. Owen Whittle in trouble with loan sharks, for fucksake. I mean, what sums are we talking about here? He went on so many bird trips, did he, that he got into debt with the kind of people who go gunning for birders? I mean, read that last line again. About as likely as Owen Whittle the housewife's choice. One fairy story after another. Let somebody else worry about it.

The teal's not on the part of the reservoir nearest the first entrance, where the ducks and canada geese gather to be fed. Takes me quarter of an hour to find it, dabbling round the roots of a tree in the water. It's probably too wary to be an escape, but we still can't place-tick the little sod. It's a fucking hybrid.

WELL, IT'S HAPPENED at last. They called me into a police
station around lunchtime. Stevie's been arrested again.

It's usually me has to go and fetch her, they're not Bish's
favourite places. Luckily I'm not working this afternoon but it's
still a pain, specially as it's not like she needs somebody to post
bail. The most she ever gets is a caution.

Still, it's a tradition by now. Stevie gets nicked, one of us goes
and meets her, tea in the nearest park. You do it because she needs
it. Moral support and not just an audience.

We're sitting outside by the Serpentine Lido and I've got us a
couple of coffees from the shop, but she bought sandwiches on
the way, humous on rye, I'm sitting here pulling the beansprouts
out. 'What was it this time, mink farms or nuclear?'

She's been on one of her marches. Anti-vivisection today, Hyde
Park to Trafalgar Square. Except they were re-routed down the
side streets and there was nobody to see them, so they're only
demonstrating to theirselves according to her. Maybe she won't
bother next year.

She got herself arrested for breaking the police cordon and holding a placard in front of the Boots in Victoria Street. I say police cordon. Two plod and a female plod, and they knew her from past crimes and misdemeanours. Not you again, Stevie.

This part of the Serpentine, there's some swans and feral greylags, otherwise not much birdlife – though Stevie and me did see our first rednecked grebe here soon after we first met. We sat there with our bins and notebooks while the tourists went past, flask of coffee like a pair of old dears. Cheese rolls because she wasn't a vegan then.

'Pochard sounds like it ought to be french,' she says. 'Like mallard. All the common ducks have names like surnames. Teal. Gadwall. Smew.'

'Redbreasted merganser. Longtailed duck.'

'Very funny. Listen, I've been thinking. This might be the last time you have to collect me from a police station, what do you think? I can't see myself doing this much longer.'

I tell her I can't imagine her giving it up. It was her who said men want to fix things and women endure.

'Yeh but it wears you down,' she says. 'Your name on police computers, people thinking you're mad every time you open your mouth.'

She lobs a bit of her sandwich into the water and the black-headed gulls come in, nabbing anything the pochards miss. They all eat well when Stevie's around, no mother's pride here.

'Don't you wish you could have a lobotomy sometimes?'

What's she talking about?

'Take out the part of your brain that notices what's going on in the world.'

'Fuck, Bus, what are you asking me for? According to you, I've already had the lobotomy.'

'I do tell you that, don't I. How do you put up with it?'

'Least of my problems. What's the matter exactly?'

'I wish I was like you,' she says. 'The way you can blot things out.'

'No you don't. You'd hate yourself.'

'I don't know any more. I wouldn't mind ignoring half the stuff I think about. I wouldn't be so fucking exhausted all the time.'

'Do it, then. Ignore it.'

'Easier said. I hear about dairy herds with chronic mastitis and suddenly I can't have a cappuccino any more.'

'Then have a decaf soyaccino instead. One-fifty in Neal's Yard.'

'Ha ha.'

'You always adapt, Stevie. What's brought this on now?'

'Nothing,' she says. 'Pressure of work.' She chucks her last bit of sandwich into the water. There's no takers among the ducks, so the gulls get it all. High-pitch squabbling all round.

'Pressure of work?'

She nods.

'Not an egg collector getting shot?'

'What's that, an educated guess?'

'Bish said you were agitated about it.'

'Bish jumps to his own conclusions,' she says. 'I've hardly mentioned it.'

'Shit, not you too. You both used to talk about Owen Whittle all the time. Now Bish says he doesn't give a toss either. I give up, the pair of you.'

She's wiping her hands on a serviette. She hands me the water bottle, but fuck that.

'Alright yes,' she says. 'It's about an egg collector getting shot. It's made me think.'

'About what?'

'About me. What else do I ever think about?'

'Too fucking cryptic, Bus.'

'I haven't got time to be anything else. Come on, let's have a walk. I've got to be at St James's Park to sketch the pelicans.'

That's an excuse you don't hear every day. We walk round the Serpentine to feed the tufties near Peter Pan, which must be the horniest statue in town. They put it up overnight so's the local kids would find it there one morning, as if by magic – but two of the bronze fairies are snogging each other and another one's got her arse in the air while she's looking up his tunic.

We break up some bread for the mallards and tufties. We never feed the captive birds in places like Regent's Park, but we do it with wild birds, which is what this lot are. They might look un-dignified scrapping for bits of bread, but only to us.

'Owen Whittle,' she says. 'You've been thinking about him too, haven't you.'

'I've been trying not to.'

'Why?'

'What do you mean why? Because he was shot dead. That puts pictures in your mind and I don't want pictures like that. What do you mean?'

'Calm down, for fucksake. I was only asking.'

'You and Bish, you never fucking change. You think you're the only ones who react to anything. You talk like I'm made of stone sometimes.'

'That's obviously not true,' she says. 'Well, well.'

She hands me some of her bread and I tear it to pieces. When I've done that, she puts her hand in mine to take some of it back.

'Right,' she says. 'We've established what you're not made of. Now tell me more.'

'Oh yeh, typical. You won't talk about it but I'm supposed to spill the beans. That's fair, is it?'

'No.'

I throw a piece of crust and it hits a male pochard smack on the back. A canada goose nips in and nabs the bread before he can turn round. I ask her if she thinks Owen Whittle was scared.

'Yeh,' she says. 'Definitely.'

'Why? They say he went out like a light.'

'They also say he bled to death. Did he wake up while that was happening? If he didn't wake up, did he dream? When you take an overdose, do you dream? If you do, it can't be the peaceful death you're hoping for.'

''I think he fell from a height and passed out and didn't have any dreams. I think he had the peaceful death we wanted.'

'We, huh?'

'I didn't want him to suffer.'

She touches my face. She can lower your pulse rate doing that, with just her fingertips. 'Don't give up the marches, Stevie. It's just a nutter with a gun.'

'What does it matter to you? You've never been interested.'

'I like knowing you're out there doing it.'

She looks at her watch and kisses me on the cheek. Time to go. She gives me the last of her duck bread, but I'm going too, I've got to be someplace else. I leave her at the tube and walk over Waterloo Bridge to catch a network southeast. She'll be using her car later on, so I can't borrow it. Hence I'm taking one of those slow trains that go out through Richmond and stop at places with wooden platforms and names like Martin's Heron.

You're never really out of suburbia out here, and the odd patch of farmland doesn't set birders' hearts fluttering. Even so, Bish and me used to do this trip a lot when we first started. I came here for my first great northern diver near Sandhurst, big primitive bird breaking blue water in bright sunshine, you could see why the canadian indians revered it. The white canadians call it a loon, for the noise it makes, fucking disrespectful all round.

I knew Stevie was on edge soon as I saw her, even though the police station's like her second home. Whereas me, I didn't bat an eyelid, despite my big guilty secret. She's arrested for standing in front of a chemist's, then collected by somebody who's getting away with murder. I almost felt like telling them, see the look on their faces. I get off the train at Winnersh and take a bus to the crematorium.

There's a cemetery attached, and when I get there they're getting ready for a burial, there's cars outside the memorial chapel and people working round an open grave in the distance. Past the chapel there's an E-shape wall with metal plaques on it. I wanted to rent one once, but I was told they're already paid for. What about those empty spaces then? Oh they're where the other plaques used to be. People pinch them for the copper.

The people standing round the open grave are all workmen, and there's a little yellow earthmover near it. One of them walks over the mound of earth round the hole and gets a long plank of wood from near the fence. There's only two other people in here. An old woman just leaving, and a fortysomething geezer who got off the train with me. Heavy and fit-looking, though you could probably outrun him. Glasses with clark kent frames.

The tombstones are bigger and posher over this side, black marble shaped like double beds, probably cost a fortune. Lot of inlaid photos, mostly italians and cypriots.

Complete contrast the garden of remembrance. A row of lawns divided by yew hedges cut into tall rectangles. They've edged the path running through it with a row of single bricks on each side, inclined at an angle of forty-five degrees so's their sides face up at you. There's a small plaque on most of them with the name and details of somebody dead, plus just enough room for a one-line message, though you need good eyesight to read them down by your feet. No wonder I tried to buy a plaque.

I couldn't get one, so my mum's on the ground next to a patch of grass with no border. I quite liked the idea of putting it close to the yew hedge, where thrushes peck under the bottom branches, but really it was just what space was available. There's no one-liner on her plaque, because I told myself she wouldn't have wanted one.

I scattered her ashes on the grass just in front. The local crem wasn't what I wanted ideally, but there was no special place she asked to be buried, so this was no worse than anywhere else. The idea of scattering ashes used to conjure up a romantic image, at least to me, like a peasant woman broadcasting seed from her apron. Instead, they give you something that looks like a kettle with a knob on top and holes underneath, and you push the knob with your thumb and the ashes come out straight down. Scattered's not the word.

I also thought they'd be something like talc, falling without making a sound, soft and elegant. But they're crunchy, hissing like hail when they hit the grass, apparently because they only give you the ashes of the skeleton, after they put it in a grinder. No meat or fat or the coffin you paid six hundred quid for, which I presume they use again.

Nothing like that for my dad, who died two years later and got an oak coffin in his family plot. She's down here, he's buried up in Cumbria. Amicable separation.

She took a year to die, him three months less, in so much pain the nurses couldn't cope with his screams. And I'm supposed to care if Owen Whittle had a peaceful death or not.

Fuck knows what I'm doing here. It's not an anniversary and I'm not expecting any comfort from her last resting place. Maybe I might've done if she was buried and not burnt, her body still there at least. Except then you'd almost want to get in the grave with her.

If she was still here, she wouldn't condone what I've done, but she'd understand it. We all walk a fine line, she said once. Cuddling your little daughter, throwing yourself under a bus for her – the difference between that and abusing her is paper thin, whatever people tell you. Shit, blood, amputation, dead bodies and animals with fur: if any of the above turn you on, it's just the luck of the draw, try and believe that. The people who store their own piss in sweet jars in their council flats, there but for the grace of god. The tightrope's so thin, it's no wonder we don't all walk straight, whatever straight means.

Just her opinion, she said. No reason for me to take it on board, but she'd be failing herself if she didn't put it in front of me. And now here I am, fallen right off the tightrope, and she's not there to say she understands.

Still, ay. Being alone is being free. Everybody you care about leaves you sooner or later, then there's nobody to answer to.

I'm squatting down to check her plaque, which looks about the same as last time I was here. I could come back and polish it once in a while. You do it for a living, so it's the least you could do for your flesh and blood. But what's the point unless you do it every month or so, it'll go green regardless. And any stray soil gets washed off by rain. If I never came back again, she wouldn't blame me.

The ripples are spreading, ma. I knew I'd make ripples, though I wasn't sure what sort. Stevie says Owen Whittle made her think, but I don't know what she means exactly. People aren't telling me things any more, which isn't the kind of ripples I wanted. Time to be getting back. I'm talking to myself here.

On the way out, I see a crowd's gathered round that open grave, plus a pair of magpies looking down from the nearest tree waiting for worms, though maybe they're hoping something bigger might be left unattended. They fly off when one of the workmen kicks his boots clean on the tree.

There's always trees in these places, and with the shrub borders and long grass they're not bad for common town birds, though not as good as some people tell you. Treat your nearest cemetery as a local patch. Oh yeh, wander around the graves with a pair of bins? They'd really think you'd jumped off the tightrope.

Anyway they're overrated for birds. If they're near the coast you've got a chance, specially places like Great Yarmouth on the east coast. Inland you might get the odd redstart or ring ouzel, but not in darkest Berks. Not that I've spent much time in cemeteries, even when I scattered my mum. She didn't die during migration.

The workman coming away from the grave passes me on his way to reception and tells me one of the sides has fallen in and they're having to shore it up with planks. Ninety-year-old nun he says, smacking soil off his hands. She taught him at primary school. Pain in the arse in life, too.

The geezer who came in with me, he's been going round the gravestones like he's looking for somebody. Me, I take the long way out, round the boundary hedge, because my eyes are filling up suddenly and I don't want people seeing it.

Here's my mum dying too young while I've got my whole life in front of me and I'm letting it go. It's about the only thing she wouldn't forgive me for.

She loved life. My mum the sad sod. How can you love it when your job and marriage and health are shit. How can people have no fucking regrets.

She used to piss me off with all her relentless cheerfulness. Hiding the worst from me I suppose, except it ran in the family apparently. Her brother-in-law my uncle was dead religious all his life, praising the god who gave him parkinson's. How fucking dare they.

My not wanting to do much or go anywhere, I probably got it from her. All her life in the same pair of slippers. Till she was about to die. Then oh fuck. Suddenly she wants it all and she wants it now. Saga cruises, two call-boys at a time, writing poetry. Some really embarrassing poetry.

What the fuck for, by then. Why not years before, when it might've mattered. Why wait till you're a dead woman walking. All that life-affirming bollocks. I hope Stevie doesn't turn out like that.

There's so many tears your nose starts running and you have to clear it on the grass. I'm well away from the main buildings, so the only witness is a male blackbird foraging under the hedge. One of those with a bill that's more gold than yellow, slightly mad eye. Perfect glossy plumage of course.

See what I mean. No good birds in cemeteries.

I HAD TO work late tonight. Mrs Chauhan needed me to do her kitchen because her son's bringing his new wife home. I don't get my full rate with her, but she makes the best channa in west London even with her arthritis, and her son pretends he thinks she cleaned the place herself. I didn't get home till midnight.

Go to the bathroom first, wash your eyes out after using solvents all day. Then pick up the post and go through to the front room. I've left the curtains open and the streetlight's coming in.

The street where I live is terrace houses like anywhere else. Some of the residents parking spaces are empty because we haven't all got cars. There's only three on the other side of the road and one of them's got two people sitting in the front. At this time of night.

It's a car I don't know. The one next to it belongs to a couple of jamaican brothers, and the other one's the new people opposite. I clean their place on thursdays.

But this car doesn't live round here, and it never stays very long once I get home. I saw it at lunchtime once, after I came back from a job up the road. I couldn't tell if it followed me or it was already there waiting.

I'm not paranoid and I'm not imagining things. The car at Barn Elms, that was just somebody putting their headlights on. Nobody followed me to my mum's grave and I don't think everybody who passes my window is a plain clothes.

But this is different. I swear I saw this car, or its twin, when I went to Lonsdale Road for the bluewinged teal. A year ago I wouldn't have noticed it, but I keep an eye out nowadays.

I put the binoculars on it a minute ago but things look even darker in bins and I couldn't tell if it was two men or two women or one of each. They'll drive off soon.

I've got two phone messages, both to do with work. I log the number of the old dear who wants me to clean her flat because she can't do it any more. Dusted her own place every day for the last fifty-three years, her message says, as if I want to know. A weird generation that was. Nobody needs to clean their place every day. Dust just doesn't fall that fast. I'll do her place twice a week and she'll probably think she's living in filth the rest of the time and wonder how her life came to this.

I open a can of beer and go back in the front room. I thought of pulling the curtains but leaving a gap, peek out to see if they get out the car when I've done it. But there are limits.

I tear a black bin liner off the roll and go round the house emptying the wastepaper bins and the one in the kitchen. The bin liner's only half full but I take it out anyway.

I drop the dustbin lid when I lift it, and it rolls across the front yard. I dump the bin liner in the bin, then put the lid back. The car across the road starts up. It doesn't put its lights on, just sits there with the engine going. I open the garden gate and drag the dustbin out onto the pavement. The car drives off.

I don't look at it till it's halfway down the street and got its back to me. The headlights don't come on till it turns the corner. Somebody steps out of a doorway and walks past on the other side of the street. He gives me a wave and I give him one back even though I don't recognize him.

I go back in and finish my beer and sort through the post. It's ten days since I heard from Stevie, and now there's a letter from her, a xerox of the speeding ticket we got on the way to the ivory gull. There *was* film in that camera.

TIME GOES BY so slow it's like being back at school, specially when you spend most of it on your own. I left two messages on Stevie's machine and one for Bish, but no reply.

Nothing on the mobile and no meeting up with anybody. There haven't been any big birds even though it's migration time. Anticyclones in the wrong part of Fenno-Scandia apparently. A serin turned up at Dagenham Chase and I crossed London to see it because it was better than nothing. Bish went the day after and I don't know about Stevie. I met Angelo there but only by accident. We used to get together not just for birds, now we don't get together even when there is one.

There's been nothing new about Owen Whittle on the news or ceefax or the internet. I'm not going to ask Bish even if he gets back to me, and if I went to the horse's mouth and asked Frostbite, they'd really begin to wonder about me.

I don't want all this time on my hands, so I've been working all hours, which saves you having to think, getting home late so there's no time to do anything except eat and crash. Doing the jobs nobody else wants, like cleaning a mobile kitchen for a catering company on a commercial shoot. It was a thai curry and toad-in-the-hole day, in the middle of a heatwave. Still better than sweating it out at home.

On the way to these jobs, I read bird books on the bus and tube. No opinion required, so there's no need to think. The couple of afternoons I couldn't get a cleaning job, I cleaned my own place. Room by room, putting it in order, getting blisters using a heavy duty scouring pad. I went for a drink with Angelo but we didn't talk about anything and I drank too much so's I'd sleep.

I didn't see the car outside my place again and I thought maybe that was the end of it. Then I came out of an office I was cleaning and saw it driving off. I didn't go home that night. I rang an agency I used to work for and hoovered a hostel in Paddington.

I came back home that morning with eyes like shit and nearly fell asleep in the kitchen except I heard a familiar high-pitch trill and ran to the window just in time to catch the arse end of a wren as it flew off my garden fence up into next door's buddleia. Nice one, a new place tick for the house. Didn't think I'd be getting any more.

It puts the house list up in the mid-twenties. Alright, twenty-six. Birders are always coy about the exact numbers on their various lists, to make theirselves look a bit less mad. Talking of which, I probably reached the nadir when I saw a sparrowhawk over the street and sprinted fifty yards to get it on the house list. There were neighbours looking, but no junkie cares about that.

I went and got my bins and watched the wren till it disappeared over the fence like a mouse with a cocked tail. Its name in polish sounds like the call it makes: *strzyzyk*. The most common bird in the country, but you clock it thoroughly when it's a tick. Story of your life if you're a birder. Spying on things with binoculars. Finding out where they live, who they eat and drink with. Keeping dossiers on them.

They don't like it any more than we do. But sometimes they get used to it. Keep still enough and they might start mating in front of you. And most of them are flight animals, whereas predators aren't programmed to deal with being put under surveillance.

The easy solution would be to go down the nick at the end of the road and turn yourself in. But I won't do that. When they come for me, I'll be ready, it's what I want. But it's against my instincts to do their job for them.

I just wish they'd get a fucking move on. I get the feeling they're playing with me, like a cat with something that's fallen out of a nest. The car's registration ended in DWL, which looked like OWL from a distance. You could almost believe somebody's taking the piss.

I GOT TO talk to Stevie at last. She's going to be doing some sketching out of town, and she asked me to go with her. It's just up the road off the M25 so I said alright. I've got a quiet day today.

When we get there, there's one other car in the car park. We walk between the river, the railway line, and a disused conveyor belt they used to use for shifting gravel, if you can picture that. Then you're surrounded by trees and nobody's going to bother you.

It's hot as hell again. The only clouds in the sky are the straight lines left by a jet, and the light's so strong the leaves on the willow trees look white on the other side of the river. I'm in shorts and baseball cap and Stevie's buried under factor twenty.

There's no birds so far, except what passes for a chaffinch's song. But we haven't reached the right place yet, and in the meantime there's reeds encroaching from the riverbank and whacking great yellow irises and buttercups the size of custard tarts. As soon as there's any shade, and I mean just twenty feet of it under a tree, you get speckled wood butterflies. Things you only start noticing when you accompany the Bus on her sketching trips.

When I say she asked me along on this one, I might've been exaggerating slightly. She didn't want me here at all. She didn't even want to tell me she was going out.

She picked up the phone for once, and I said we ought to meet up, it's been ages. I knew Bish was away rehearsing, so she wouldn't be seeing him. I told her I wasn't doing anything today, which wasn't true. I had to rearrange a full day's work, it nearly cost me a new client. She said she wouldn't have much time to natter, she's got a whole chapter of drawings to do, for a new field guide. But come along if you want. Fucking good of her.

The path comes out through the first lot of waterside trees and runs along the edge of a flooded gravel pit. The path's better here because the fishing club maintain it. They nod at you sometimes, or tell you they've seen a kingfisher, like they think we're all on the same fucking side. There's none of them here today.

You've got swallows and sand martins chasing insects over the lake. You always check if there's a hobby up there, hunting them like a scimitar, a bird that makes the word falcon so good. Respect to the small but perfectly formed homicidal maniac.

The path takes you away from the lake and through some open grass with rose bushes the size of your garden shed, some with pink flowers, some with white flowers with yellow centres. Willow scrub and the odd poppy, a primeval look to it, dead white branches sticking up out the grass like antlers. I say primeval. The burnt out car's been there since I started coming, out of place here where hardly anybody goes. The locals walk their dogs somewhere else.

So there's no litter and everything grows to sizes you don't normally get. Dock leaves five foot across and mega daisies and the grass never gets cut. Leave it fifty years, they say, and the whole country turns to forest again. This'll do, says Stevie, and we sit down in a gap in the scrub by the side of the lake.

She's not here to draw birds this time. The surroundings instead, for those pencil backgrounds you get in bird paintings. She's sitting with her back against a tree while I'm looking around but only now and then, there really is fuck-all about. This is one of the few places in England you can guarantee smew in winter. Tiny white ducks like porcelain in all that excalibur green. But not this time of year, when there's nothing on inland waters except coot and great cresteds. Lie back and sunbathe.

Meanwhile her pencil's an extension of her arm. She's like Bish's drummer like that. Drummers can't stop drumming. Give him a biro and he'll do triplets on his thighs, or coffee cups, or the steering wheel when he's driving and you're in the back.

Same with her and her sketching. On the tube, in a caf, in the bath. The first time we met, she was doing speed drawings of a great spotted cuckoo on the south coast, a life tick for both of us. I introduced myself by showing her my own sketch of it, two circles for the head and body and a long rectangle for the tail. Perfect, she said. It's all you need for field notes. Michael fucking angelo.

It was Bish who christened her Red Bus Oxford. He couldn't be arsed to remember her surname and she was working for a wildlife mag at the time, catching the Oxford Tube bus outside the Ken Hilton.

Since then we've had all the comments. What the three of us get up to. Everybody wants to be around Stevie and her red hair. But it's like Bish said: she's one of the boys, so you can't think about her that way. Allegedly.

Maybe I've been giving the impression she's some kind of self-taught amateur who got into illustrating by accident. Actually she went to St Martin's School of Art and had paintings in the academy exhibition. Then with a career in front of her she suddenly packs it in and starts drawing blackbirds instead. Three months working on a book of garden birds.

I never understood why. That's my fault probably, but you should've seen her before. I was there when she'd get skunk drunk and smash beer glasses on pub tables. For the randomness of it, she said. What shapes came out and whether she got arrested or not. Then she'd do something not random with the pieces. Her graduation show had a ten-foot sculpture made out of broken glass. Bish spent half an hour staring at it –

She's put her bins up suddenly. So do I, but you can't see much through all this greenery. Take the bins down and wait for movement with the naked eye. What did she see?

'Fat bloke,' she says. 'Watching us with bins.'

'Another birder probably. Where was he?'

'Other side of the gravel pit. I've lost him.'

'No, he's there. See the tallest tree. Left of that. In the round gap.'

Birders get good at giving directions. If there's a rare bird in a bush, you put people on it quick or risk getting lynched. So this fat bloke's easy. Specially as fat's the operative word.

Even at this range, with bushes in the way, you can see he's twenty stone, you could fit both your thighs in one leg of his shorts.

He's kitted out like a great white hunter and his safari shirt's sticking to him in this heat, a floppy hat hiding his face. His bins cost seven hundred quid, except he's wearing the case as well, like somebody who's bought expensive bins before he's seen many birds. He disappears in the trees and doesn't come back though I keep a look out. My bins cost a fraction of his but they're alright for spotting fat blokes.

'Are you sure he was watching us? Not just looking this way?'

'How would I know?' she says.

'Well how long was he looking?'

'I don't know that either. He was already using his bins when I saw him.'

I keep scanning the far bank, but the plant growth's too thick. I tell her he's probably checking if we've seen anything. He doesn't look like he finds many birds for hisself.

But I'm already talking to myself. She's buried in her sketch-pad again. She's already scrunched up a couple of sheets of paper and dropped them on the grass, which is unusual for her. Normally she just turns over the next page and starts again.

She's probably in a hurry as usual, there's always a lot to fit in. She does a full day's work on the illustrations and she's got a social life worthy of the name. Plus, unlike Bish nowadays who just moans about the state of everything, she actually gets out there and does something. Shaking cans outside tube stations, manning stalls at environmental fairs, the odd demo. Sometimes very odd.

When she found out mcvitie's used fish oil in their biscuits, hoovering up the sand eels puffins feed on, she went to a rally outside their head office. Other people went too – but only the Bus walked there through the City wearing fishnet tights and a giant mask shaped like a puffin's head, asking directions on the way.

Here she is with a life full to the top, and mine's always been the opposite – so why do I always feel like putting an arm round her?

That difference between us, I felt it most when I was standing in front of her sculpture made out of broken glass. Her graduation show was about sacrifice, something that went back to the pair of cousins who gave up their way of life to bring her up when her parents died. I wasn't there the day the cousins came down for the exhibition.

There was one piece she made out of parallel strips of metal you were meant to run your hands along, with different numbers of spikes. For two different kinds of sacrifice, the blurb said. Men traditionally fight wars and go back into burning houses for their kids, whereas women make small sacrifices every day. But the next piece contradicted it, a photomontage of the first woman suicide bomber in Gaza, an ambulance driver routinely shot at by israeli troops, same age as Stevie when she died.

Meanwhile the glass sculpture was about giving everything up for something you badly wanted. A bit of a crude idea, she said, which we all thought was false modesty once we saw the piece.

The broken bottles were fixed together with their jagged edges facing you, so's you couldn't touch any of the smooth sides without cutting yourself. You'd see people reaching over the rope barrier then whipping their hands back, all aware of our bodies suddenly.

Bish stood there staring, and everybody assumed it meant more to him, being an artist of sorts. Except it was me who never got it out my head. I didn't say anything at the time and I can't tell her now, specially as she doesn't want to talk and her sketching's shutting you out. Sticking her tongue out in concentration, her pencil attacking the paper. Busy busy busy, keep back keep back. Tell me how you break through all that.

I might be able to if I was sleeping with her. I believe that. She'd talk about anything then. If I'd woken up with her red hair in my face recently, Owen Whittle might still be around. That's one theory.

It's a bit late for that, so you might as well take what you can. 'Stevie, I need some sleeping pills.'

'Here we go, only calling me Stevie when you want something.'

'Bollocks, Bus.'

'If you want sleeping pills, go to the fucking doctor.'

'I don't want him asking a lot of shit questions. You must have a week's worth someplace. And not those fucking herbal sachets. I want to crash out properly.'

'Pills give you a desperate sort of sleep,' she says. 'Anyway what do you want them for? I didn't know you used them.'

I tell her the job's been getting me down and she says so that explains it.

'Explains what?'

'The way you've been recently.'

'The way I've been? It's the way you've been. What do you mean recently? How recently?'

'Couple of months,' she says. 'It feels longer.'

'And what have I been like?'

'I haven't got time,' she says. 'I've got to finish this by tomorrow or they won't pay the next instalment.'

'Two fucking minutes, Steve.'

She stops drawing and wipes her hair away where it's sticking to her neck. 'Distant,' she says. 'Remote. Self-absorbed. Taciturn. Twitchy. Uninterested. Forgetful. Mean with your time. Slightly underweight. I haven't stopped, I'm just pausing for breath.'

'Fucking hell Bus, no need to sit on the fence. You've been thinking all that? I didn't know I'd been any different.'

'Well you wouldn't would you. You've been distant, remote, self absorbed . . .'

'Yeh. I suppose I have.'

The sweat's tickling down my back. The sort of weather that reminds you you've got a coccyx. The side of her hand's leaving sweat marks on her sketchpad. She asks me if it's really the job that's getting me down.

'Yeh, what else?'

'It's been bothering you so much you need sleeping pills suddenly? It's not exactly a job you're in love with. Why's it getting to you now?'

'Twenty-fifth birthday. Rest of my life as a fucking cleaner. Can't be that hard to understand.'

'Can't be that hard to talk about,' she says. 'Better than swanning around on the surface and paddling like fuck underneath. You could've said something.'

'Bus, you've had something on your mind too. I honestly didn't think you'd have the time.'

'Of course I've got time,' she says. 'What did you think I was going to do, laugh at you?'

'No, you wouldn't laugh.'

She rubs her fingers on her sketch to do some shading then looks across at me, but I'm making a daisy chain. 'Go on,' she says, 'tell me.'

'Drop it, Stevie. It's only the job.'

'I want to hear about it,' she says. 'Except not now, I've got to finish this by six-thirty. I'll make room for you later. Fuck, that didn't come out too well.'

'It's alright. Let's go, you've done that drawing to death.'

She puts her stuff back in her bag and gets up. She says she's not giving me any sleeping pills, they're fucking dangerous. Let's go and find the groppers, they ought to be showing soon.

We're walking beside a stream where there's reeds in the water as well as on the bank. So much veg the reflections make the water look dark green even at close range.

We cross the stream on a fallen willow trunk. Soon there's a big hedge of rose bushes in among some hawthorns, which makes it a really thorny place, you catch yourself on assorted things spiky. But once you're through you're in a semi-enclosed space, size of a small garden, marshy most of the year but dried out today. Small rose bushes and tussocks of tough grass, the secret place where the grasshopper warblers live, groppers in that irritating shorthand birders use, the birds we've come here for.

I'm wiping the sweat and sunblock off with my cap. There's a mixture of sunlight and shade in here because the rose bushes are different heights. Stevie sits down and starts sketching again while I open my rucksack for something to drink. We listen out but there's just the gruh-gruh-gruh of a reed warbler in the distance.

I put the bins up. Not for the reed warbler but in that direction, following the gaps between the rose bushes. Have a swig of water then stand up for a better look. Stevie's got her head down sketching. I go out the enclosure and follow the stream under the trees.

I'm back in the area of grass and bushes and branches like antlers. Nostalgia written all over it. This is where the three of us saw our first scrubland birds. Whitethroat and lesser whitethroat, a great grey shrike one winter. And I thought I'd died and gone to heaven when I found a river warbler at the end of my first summer.

Lifers fall into three categories. Tick (because you tick it on your list), supertick, and fuckinghellwhatsthat. River warblers are definite fuckinghells in this country, really rare vagrants from eastern Europe – and nineteen-year-old beginners are *not* supposed to find them for theirselves.

But I did. Definitely. I recognized the song and tracked it to a particular bush and made all the mental notes and ran back to fetch Stevie and Bish. Naturally by the time they got there the little darling had flown off – and they weren't in a hurry to believe me. I'm still waiting now.

Fuck off the pair of you. I saw the undertail and everything.

What did it look like?

You know what it looked like. Scalloped all the way down. And I had the sun right behind me. You're not talking me out of this one.

Grasshopper warbler's got a scalloped undertail.

But the tips aren't as pale, are they. Anyway I heard it call. Zit-zit, zit-zit, like those sprinklers in Hyde Park.

Grasshopper warbler can sound like that. You know how ventriloqual they are.

I tried telling them I knew it was a river warbler by its jizz, just its stance and behaviour, you could see it was a locustella not an acro. But they wouldn't have it. They said I wasn't experienced enough to be certain. Stevie of course, she'd sketched river warblers in Romania.

God dear, was I furious. Bish saw the look on my face and gave me a wide berth. Even now I'm thinking how dare they not believe me. And I don't buy that talk about me being inexperienced. Deep down they still think I was stringing it, telling a deliberate lie. And for what, pray? To impress the perfect pair? Prats. Just as well I'm the forgiving type.

I've reached the stream again. I've never stopped scanning with the bins – and now there's something at last, the reason I came back out here.

Our fat bloke's reappeared, walking on the waterside path. Now you see him now you don't through the trees, but he's a lot closer this time, you can see his safari gear's got a sort of army camouflage effect with all the dark sweat patches. I come out onto the path by the stream and let him see me.

We never get close enough to have to nod to each other. And he stays on his side of the river and I stay on mine. His hat's still hiding his eyes but you can see his mouth's permanently open in the heat. He disappears again. When he comes back out through a gap in the hawthorns, he finds me walking almost parallel. When he crosses the next patch of open ground, he sees me picking black-berries. In the end, he starts making his way back to the car park. The last time I see him, he's a long way off, the sweat patches still showing, in and out the trees like a speckled wood.

You could hit those patches from here, he's that big. You could use them like targets. They say when you shoot somebody the body sort of breathes out. You can hear the air escaping if you're close enough, feel it on your face even. This huge sod would be like pricking a zeppelin, so you'd want to be this far away.

And that's me all over. I don't do close-ups. I wait till you're a safe distance away with your back to me. Then I leave you lying there haemorrhaging, with fear in your dreams. And tell myself it's all in a good cause.

A cormorant's flying across the next flooded pit, craning its neck like a black concorde. On the way to stuffing its face at the nearest trout farm presumably. Fuck their profits up a bit, though not as much as they claim. Go on, my son. Get some in before they pass the ammunition.

With the bins, you can see Stevie before you get back to her. She's put the sketchpad away and she's lying with her eyes shut, frowning in the sun like a little kid. She's lying on her side and I can see she's wearing one of Bish's earrings.

I never like keeping my bins on people for long. It's what made me nervous with Owen Whittle. Smacks of peeping through some-body's bedroom curtains, and you always think they can see you as close as you can see them. But she's still got her eyes shut, so I keep watching her.

I prefer her like this. I used to worry about thinking that, as if I liked her better when she looked like a little girl and wasn't talking. But it's not about that. When she's like this she's peace-ful, and I've never thought of her as peaceful.

I get back to the enclosure and sit down next to her. She doesn't wake up, so I pick up the bits of paper she's screwed up. Two half-finished drawings of pelicans, obviously the ones from St James's Park, curled up with their huge beaks under their wings. I scrunch them up again and leave them there, then lie back and doze. I must actually fall asleep, because when I look up next she's dripping water out the bottle on the palms of her hands, rubbing them together and patting her face. She holds out the bottle for me and gives me a smile, like she's about to start trying harder.

'Are you sure the groppers are here yet? I didn't hear one while you were away.'

I tell her it's alright, Frostbite saw one at the weekend.

She takes the water bottle back and has a drink then screws the top back on and wipes her mouth. 'What do you think,' she says. 'Should I pack this job in?'

'Here we go again.'

'Yeh well fuck you too. It's alright for you to tell me how shit your job is, but when I do the same you turn your fucking nose up.'

'And you're fucking surprised? Look, on the way back here I

told myself I'd listen. Whatever's on her mind, pay attention and don't get pissed off. And then you start by talking about work and I think shit I've heard it all before.'

'You poor thing.'

'We go through this every couple of months. Last time it was your job's no better than mine, the hourly rate's about the same. This time: fuck knows. Stop me, Stevie. I'm not being fair.'

'No it's alright,' she says quietly. 'Looks like neither of us can handle anybody else right now. For the record, I only mentioned my job because you wouldn't talk about yours.'

'Right.'

'And I thought if we started talking about mine, we'd get back to yours in due course. The conversation would have a natural flow to it. The best laid plans, ay.'

'Do it, then. Tell me why you want to pack yours in, and we'll talk about mine after.'

'Good,' she says. 'I get to talk about myself first.'

This time her smile makes you want to kiss her. Try that, why not. Kiss the face off her. That red mouth that never needs any lipstick. That anger of hers would turn to oomph soon as you touched her. Seize the fucking moment for once, you know she wants you to.

Yeh, well. Have an apple instead. Go on then, why does she want to pack the job in?

'Owen Whittle,' she says. 'Since you already know.'

'I only know what you told me, which is nothing so far.'

'It's very simple and very stupid,' she says. 'It's made me question what I'm doing. Somebody feels strongly enough to shoot an egg collector out of a tree, meanwhile I'm drawing pictures of birds for a living.'

There's a family of longtailed tits jumping from tree to tree. Tails as long as their bodies and no beaks to speak of. A breeze starts moving the willow leaves in the distance, but it's not reaching us. I undo the water bottle and spill some down my front.

'They don't know Owen Whittle was shot because of the eggs.'

'Yes they do,' she says. 'They must do. Nobody buys this story about jealous husbands.'

'Alright, but listen to yourself. Somebody shoots him and suddenly there's something wrong with drawing birds? You're not the useless one in that scenario.'

'Yes I am. I've always thought I was wasting my time. This has just confirmed it.'

'It's something you do really well, Steve. I thought that was enough.'

'That's because you're no good at anything.'

'And that makes me the lucky one. I know, you said.' I have another bite of the apple. What's she going to do, give it up?

She shakes her head. 'It's the only way I can earn a crust,' she says. 'I'll just have to live with it. I don't like the thought of you paddling under the surface.'

'This is where we talk about me, is it?'

'It's that part of the flow.'

'No, it's too sudden. You can't just say a few words then hand over to me. You must've thought about it deeper than that.'

'Let's just say I've distilled my thoughts into very few words.'

'Too slick by half. You're doing it again, avoiding the fucking issue.'

'God,' she says, 'why does it matter so much? What do you want me to talk about?'

'Everything. I want to know exactly how a shooting can make somebody question the work they do. I want to hear what you think of whoever shot him. If you've got any mixed feelings about it. And why it's so hard to talk about.'

She's been fiddling around in her bag like it's a place to hide. She emerges with a small tupperware of black cherries and shares them out. They work. They shut me up. I eat two at a time and throw the stones under a bush. You never know, a hawfinch might find them.

'Your paddling under the surface,' she says. 'Did Owen Whittle make you think about your job too?'

'In a way.'

I look across at her but she's got her sketchpad out again. 'Are we ever going to talk about it, or don't we do that any more?'

She's squinting up at the treetops. 'I don't know,' she says. 'Things never stay the way you want them to.'

'And that's my fault. I know.'

She shuts her eyes at the sun and pulls her hair back, using the sweat to stick it behind her ears. 'Me not talking to you,' she says. 'Does it make you feel lonely? Worse than being on your own?'

'Yeh.'

'Is that why you went for a walk just now?'

'I was keeping an eye on fat bloke. He's gone now.'

'What for, if he's only a birder?'

'He's an egg collector. I wanted him to know I was onto him.'

'An egg collector? What did you do?'

'I tracked him. He saw me watching him, so he left.'

'You tracked him?'

'I let him see me.'

'An egg collector,' she says. 'And you let him see you. That constitutes a result, does it?'

'What do you expect, a fucking citizen's arrest? You saw the size of him.'

'Where's he gone?'

'Fuck should I know?'

'He's looking for nests someplace else,' she says. 'All you've done is stop him looking for them here, for one day. Were you just talking bollocks earlier on? Did the whole Owen Whittle thing pass you by?'

'You'd rather I had a gun, would you? That would've stopped him collecting any more eggs. The Owen Whittle solution was alright by you, was it?'

What's that look she's giving me. Why do people give you looks? They expect you to skip a beat, do they? 'Letting him see you,' she says. 'It just doesn't seem enough.'

'I know. That's why I took his car number. I'll give it to the police on the way back. I know their environment people.'

'You arsehole,' she says.

'You don't approve of that either?'

'Letting me give you grief like that. And all the time you've got his car reg. You tosser.'

'I would've told you earlier but you jumped down my throat.'

'You total tosser. And you call *me* a drama queen.' She has another swig of water like she's angry with it, then turns a page in her sketchpad like she wants to inflict pain on that too. Smile if you think you're hard enough.

The steam's stopped coming out her ears. 'How did you know he was an egg collector?'

'He had his binocular case on him.'

'Tell me more, detective.'

'Only egg collectors carry them around like that. Like Owen Whittle.'

'Well well.' She has a swig of water and starts tying her hair back. 'He must be mad,' she says. 'Fat bloke. He must be very brave or thick as shit.'

'Why's that?'

'Going around looking for eggs when Owen Whittle was shot dead not a million miles from here. You'd think he'd stay indoors, the fat fool. One dead egg thief should be enough of a deterrent.'

She hands me the water bottle. 'You did good getting his car reg. Listen.'

'Apology accepted.'

'No, listen. Gropper. He's been singing the last couple of minutes.'

'You daft cow.'

We stand up to get a better view over the enclosure, staying where we are even though you're always tempted to shuffle the bushes and get them to show theirselves. Grasshopper warblers can sit deep in scrub for hours. This one's bolder, probably because it's too cool in the shade. In five minutes he's perching on top of a rose bush, mouth wide open for an eternity, turning his head for the ventriloqual effect.

All our breeding warblers come from Africa and Asia, and they're all dull to look at, not like the americans. But they make up for it with distinctive songs. Grasshopper warbler sounds like what you might expect, a buzzing trill like a high speed drill in the distance. It's apparently the first kind of sound you lose when your hearing starts to go.

This one turns to face us sometimes, showing his big orange gape. Oily olive plumage, streaks on the back, that subtle lemon throat. Like raptors but in a different way, you never get tired of seeing them. Stevie agrees.

She started sketching it soon as it appeared, getting it all down before it dropped out of sight again, her eyes going up down up down. Then it's gone and she stops drawing and says good, now come on, I've got to be somewhere.

It's cooler on the way back, the shadows are longer. The other car's gone when we get back to the car park and she comes over to me with her sketchpad.

'I really do need to get back,' she says. 'Otherwise I'd stay and talk. Can we take a rain check?'

'Yeh, whatever.'

'No, not whatever. Can we?'

'Only if we talk properly. You still haven't told me everything.'

'Getting fat bloke's number,' she says. 'Here's your reward.'

She's showing me what she's been drawing. Everything she does is good, but today she needs me to say so. 'It's brilliant Bus, really great.'

I take it and turn it the right way round, and it's a drawing of me, head and shoulders in half-profile. She's dolled me up a bit, but otherwise perfect, and all with just a few pencil lines. I say so myself, but it's the best thing she's ever done.

'I couldn't get your legs paddling under the surface,' she says. 'But the rest isn't bad. You should cut your hair though. Remember I used to like it short?'

She's standing close up. Hot body smell, sweat under her nose, the greenest eyes. One of the boys, my arse.

'You know what?'

'Tell me,' she says.

'It *was* a fucking river warbler.'

FUCKING TYPICAL. I was so worried about being late I got here too early and had to kip in the car. Then I overslept and didn't wake up till the sun was out, and now it's probably too late. Waste of a day when you haven't got many left.

I've parked in a dirt space by a metal gate separating two fields. The sun's still low and cold, sending my shadow across the road, up the hedge and into the field beyond. I put my jacket on and stand looking over the gate with my bins.

I hate places like this, specially so early in the morning. Acres of rye grass and terrible yellow rape. They get paid for grubbing up hedges and paid for putting them back. Except the ones they put back are thin and crap for wildlife. They only do it so's they can collect another subsidy. They'll leave a stubblefield and tell us it's good for winter birds, except they spray it. They spray everything.

So what am I doing here if it's such a hell hole? Well, even our fucked farmland occasionally turns up important birds. This is one of the top places in England for seeing honey buzzards. There's a famous watchpoint up in Norfolk, but we leave that to the beginners. This is more secret and we think of it as ours.

It's one of the best names on the british list, honey buzzard, though it's a bit poetic for what they actually do. They eat the bees not the honey, and even that's not their usual grub, they mostly feed on ants and ant larvae. When they find an ants' nest they don't eat them all, they leave some to multiply and restore the population. Farming them, in other words. Smart birds, a lot of people's favourites.

That's down to the usual combination of being rare and hard to see. We've only got a few breeding pairs left, and you only ever see them in flight. I don't know anybody in Britain who's seen one feeding on the ground. We've all seen them on video, digging out a nest or circling on the thermals over Sinai in their thousands or shotgunned out the sky over the Straits of Messina.

I even know their name in polish, courtesy of Bish. *Pszczolojad*, from *pszczola*, a bee. Or *trzmielojad*, from *trzmiel*, also a bee. Very helpful. I stand around scanning the sky for twenty minutes, even though I suspect they're not around any more. I'm here as a monitor.

They haven't been seen since they arrived in spring, and rumour has it that the farmer's had his way with them. Poisoned them on the nest, most likely. He wouldn't risk shooting them in broad daylight. He's been seen going into the wood where they nest, and there's only one reason he'd do that.

Honey buzzards eat insects like I say, not his precious pheasant chicks. But nothing surprises me about landowners any more. If you're a bird with a curved beak, you might as well have a target tattooed on your chest.

The morning's getting warmer, hence the male yellowhammer that's started singing in the nearest hedge. Nice bright yellow, but not what you want right now, specially not if it's going to keep this up all day. Tweedle tweedle tweedle twee. Torture. It's listed as a-little-bit-of-bread-and-no-cheese in the books, but whoever wrote that must've spent a night spliffing with Bish.

A car slows down for the crossroads round the corner. Silence for a bit, except a sound so far away you can't tell if it's a tractor or a four-wheel-drive. I get the rucksack out the back, lock the car, open the gate and go into the field. I've got a baseball cap to keep the sun off, and enough food and water to last. Vigilante with salad sandwiches.

I don't bother putting the bins up straight away. Honey buzzards are big enough to see with the naked eye. Sit by the hedge and contemplate the glories of England in summertime.

I really do hate it out here. You do most of your birding in the countryside, but everything I'll miss when I go is in town. The way a London hoppa bus cuts its engines when it takes a long bend, the world war statue at Paddington, crossing Battersea Bridge after playing poker all night.

But it's easy making a list like that. Truth is, the city's got nothing to beat. What they don't tell you about the country is how downright fucking *boring* it is. If I lived here, I'd have topped myself years ago. Stevie says when she paints in London she's always finishing off with the colour black. Out here it's blues and yellows, by the sea it's mostly white. But both of us prefer the black.

I get the water out the rucksack and have a drink. The first birds appear in the distance, flying across the top of the nearest wood. But it's only rooks. Might as well fast-forward, there's only going to be more of the same.

I'm pretty sure I fell asleep with my eyes open this morning. I know I never took them off the sky. With a species like this, you have to keep looking, you can't rely on hearing them. Birds of prey do call, high-pitch and peevish, not a sound you'd expect from something that can tear the liver out of things. But I've never heard honey buzzards make a sound – so I've been putting my bins on every bird I couldn't identify immediately. Anything flying in the distance looks like a raptor, woodpigeons being the worst culprits. I've had my sandwiches and chocolate and half the water and been for a slash three times. Sum total of the last five hours.

A car drives up from the main road and stops next to mine. I'm looking through the binoculars and nobody gets out. It stays there with the engine on for a second, then drives on round the corner. I check my watch, put the rucksack on my back, go over to the metal gate, and start walking across the next field.

I'm keeping to the edge like I always do when I trespass. Some countries in Europe, you're allowed on farmland, but it's never been like that here. Nearly all the land's privately owned, so you have to hop over hedges and sneak around your own country. Anybody sees you, they could use their criminal justice act on you, but even they know that's a hammer to crack a nut.

At the end of the second field, there's a small wood. When I get near it, I flush some birds but they're all female pheasants running back into cover. There's some movement at the corner of the wood. I wait and see if anybody shows, then walk over there along the side of the field. Just a group of cows. You can see my car from here. The sun's still warm on your back. A landrover starts up and I walk towards the noise, still hugging the wood.

Far end of this latest field, there's a hedge that's so thin you don't have to go right up to it to look through it with bins. The landrover's parked in the field the other side, but I can't see the driver. Scan around and still nobody, luckily no dogs. I stay where I am and eventually somebody comes out the ditch the other side of the front wheels.

That's got to be him, the farmer. Flat cap pulled right down. They told me he's losing his hair, so I presume he's protecting his head from the sun. Except he might be casual labour for all I know, I don't know enough about the workings of a farm, like who's allowed to drive the landrover. He gets a rake out the back of it and disappears down the ditch again. I walk round to get the sun behind me.

He might stay there another hour for all I know. Somebody else might turn up to help him. I'm looking for a gap in the hedge when he comes back out the ditch, wipes his hands on his vest, throws the rake in the back, and drives alongside the ditch till he gets to an open gate, then out. I follow the hedge round and cross the farm track on the other side of the ditch.

He's only gone as far as the next field. It must be his day for working on ditches: by the time I get there he's poking around in the bottom of another one. I'm looking along it and he's got his back to me, sweat in the body hair between his shoulderblades. Then he stops what he's doing and comes back to the landrover.

And I know it's him now, definitely. He's taken his cap off to wipe his head, and he's balding from the front.

This is Fredu Caruana. He used to run a bar in Malta but he sold it to buy this small farm. Soon as we knew he was maltese, we thought: trouble. They shoot everything that moves over there. The place is littered with shotgun shells and you're lucky if you see a single wild bird, no exaggeration. Looks like he's after ours now.

If he's already shot these HBs, then shooting him won't save them, obviously. And I don't believe in punishment for punishment's sake. So what do we call this? My attempt at a deterrent?

I mean, Stevie was right about the fat bloke we saw at the grasshopper warblers: you'd think he'd be more careful. Egg collectors have the same sort of network as birders, and fat bloke would have known all about Owen Whittle being shot. Yet there he was, not long after, back out there feeding his addiction. Same with our maltese friend here. So maybe one dead villain isn't enough.

Except I'm not sure that's it either. The fact is I don't know what I'm doing here. I seem to be evolving from deranged egg protector to Confused Of Shepherd's Bush. I've even started daydreaming of getting away with it and carrying on like nothing happened – but then I also put the gun to my head once, at the kitchen table, staying there so long I had to put it away because you feel a bit daft after a while. I've tried imagining what a police marksman's bullet might feel like. Head as well as chest.

This is something they don't tell you about. You hear of people getting a taste for it once they've fired the first shot, and I wondered if that might happen to me – but nobody tells you it could end like this, in simple fucking confusion. The real reason I'm out here right now? Fuck knows. Because he's there. And the honey buzzards aren't. I don't know the reason. Fuck the reason. What difference would it make to him, knowing the reason? What matters is here I am. Here I fucking stand.

Fredu Caruana's round the other side of the landrover and I can't see him for a second. I'm assuming he might be changing his boots, but when he comes round this side of the landrover he's holding a pair of bins in both hands, giant twelve-by-fifties by the look of them.

In the back of my mind, I'm already planning what I'm going to say when he comes and feels my collar. Except he's not even looking this way. He's pointing his bins up in the air. When he keeps them fixed on one spot, I follow where he's looking. Takes me a while to see anything more than clear blue sky, but then I fix on a pair of birds right overhead, so high they're just dark dots.

Common buzzards. I don't know if he knows that, but I do. The way they hold their wings in flight. More birds with curved beaks. He's probably wishing they were in range.

He puts his bins in the landrover and drives off again. Christ, where to now? Whatever he's been doing in these ditches doesn't take very long. I follow him in my bins in case he comes straight back, then I set off round the next field. I called this a small farm, but it's not if you're on foot.

I don't like where this is leading. I can see the farm buildings from here. The palms of my hands are sweating onto the bins as I keep scanning the skies in the faint hope.

There's nothing up there and fuck-all on the deck either, where all the life's been nitrogened out. This latest field of short corn is like a scalp that's been treated for nits: no insects or voles and therefore no birds. Compare and contrast places in the med, where there's so much insect life the swifts come down to strafe the tree-tops and the birdsong goes on all day. In the great british countryside, the silence has you looking over your shoulder.

I can hear the landrover stopping again, just round the last copse before the farmhouse. Because of the way he's laid out the barbed wire fence, I'm having to walk out in the open to get there. What if he's watching me through those massive bins. He might have a shotgun on the back seat. My pulse is finding some novel places behind my ears.

I follow the barbed wire round the edge of the copse and stop at the far end. I can see the landrover but there's no sign of him. There's no ditch here, far as I can tell, so what's he doing? Stay where you are and use the bins.

I still can't see him – then there's a sudden movement to the left. Just a male pheasant creeping out the copse, but it scares the christ out of me for a second. Piss off my son, before somebody shoots you.

I'm following it with the naked eye – and that's how I see friend Fredu again, through the long grass round the edge of the copse. Sitting with his back to a tree, shoes and socks off in the shade. Having his tea.

I'm shooting him left profile. Bending over his food gives him a double chin that makes him look older. His stubble used to be black probably. In the bins, I can see he's got half a ciabatta and a piece of salami and some cheese with holes in. He's cutting the bread with a penknife, for all the world like some peasant in the med – which is what he is, I suppose. Vest and hairy forearms. There ought to be vines and olive groves, not a birch copse he planted for the subsidy.

He looks knackered. This is a small farm and he works it with his hands. There's a wife and kids in the farmhouse and I saw a common buzzard earlier on. They're coming back to this part of the country because farmers aren't shooting them so much now. Put your rucksack away and piss off back to the car. You'll want to miss the traffic back to London.

Yeh, well. Have a listen before you go. You won't hear anything, the birdsong died out years ago. Most of the birds on our red alert list were put there by farmers. Partridge, corncrake, corn bunting, stone curlew, lapwing, turtle dove, barn owl, song thrush, skylark, tree sparrow, linnet, our friend the yellowhammer. Told you birders need lists. Stevie and Bish know this one backwards.

Add honey buzzard to it, it's rarer than goshawk. Fucked by agrochemicals like everything else, or by one man's poison. Bish came here last week. Frostbite's been here, and most of the others. We know the birds arrived in the spring and now they've disappeared. So I'm not being judge and jury on the evidence of a single morning.

The sweat's coming in at the sides of my eyes. He's unscrewing a bottle of tango apple. Somebody opens a window in the farmhouse and he looks up. The rucksack weighs a ton and my fingers feel like quarterpounders when I take it off.

I'm squatting with my back to the line of trees, so I'm facing back across the field. I can see him out the corner of my eye. I'm kneeling down and opening the rucksack, and I'm looking into the sun, so anything that moves is just a silhouette. But silhouettes are alright in this case. I glance up – and get hit right between the eyes.

I don't need my bins. I said this species is big enough. Big and unmistakable and a fucking godsend. The relief comes up and squirts blood into your face and fingertips.

In the books, they don't look very different from common buzzards. In the field, only beginners confuse them. Buzzards fly with stiff wingbeats, kill-that-rabbit, kill-that-rabbit. Honey buzzards can't be arsed with all that. They go around like aerial lounge lizards, wings flopping like fops, loose and louche, as if they're only out hunting because it's the servants' day off.

There's two of them too, so it's the breeding pair. They must've moved their nest site since last year, so you can only see them if you trespass deeper into the farm. If he'd wanted to poison them, nobody would ever have known.

Instead he kept quiet about them so even the birders wouldn't disturb them, and now they're up there as living proof, Mr Cool and his Mrs, the best two birds in the world.

They're only visible for twenty seconds, and they're too far away to see any colours or the stitching on their undersides. But that flight pattern's more than enough. Relax, everybody, the cavalry's here. They'll never know how glad I was to see them.

When I get back to the other end of the field, I look through the bins, and our maltese friend is cutting hisself a piece of salami, concentrating hard on the task. Twenty years working all hours in a smoky bar, in a country where there's hardly any soil and they kill all the wildlife – you'd give that up for this. Daily bread, sweat of your brow. I can hear a woman's voice calling him from the farmhouse when I climb over one of his fences and walk back to the car.

I'm in no state to drive just yet. I take the baseball cap off and pour half a bottle of water over my head. I take my top off and use it to wipe myself all over, then put a new one on from the back of the car. I take my shoes off and stick my socks on the car roof, then dribble some water on my feet and wipe them too.

I get some sunglasses out the glove compartment. An old pair of Bish's, big like flies' eyes. I sit on the driver's seat with the car door open and my feet out on the grass verge. I drink the rest of the water and eat all the food: an onion bhaji and a crunchy oat bar and two bananas, whacking the body sugar up because I never felt so fucking shattered.

I'm staring ahead. The far corner of this field's turned into a mini replica of an ancient hay meadow. Longish grass, some cornflowers and poppies. Walking about in it, just their heads showing most of the time, there's a pair of grey partridge.

Common as pheasants once upon a time, but not since farming practices changed, now you're lucky if you ever see any. There's not much grey on them. The male's got an orange face, red-brown stripes down his flanks, and a purplish horseshoe mark on his belly. You flash sod, you. The female's dull and brown as usual.

I go over to the hedge and (how's this for fieldcraft) I puke quietly so's not to scare the partridges off. I puke three times and stay there because I've got the shakes. Eventually I go back and swill my mouth out and sit in the car.

Call that the relief gushing out. And the horror. I didn't feel like a monster after Owen Whittle. I tried to, how's that, but I couldn't. But now, after what I was planning to do, without a scrap of evidence – imagine if I hadn't glanced up at that moment, or if I'd seen the honey buzzards after I'd done it. God above, how did I get like this? Go into a police station when you get back and turn yourself in. Or get the gun out at the kitchen table and go through with it next time. Before you do any more damage.

The landrover's back, accelerating somewhere behind the trees. I have a last drink and get up when the socks are dry. Shut the car door quietly before you drive off, but the partridges are on the move anyway, heads bent as they creep off through the long grass with the sun going down, another species on its way out.

I know the feeling, fellas.

I DROVE THE rest of the day. By the time the sun went down, I was down south again, going up a half-hidden track onto one of the Surrey commons. The car park's a patch of cleared dirt inside a fence made out of pine branches. From here you walk up onto the ridge and you can see halfway across the county. Me, I always stay close to where I've parked, looking down the path through the heather towards the conifer plantations.

I'm a bit early and there's an untidy sunset at the end of a day when the rain's only just stopped down here. A magpie's been doing its castanet cackle since I got out the car, but that's not exactly what the doctor ordered. I'll probably have to wait another twenty minutes and even then what I'm waiting for might be gone by now. I'm useless at dates.

Ten minutes later another car comes up the slope and parks near mine. There's always families coming up here, or birders look- ing for the same thing as me, but that's normally earlier in the year.

There's two of them getting out. They're both younger than

me, looking like they might be students. One of them's really tall. It's darker now, the sun's gone behind the conifers, so these two get very close before you can see they've both got bins. One of them asks me if there's been any sign.

'Not yet. They're still here then?'

'One was seen yesterday,' he says. 'Briefly in flight, not on the wires up here.'

I ask him what time is it and he looks at his watch. 'Twenty past eight. Apparently they usually show by now.'

'It's so light they'll probably wait till quarter to. Where's the best place nowadays?'

'Could be anywhere,' he says. 'This is as good as any, but we'll have a look up on the ridge. If we see them first, we'll give you a shout.'

'It's alright I'll hear them from down here. Thanks.'

They walk up over the top of the hill. I wait a minute then move along the fence, looking inside their car on the way. I've got the feeling I've seen the tall one before. Probably some bird reserve somewhere. I come back to the fence, face downhill, cup my hands over my mouth, and make a purring trill by rolling my tongue.

Birders are always doing this kind of thing, trying to attract birds by imitating them. Warblers are supposed to be the most susceptible, they can't resist pish-pish noises apparently, though I never understood why: it's nothing like any warbler I've ever heard. Which is probably why it doesn't work. Which never stopped anybody trying it.

The sound I'm making isn't right either, but it's worth a try sometimes. If you want birds to come to you, it helps if you speak their lingo. Mind you, the right accent obviously helps: nothing's happening here. Plan B with this species is to put a handkerchief down on the ground and clap your hands, and I'm not making this up. The clapping's like the noise they make with their wings and the handkerchief's supposed to remind them of the white patches on their wings. I've never tried it myself and I'm not going to start now, specially not if these two student types are looking. I walk in the same direction they did, up the steps and onto the ridge.

From here the hill drops steeply on the right, down to some army buildings surrounded by a wire fence, out on their own in a clearing like the alamo. Beyond the buildings there's a hill going up to another ridge, everything covered in heather and short pines, divided by sand tracks that look very white in what's left of the light. No sign of the two birders. Scan with the bins but it's too dark by now, just a reddish glow between the clouds low down, like light through a mouse's ear.

Then the great sound starts up at last, what the books call churring though it's nothing like the noise you make by rolling your tongue. Imagine a geigercounter going a hundred miles an hour, really odd and unearthly, you'd never believe a bird could sound like that. It's coming from where I was standing in the first place, so I go back to the car park and listen.

The geigercounter's stopped, which is always good because it means they're about to fly. Sure enough, the first wingclaps start up not far from the fence, and I can just make out the pale patches when one of them flits across the front of the conifers. I manage to get my bins on it just in time to see it flip over the treeline.

The white marks on its wings and the tips of its tail sides look like the lights on a plane. Nice one. My first nightjars for two years, with all the usual oomph.

They get the name from the noise they make (night chur). There's more of it in the distance, and I climb over the fence and follow the path up. The sand's damp from all the rain.

The sound's coming from a small patch of pines on the right, a place you can't get to without walking through the heather, so I stay on the path till I get to a crossroads, where the sand's ankle deep. The trees are silhouetted against what's left of the light, and I can see one of the birds perched on the highest branch, no more than a shape, balancing with its long tail. Then the sound stops again and it flies but I can't see where.

I'm trying to follow the direction it took when one of the two birders appears in the bins and I take them down from my eyes because I can't see where his mate is. This one's coming over towards me and I start walking in the opposite direction till I've got a line of trees at my back. Now turn round and scan like I'm looking for the birds. He's gone and I stand there and wait.

It's always quiet up here, just the rurring of traffic in the distance and a dog barking down the hill. The heath at dusk, its best time of day.

One thing these two students aren't is egg collectors. The nesting season's finished and anyway they're not carrying any of the right gear. So where have I seen the tall one before? Where's the other one gone? I don't remember them on a twitch –

Suddenly, out the darkness right behind me, there's this almighty terrible scream. Alright it's more of a loud too-ook, but it still scares the fuck out of you. Your heart really does smack into your throat. I turn round like the victim in a horror film, listening for every creak in the dark, only to be terrified by something harmless like the neighbour's cat. I forgot nightjars make this weird noise when they fly.

There's two of them right here, flying round and round me no more than twenty feet away, that famous bouncing flight. Again, the books don't quite get it right. Like giant moths, they say, which is close enough – but really they're like those terrible cheap effects you get in science fiction films from the fifties, bobbing up and down on invisible elastic, wings held up like rabbits' ears. Clapping and geigercountering, birds from another planet.

Just now though, at these crossroads, places where ghosts met up in medieval times and blues singers sold their souls to the devil, you can see why people used to imagine they were spirits of the dead, specially when they whoo as they float past. But friendly spirits and sort of vulnerable, like everything else on the heath.

And they do their bit in exchange. I heard somebody say once: you can't think about your troubles near water. Me, I can't feel low around birds. It wipes your mind clean just watching them. I used to come up here when I was at school. Two trains then hitch a lift. Something thrilling about birds that only come out at night. Catching a night bus home, you felt you were one of them almost.

I came out here with Bish once, in the days when he actually did anything. He spent a fortnight guarding their nests at night. I did it just the once. Too much like hard work. With all the birds you can see on long summer days, he brings me out on the graveyard shift.

116

I asked him why he did it, him and Stevie. Why campaign for birds and beasts when there's so much human shit going on? Poverty-related diseases in London and we're supplying half the world's landmines. Meanwhile him and her are guarding nightjar nests.

Look at it this way, he said. We might think experiments on animals are acceptable, right? If they lead to a cure. But that's only our view, as humans. The animals presumably don't agree – so do we win the argument just because they can't take part in it? Who stands up for them if we don't?

I said animals don't expect anybody to stand up for them. In the survival of the fittest, they're at our mercy – and that's the view an animal would have. That's not as clever as it sounds, he said. It's an excuse for standing by and doing nothing.

I'm standing still so's not to spook these two nightjars, and they fly off in the end. Another one starts churring in a different part of the heath. They seem to be the only ones left, which is fine, three more than I expected at this time of year. I thought they'd be back in Africa by now.

Nightjars aren't fuckinghells in most people's book, you wouldn't normally travel hundreds of miles to see one. But then again you can get tired of big ticks all the time, they don't really add much emotionally. You can't share a sense of place with a species that's only been here four or five times. Good for your list, but that's about it.

Plus a lot of the rare migrants you go and see are dying, flopping to earth after crossing three thousand miles of ocean – and you're watching them in their last throes. You'll get four hundred people crowding a country lane on Scilly, scrummaging for a view of an american cuckoo, knowing it won't last till nightfall because its stomach can't cope with european caterpillars. You'll feel genuinely sorry for it, but that won't stop you writing it up in your notebook. Ghoulish. Oh well, they die whether you're watching them or not, so where's the harm, I suppose.

Nightjars are a different category. Not rare strictly speaking, but uncommon, and summer visitors only, to a limited habitat. Like the other heathland specialities – hobby, woodlark, dartford warbler – they're barely hanging on here as breeding birds, so it's always a relief when you see them. And they only come out at night, so you get a touch of mystery thrown in. People used to think they drank the milk out of livestock (their latin name means goatsucker). That's the sort of thing they believed in the countryside. And they keep telling us to leave it in their hands.

The sun's completely gone by now, black clouds streaked over a paler wash, silhouettes of pointed trees. Stand still and listen out, but there's just an itchy silence, like being back at the office on your night off. I put the bins on what might be a nightjar in the middle distance, but turns out to be a bat close up. You'd have to ask Stevie what species. I'm watching it flying around when there's some scrunching in the heather and one of the birders, the tall one, steps out in front of me.

I'm standing where I can look both ways along the path. The other one's still not showing, so I ask him where he's gone.

'Over the other side of those pines, for a closer look at one on a branch. Did you get good views?'

'Had them flying round my head.'

'Oh brilliant,' he says. 'Got quite close myself. I forgot they make that strange call. Actually I've been coming here a week and this is the first time I've caught up with them.'

'What, anywhere?'

'Oh no,' he says. 'But I've never found any on this common. My girlfriend lives nearby, so I really wanted to see them here. Looks like you brought me luck.'

'Right. Hope your friend gets his close view.'

'He's been seeing nightjars here for years. This might shut him up at last.'

He walks past me and disappears in the dark near the cross-roads. I stand and watch then carry on walking up the hill.

I've got close to the nightjar in a tree, it couldn't hear me walking in the sand. It's silhouetted on the end of a branch, such a big head it looks top-heavy, like it might snap the twig and fall off.

You can smell the change in the conifers since I got here. A by-product of birding is you learn to use your senses more. You can smell these trees drying out, unlike the Owen Whittle planta-tion. You scan horizons, which you never do in town. You notice changes in wind direction. You can hear an ant pissing on moss at fifty paces. Alright I made that one up.

Weird, but I don't know if this bird can smell me coming. I've never heard of a bird hunting by scent. You can fly, goatsucker, and we've all envied that in our time. But can you smell the roses, we wonder. Too busy counting moths probably. Another hundred tonight or you won't get your body weight up for migration.

This is the closest I've ever been to a nightjar, I swear I can feel the draught of its wings and see that fucking great gob open as it flies off. It does one more fly-past over my head then flutters off into the night. I start walking back towards the car park.

So was the old mojo working tonight? Well, the souls of the blues singers did their best, with their wingclaps and crazy whoo-whoos. But it was too much to ask and I'll have to look elsewhere. There's something I should've done ages ago.

Back in the car, I don't put the headlights on till I've finished reversing and turning round. On the way down the hill towards the road, I see the other geezer at last, caught in the lights on the side of the road. I check him in my rearview, and he's watching me all the way down the track till I'm out of sight.

I come off the M4 after Heathrow and end up down a short street with a narrow house at the end. There's a rugby pitch behind it, a backdrop of trees, and just one light on, like one of those ads for scotch in the highlands. When the front door opens, it feels like walking into a seedy motel room but with the smell of bread baking.

I'm looking at a pair of marigold gloves and a face at the end of its tether, which gives you hope.

'Fuck this, Stevie. It's time we started sleeping together again.'

WE'RE DEEP INTO summer now, but the mornings are still monkey cold sometimes, specially in this steady easterly that's been blowing the wet in off the North Sea. A really faint drizzle, like an aerosol, the kind birders hate because it gets into *everything* – gloves, bins, every seam in your clothing – while you stand there and take it. We're doing that right now, standing around taking it, even though the bird we came here for is either long gone or was never here in the first place. So naturally we ought to be pissing off home where it's dry. Ha.

There's thirty of us left, hard core only, the ones who'll still be hanging around hours after the bird was last seen. We're standing in a single line looking out over a flooded pit, a few still checking its shoreline but most of us stamping our feet in the shingle or getting mars bars out, swearing at the weather. Scopes and tripods lined up like artillery even though the little gem's probably somewhere over Biscay by now. Not for the first time, we're getting rained on for nothing.

Two more people show up, at the mouth of the footpath

leading from the lane where everybody's parked. They're hurrying over, undoing the legs of their tripods, and even when they realize nobody's on the bird they don't slow down, they'll be telling theirselves we've seen it so well we're resting our eyes. Even when they know the truth, they'll still stand around, sharing the disappointment as much as anything, which is something you can handle if it's communal. The one thing you *don't* want is to get there and be gripped off, every other fucker seeing it just before it disappeared.

The two of them are setting up their scopes and asking when was the bird last seen. I don't recognize them, so they're probably local dudes, the kind that always look nervously optimistic, scopes with the latest goretex covers. They know enough of the dos and don'ts not to be seen looking through a field guide, but they keep one in the car.

The heavy birders meanwhile, we look like a different species with our shit-coloured clothes and our scopes covered with masking tape or even plastic bags. And you can spot us without all that, we're the ones who've learned how to look like we don't give a toss, standing around chewing the fat as if we've seen the species a dozen times – when in fact we're the ones who drove halfway across the country for it.

Frostbite Temple's here for instance, the ace hitch-hiker, who's seen every rarity in the last six years though he's on the dole. He's been getting lifts by faking that limp so long it's probably become a real one. Next to him, Terry Chai the bird illustrator, swearing in chinese, then Angelo Cane who does his own tattoos, including the rock thrush he found in Suffolk, except he got the colours back to front because he had to be pissed to do it. And the one and only Jace Babb, biting his nails down to the moons, his weekend already ruined.

Most of us who do this hobby are mildly stark staring, but Jace is the undisputed king, completely fucking radio. He's the only one I know who collects dead birds as well as ticking live ones. He keeps their remains in a glass cabinet, seventy species so far, pigeons' heads and massive great gannets' wings and his prize possession the torso of a fox sparrow. He asks people to save him anything their cats bring in.

He even named his daughter after a rare bird. Isabellina Oenanthe, an izzy wheatear, he took her to see one when she was eight months old, holding her above the crowd in the rain at Portland Bill. His wife pleaded with him to christen her Penny if he insisted on a bird's name (Penelope's the latin for wigeon) but he said no it was too ordinary. She stopped having kids after that. It's useful having Jace around, reminds us how we could turn out if we don't keep the brakes on.

Mind you, it's probably hereditary. His mum called him Jason because it was the first letters of every month from july to november, and his three sisters are called May, June and Julie. They never go out together. He's trading bird tales with Bish right now, I can hear them from here, both bareheaded in the rain.

I've been wondering where Bish keeps disappearing to. He's come back from the other side of the hawthorn hedge this time. You'd assume he's been taking something, except he's always been happy to share that around, and today he's been going off on his own.

I turn round and scan the edge of the pit on the off chance. The bird we're here for is the kind you can miss in all this shingle. A solitary sandpiper, all the way from America. Stevie's already seen one, the jammy cow, so she didn't bother coming. She's had four more lifers than me in Britain, so this was one I was hoping to get back. If I don't, the worst thing is having to face her fake sympathy when I get in.

We hate this bird by now. For not being there, for the fact it can fly away, the vacant look on its face. Even its name: solitary sandpiper. Most sandpipers are fucking solitary.

Days like this remind you you don't even like birds, if you're honest, you only do it because they're convenient. You'd rather do mammals, but there's not many species and they're mostly nocturnal because of what we do to them. Butterflies: even better. You could almost believe in a god because of butterflies, why else are they so beautiful. Except there's only sixty on the british list and they only come out in summer. There's too many moths, and some dragonflies you can only tell apart by their genitalia, and even I'm not that sad.

I wander over to tell Bish I'm going for a walk. There's a couple of small pools on the other side of the shingle ridge.

'No bigger than toilet bowls,' he says. 'I've had a look, don't bother.'

'Makes a change from standing still. I'll shout if I see anything.'

Now the mist's gone, you can see the horizon all the way round, though horizon's a fancy word for acres of shingle with a few hawthorns and dwarf willows, the whole place still looking like the gravel workings it was till recently. Beyond the horizon, there's a track the gravel lorries used to use, with a few miniature pools at the end. Like Bish says, useless for waders, but you never know. That tiny bit of hope is what keeps you playing the game on days like this. Birds fly away but they sometimes fly back.

Crunch through the shingle then. Find a hawthorn big enough to stand under, and leave the bins under your waterproof. You didn't come here to look for the bird, just to have a few minutes to yourself.

I'm no good in a crowd suddenly. Specially this crowd. Forget everything I've been saying about them, these are normal people. They run their own business or they're somebody's dad, they live by moral codes. I dread them thinking ill of me.

Except they would and they wouldn't. They're friends of mine. They'd be appalled by what I've done and never forgive me, but they'd also let me use their priest holes. I've been lucky in a lot of ways.

I could do with a fag. I don't smoke, one of the million things I never bothered trying, but I wouldn't mind starting now, I gather they keep your pulse rate in order. And my shoulder's killing me from work. Buy a nicotine patch on the way back.

Or see this solitary sand instead, that would do it. Birders talk about needing a bird. They don't ask you if you've seen a solitary sandpiper in Britain, they say 'do you need solitary?' And we do need solitary. Just when you let yourself believe birding's the new rock and roll, you're reminded what a stupid kids' hobby it is, no better than stamp collecting or coins, which is definitely not the next big thing. You put a spin on it by linking it to the hunter-gatherer instinct, but you're not convincing anybody.

Why does somebody like Stevie do it? Keeping these stupid lists. I thought artists were supposed to be above all that.

Fuck no, she said. They're the *real* list-makers. Rows of soup cans and marilyn monroes, self portraits at different stages in your life.

So I'm an artist then, am I?

You're a collector, she said. An artist's best friend. I'll paint that solitary sand and you can buy it.

Back to the present – and there's no sandpipers to paint. Plus the drizzle's the same over here and I've had my break from the madding crowd. Time to rejoin the other planespotters.

A bird photographer's turned up with his monster lenses, heroically optimistic in this weather. Plus a couple of the new young turks, all going over to Bish, who's plentying as usual. He's hot under his rain gear apparently, he's been telling everybody his scrotum's sticking to the inside of his thigh, more information than we strictly need.

Look at the way everybody behaves round him. I get on well enough with them I think, but with him it's actual hugs and kisses, like they'll be healed by touching him. Partly it's because they know he'd give them the shirt off his back, which he did on Shetland once when they left Terry Chai's luggage behind. I'd do the same, except they'd suspect I'd want a receipt.

Typical birding crowd when you look at it. No women, no blacks, couple of them still doing it in their sixties, still not modifying their behaviour, still farming their women. Hope to die before you get old and end up like this.

Mobiles and pagers keep going off, but the birds are all crap.

Nothing more irritating than seeing semi-common stuff on a pager when you're dipping on a mega.

'Alright, bed wetter?'

This is Frostbite's traditional greeting for me when there's an audience. Jace Babb offers me an extra-strong mint. They're in the middle of another stage in dips, discussing previous twitches. Bish is giving them an extended rundown on the ivory gull, what an easy twitch it was, just sitting there waiting for us. The congregation are all smiles because they've seen one too.

And you remember why you do this, in all the rain and lunacy. For a few hours every now and then, you're not a cleaner or a telephone banker or somebody who drives cars to showrooms. You're free of shit clients and ungrateful kids and partners who won't go down on you and debts. Your opinions count here, you're an expert. You're a bed wetter because of ten cans of lager and a sleeping bag in Shetland, not some childhood affliction. Angelo Cane says hello hello in a music hall voice. What's all this 'ere then.

He's looking across at the top of the ridge, where two police are suddenly walking down the shingle. Flat hats and waterproofs. Bish tells me they've come to arrest me.

'Fuck off.'

'For impersonating a birder.'

The two police walk along the edge of the pit and round behind the line of birders. By the time they start coming down our side of it, Bish has gone again, over a hump of long grass behind us. Like I knew he would.

People used to think Bish was always on the brink of topping hisself, by any means possible. Keeping tippex thinner in his pocket so's he could sniff it on the way to school. When somebody told him six hundred mils of alcohol is enough to kill you, naturally he took six hundred and fifty. I never took drugs like Bish. Bish never took drugs like Bish.

He won't live to be thirty, they said, specially when he took up base jumping for a while. You put a mini-parachute on your back and jump off something like the Park Lane Hilton, anywhere that's only just high enough to survive. They had to dodge security to jump off the Nat West Tower. He could've gone to Norway, where it's legal and they jump off enormous great cliffs, but that was too easy.

And he was never stoned when he did it, that would've been missing the point. Me, I used to pretend I didn't believe he ever did it. They didn't make a chute big enough to take his weight. Come with us next time, he said. I'll give you a piggyback.

How could anybody think this was some kind of death wish. It was the opposite. Obviously. Bish thinking he was untouchable. He'd live for ever and the parachute was just a fashion accessory. I used to feel small and pale around him, proud he wanted to know me, though you'd die rather than tell him that. And now look at him.

I've been concerned about him since we were kids. Take any subject you like. When he does session work, for instance, they pay him less than the going rate if they can, and he just accepts it and turns up again next time. Be my manager if you're so bothered. Thanks, I already clean up enough people's messes.

Women too. According to him, they only have to hear him

play to go down on their knees in front of him, he's forever giving you all the gory details. But I worry it's never going to happen the way he wants, he usually finds some way of cocking it up.

Case in point. There was one he really liked. She was talking about marrying him and I think he was up for it. Then one night he asks her to take her cap out while they're in the middle of it – the most romantic thing anybody ever asked her, she said. Except it turns out it was hurting his dick – and next day he tells her he doesn't think he'll ever want kids. Then he wonders why she won't see him again. What an einstein.

He comes back while the police are still here. You can only see their hats in the crowd. He comes over, wiping his bins and putting the rainguard back over the lenses. What's he been looking at?

'Fuck-all,' he says. 'Chiffchaff while I was having a slash.'

'Is that why you've been disappearing all day? Having a slash?'

'Come and check next time.'

'Answer the question or talk to somebody else.'

'Yeh,' he says, 'having a slash. One slash after another. Happy now? Six at the last count.'

'But you haven't been drinking anything. Have you got diabetes or something?'

'Cystitis, since you ask so nicely. Had it since this morning.'

'Cystitis? What, as in cystitis?'

'As in fucking agony,' he says. 'What are you smiling about? Don't tell me you never get it.'

'You can't get it. I thought only women got it.'

'Alright then I'm a fucking woman. I get it after sex sometimes, or too much salt in my food. I'm dying for a slash all the time, then nothing comes out.'

'This is your way of telling me you had sex this morning?'

'My cock's on fire,' he says. 'You're supposed to drink gallons of water, but it makes you want to piss even more. If that solitary sand doesn't come back, I'm going to kill somebody.'

'Here.' I hand him my water bottle but he can't face it and I put it away. 'Don't tell these cunts,' he says. 'I'll never hear the end of it.'

The two police are talking to somebody in the crowd. Jace Babb comes over and says it's probably somebody's car blocking the road, there's no room in these country lanes. One of the birders goes off with the police. That's who we should be shooting, says Bish, not the Owen Whittles.

'Owen who? Here we go, the Bishop's in his pulpit again. Put the police up against the wall.'

'Yeh, do that,' says Bish. 'Who do you think the landowners call in to keep you off their grouse moors? When the foxhunts stop you using rights of way, it's these fucking stormtroopers who turn a blind eye. The boys in blue that's really black. Try it one day, see what kind of country you live in.'

'You're all talk, Bish. Shit, here it comes.'

It's raining now, the real thing, coming down so hard it makes a drumming noise on the waxed jackets and machineguns the lake. Everybody's swearing and getting under cover best they can, and it makes people's minds up for them. The dudes all leave, sheep from goats, and there's less than twenty of us left, some of the teenagers coming over to be near the inner circle.

But even we can't take much more of this. The solitary sand's gone and the rain's giving us an excuse to piss off. Normally we'd stick it out, three hours in a downpour if need be, on the basis that you've got to be in it to win it. But today it's fuck this let's go, we can always come back if it's relocated.

We start undoing our tripods, shaking the rain off this and that. 'Hey,' somebody says, 'where are we going to go? Better be somewhere with a hide.'

'There's two shore larks up the coast,' says Jace Babb. 'If they're not showing, there's always a chance of some vizmig with all these easterlies. They've got a hide there.'

'Some what? Talk english, Jace.'

'What did I say? I can't open my mouth these days. What did I fucking say?'

'When did you start using words like that?'

'It's the fucking argot, you ignorant twat. The necessary jargon. Vizmig. Visible migration. Everybody knows that.'

'We know what it means,' says Bish, winding the key. 'We're saying it's bollocks. It's what new birders say when they want to sound smart.'

'You hypocrite prick,' says Jace. 'You say beemac, don't you? You don't say bimaculated fucking lark. You say RB flicker.'

'No I don't,' says Bish, 'I say redbreasted fly like everybody else. Vizmig, what's that? A new kids' comic?'

This causes Jace to emit a few of his favourite phrases, which has everybody falling about as always, specially when somebody tells him they're saving him a dead blackbird they found in their guttering. Little things and little minds I suppose, but you need it sometimes. Bish is carrying Jace's scope for him while he puts his rucksack on.

Everybody starts trudging off down the lane leading back to the cars, the rain hissing through the hawthorns. Angelo's pissing everybody off with his descriptions of the solitary sands he's seen in Ontario.

Frostbite comes up alongside me. 'Here, the Bishop's not ill is he? He hasn't got fucking bulimia or something? How much *has* he put on, the fat cunt?'

'Half a stone in the fists alone,' says Bish behind him, smacking his head with just enough force to flick his hat sideways. Then he turns him round and holds him by his collar. One hand's enough to tilt him sideways.

'Don't call me a fat cunt any more,' says Bish. 'Cunt will do. I mean, a cunt is insult enough, yes? Cunt is worse than prick. What does fat add to it? Fuck the fat. From now on just call me a cunt, alright?'

'Anything you say, Bish.'

'No, you say it. You're a cunt, Bish. Leave the fat out.'

'You're a cunt, Bish.'

'Thank you. Now go and order me a pie in the pub. Better have one yourself, your ribs are showing through your jacket.' Frostbite waits till he's a safe distance away before muttering about taxpayers' money and harmonica players moonlighting while they're drawing the dole.

'Here,' says Bish.

'What's that?'

'Those pills you wanted.'

'I don't need them any more.'

'Have them anyway, our bass player won't miss them. Just don't take them all at once. Come and see us play for a change. You'll like it, they've got a late licence and clean bogs. We might even do requests.'

We're nearly back at the cars when a lightbulb comes on over Jace Babb's head. 'Hey wait a minute, you said LRP an hour ago. According to you, you should call it little ringed plover every time.'

'Ah yeh,' says Bish, 'but rules are for the use of wise men and the guidance of fools.'

'Oh really? Well sit on this with your wise arse. And keep an eye out for visible fucking migration while you're at it.'

Even in summer, if you've spent half the day getting soaked to the skin there's nothing like a hot bath. Right down deep in it, with only your head showing. You're full of tabouleh and custard apples and there's a bottle of southern comfort by the bath. You want another ten minutes of this before facing the world, but the world comes in and starts taking her dressing gown off. 'Oh no Bus, there's no fucking room. I want to keep my shoulders under the water.'

'Poor baby. One day I'll call your bluff and leave you in there on your own.'

'Shut up and get in.'

She wasn't there when I got back, and the first thing she did when she came in was head-butt the kitchen door. 'Don't come near me,' she said. 'They've cancelled the commission.'

'Fucking hell. They're still going to pay you, aren't they?'

'Too right they are. But I was hoping it would lead to more work. I need the money. Cunts and fuckers.'

She'd already chucked her coat on the banister and unpinned her hair, and she started doing a striptease as she went up the stairs, dripping molten lava on every step. 'That's the second cancellation this year' (takes her top off). 'Maybe someone's trying to tell me something' (tights, almost tripping over the top step). 'Bunch of suits deciding my future prospects. Fuck this thing' (undoing bra). 'Meanwhile I can only afford my own place because my mum died. It's not even work I want to do. What are you following me upstairs for?'

'Admiring the view.'

'Idiot. Where's that bath oil I gave you?'

'I let Jace have it.'

'What? Don't do things like that, it's like giving chanel to a chimp. He'll probably drink it.'

'His wife liked the sound of it. And I don't use bath oil.'

'Now you fucking tell me. That stuff costs money.'

'That's better.'

'Yeh,' she said, 'me with no clothes on. Get out of here, I'm filthy.'

'You're angry again, that's better. Pack it in because the job pisses you off, not because it beat you.'

She turned the taps on then walked towards me, flicking her fingers dry.

'You agree I should give it up, then? You could cope with that, could you? I'd be hanging round the house all night.'

'It's alright, so would I.'

'Drive you mad.'

'Do that already.'

Her forearms were wet on the sides of my neck. 'I'll have a bath after dinner. What are you making?'

'I only just got in, I'm knackered.'

'You've been twitching, I've been working. What are you making?'

'Couscous and three veg.'

'Not bad for a beginner,' she said.

'I'd better have that kiss now, before you taste it. And stop moaning. You never have any trouble getting commissions.'

She flicked water in my face and I went downstairs to make the sauce. If Bish could see me now.

I'm sitting up to make room for her now. She's bought some fig soap, which is all well and good except the fig grains scrape your arse in the bath. She's brushing her teeth, but not with normal toothpaste because it's made with cows' hoofs. Hers has got myrrh in it, like the three wise men. Even her washing-up liquid's made with aloe vera, so there's no escape.

She gets in the bath and puts her hair up and lies back facing the same way as me, back of her head under my chin while I'm ladling the water to keep her tits warm. She takes a sip from my glass of southern comfort and warms it in the bath.

If moments like this glue you together, it's because they're underpinned by the familiar marathon sessions in bed, trying to do everything all at once, as if each one's the last chance we'll get. Which, when you come to think of it.

'What do you think of Suffolk?'

'Good birds, shit public transport. Why?'

'I'm thinking of moving,' she says.

'Not all the way up there?'

'Not anywhere yet. I'm just thinking about it. Anyway I can't go just now, there's still some work to do.'

She picks a jar of arnica up off the floor and starts rubbing it into my arm. She's gentle enough but it still hurts, the result of scrubbing somebody's bathroom with a green pad yesterday, the same action over and over. The muscles in my forearm feel like they've been pulled out, a real geriatric injury. 'Ooh, so butch,' she says. 'And you say you never bring your work home.'

She puts the jar down, turns round and lies along me with her chin on my chest, looking up. It's so steamy I can't tell if it's drops of sweat or water trickling down her face. I try wiping the hair off her forehead but it's sticking –

'Want to live together?'

'Yeh.'

'Right,' she says. 'Then we ought to start looking for a place.'

I've had some of the best times of my life in her house, and it's not like we need a fresh start. But she insists we need a place that's ours not hers.

'Like where?'

'I thought maybe Benacre,' she says. 'Those easterly winds and different habitats. There must be redstarts and bluethroats cascading into those coastal bushes, and rarities nobody sees because it's under-watched. We'll find our own black stork and olivaceous. Cottage with roses round the door.'

'And what are we going to do for work? Since you won't be painting redstarts any more.'

'I'll send you out cleaning. All those other cottages with roses round the door. I don't know, live off the proceeds of selling our places. We'll think of something.'

I tell her I don't know if I'm ready to leave London yet.

'Because of Bish?'

'Because of London.'

'I think you could be persuaded,' she says.

I'm holding the glass for her and she has a slurping sip then takes it off me and puts it down next to the bath. She lets the southern comfort dribble out onto my breastbone then starts licking it off. 'I think you'd like it on the coast,' she says. 'We might even find you a solitary sand.'

'Thanks a bunch.'

'They're amazingly tame sometimes. The one I saw was down to twenty feet.'

'The distance shrinks with the telling as usual. It was thirty yards last time.'

'The sun was in the right place,' she says. 'So you could see the subtle difference between the colours on the tertials.'

'Cow. What are you doing?'

'Can't you tell? Gripping you off.'

Her tongue's slipping and sliding. I tell her she'll get water up her nose, she'll fucking drown.

'When it's that close,' she says, 'you can tell it by its jizz, the longer primary projection. You don't need to see the white rump. Mm, I see you're still paddling below the surface.'

Her shoulders are freckled all over, and Bish was right about her other ones, except they're mostly in a cluster on her lower back. I'd be able to see them better, on her white rump, if the bathroom mirror wasn't so steamed up.

If anything's going to split us up again, it's probably her snoring. I remembered it as being quiet and cute like a kid, but it's like one of those suction things dentists put in your mouth. Roses round the door if she wants, but I'll need a chemist's nearby for earplugs.

It's one of the sounds I missed. Her falling asleep feeling safe because you're there behind her. Nights lying around in slow chatty sixty-nines, putting the world to rights.

It was all a bit pissed this time and we were giggling like in a bad film. She's kneeling over me and I'm opening her pussy lips with one finger each and she's soaking my chin and making noises like small coughs and saying oops I'm dizzy I'm falling hold me up, and muffling me when I laugh.

And there it all was. The buzz of keeping my t-shirt on while she was naked, the rude food, and the feeling I never thought I'd have again: being back home.

Her hair's invading the pillow now. I still go careful in her hair. She used to pile it on top of her head and keep it in place with hat pins, there were so many she couldn't retrieve them all before she went to bed. Number of times I put my hands in while she was asleep and spiked myself on one of those secret weapons. Jesus christ Bus, I need a fucking metal detector. You nearly put my eye out.

I tuck her hair behind her ear to keep it out my nose while I search her face, looking for something smaller than freckles. Tiny dark dots she gets when her orgasms are particularly powerful, bursting the blood vessels just under her eyes. They're hard to see at the best of times and you have to imagine them in this light.

I hate moments like this. I always hated them. When we first went out, I used to miss her even when she was asleep – and I missed her so much I resented her. It was like she wanted to be anywhere else except be with me. I used to wake her up some-times. Not completely, just a nudge to make her grunt, so's she'd be back with me for a moment. I never did it when she had an early start, though. I'm good like that.

Back then, I wanted to have known her all my life. I wished I'd met her when we were five. I wished we'd sat next to each other in class and been round to each other's mum's for tea every friday. I wished we'd lost our virginity to each other and never slept with anybody else. She made the last twenty years seem like a waste of time, and I'd only had twenty-two.

It was like I'd found something I was good at finally, look-ing out for her while she laid her burden down. And I didn't have to feel guilty about preferring her like that, soft and quiet and like a kid, because I think she preferred it too sometimes, shed-ding the outer layers for a moment, being a girl again. Almost peaceful.

All very well, she said, but she wasn't going to stay with me if I was going to get to five hundred and top myself. That only gave us five years together.

That fucking Bish. I told him in confidence.

We'll see our five hundredth together and go for five-fifty. Agreed?

She made me feel alive for the first time in my life, i.e. jealous and sick and depressed and too stomach-cramped to eat or sleep. The state we all want to be in. Two months after we started, I broke it off.

That was my litmus, you understand. The proof I could show to people. They'd see the feeling wasn't something I could just fuck out of me, it wasn't going to go away just because I had a lover.

And what a lover I had, which meant I had it all. Place of my own, money in my pocket, somebody to roam the streets with like tigers, turning heads. If a woman like that doesn't give you a reason to live, well.

When I walked out, the cold turkey was black as a hole, just impossible to bear. I nearly rang her a hundred times. I'd sit by the phone and not call her for an hour at a time. Loneliness like you can't imagine, even when you've been lonely all your life. And I'm describing how she felt, too.

I didn't think she'd take it as bad as she did. I mean, I never really understood what she saw in me in the first place – so I thought she might even just shrug it off and move on. Instead, picture this. She actually fell on her knees. Try equating that with the Stevie you've seen so far. I had to hold her all afternoon. Once she'd cried herself to sleep, I walked out.

She healed in time, she said. We can go out birding again, she said. And since then, I never once caught her looking at me in a certain way, or heard a catch in her voice, so I allowed myself to believe her. But when I knocked on her door and said we should get back together, I knew she'd say yes. We all need somebody who reminds you of your mortality.

She's snuffling in the pillow right now. She'll start talking in her sleep if past experience is anything to go by. Sweet dreams now I'm back. Which just piles on the guilt.

She'll hate me of course, when she finds out what I did. That's only right and I'm ready for it. What I can't bear is listening to her making plans for us together, when I know I haven't come back for long. I'm gambling she'll understand. I did take her feelings into account, but my need was greater. I hope my arms round her, even briefly, was fair exchange.

I'm tucking my knees into the back of hers, another thing that pisses me off. The way our bodies are made so's you can only sleep comfortably when you're not facing each other. She clacks her teeth when she yawns in her sleep. Outside, somebody's coming home late, coughing when they cross the street. I wait till I hear their front door shut, then I let myself fall asleep.

I FEEL LIKE I've known this can of coke all my life. Nothing new in that. Birders spend hours in cafs, usually when they're waiting for a rarity to reappear. But you don't normally do it on your own, so this is a new experience for me. I don't know how long I've been here. I've been watching the clock but only the big hand.

You'll try anything to pass the time. Compiling a bird list that's barely worth the name. Swifts up there, house martins down here. I watched a wasp climb up the window pane, get to the open bit at the top, then walk all the way back down, then back up. The silly sod was exhausting itself in this heat, so I scooped it up with a serviette and flipped it out the top.

Then I did what I do with every room: look around to see how I'd clean it. The grease round the edges of the tables has been there so long it's turned into bakelite. But this place is better than some. You can smell traces of the vinegar they clean the windows with.

I even had something to eat. Dry mushrooms on toast, no butter because I can feel Stevie looking over my shoulder and they don't do soya marge. Black tea because they don't do soya milk. I've got this can of coke now and a field guide open in front of me.

It's hot sitting right by the window, but I want a view of the other side of the street. See the world go by, including some of it that comes in here. Old ladies and girls my age and an australian in a yellow brazilian football top. Support your own country, mate, and take the hits like the rest of us. Unless you support Brazil at cricket. A blind man's come in with his guide dog. The caf owner says hello Christian and asks him if he wants his usual, and I realize he's talking to the dog.

A car stops on the other side of the road and somebody gets out. I watch him walk down the street but he turns into the newsagent's, the last shop before the line of houses. When I got off the tube, I went straight to one of those houses and knocked on the door. Nobody at home. Since then, nothing but people walking past and vans getting in the way when they park. Almost wish I'd brought my bins. And some puff. My nerves have been through the shredder and back.

When Bish gets nervous before a gig, he calms hisself down by doing everything at half-speed. I tried that earlier, but the food got cold and the coke went flat. I probably shouldn't have had the coke.

There's a cat sitting in the sun outside the pub next door. Public enemy number one. People with bird tables want to cull magpies and sparrowhawks and meanwhile their cats are slaughtering a hundred million songbirds a year, conservative estimate. Set the fucking guide dog on it.

It's quiet this time of day, so the caf owner doesn't hassle you when you spend forty minutes over a can of drink. He hasn't asked me why I've been here this long, he's probably used to people whiling away their afternoons.

He came over to clear the table earlier. Greek cypriot, he said. 'Somebody tried to kill an asylum seeker, you know. Right outside the caf. I see it myself. Hit by a car.'

'And it wasn't an accident?'

'Accident no. The car goes on the pavement and smack. Iraqi man walking with his wife.'

'What happened to him?'

'Broken hip', he says. 'It wouldn't happen if they stayed in their own country.'

'Did you come over when the turks invaded?'

'Yes', he said, 'but there's too many here now.' Surprise surprise, somebody else who wants to pull the drawbridge up once he's got in.

There's two women walking past the houses, but they keep going too, right past the caf window. There's nobody else in here now except the blind man, having a rum baba while his labrador's snoozing under the table.

I wish Stevie was here. I miss her courage. She could stay here and order me a tea and I'd be back before it got cold. Get back to your field guide.

I brought it because I knew I'd be waiting around. I've been here so long I've looked through it cover to cover, you've got to refresh the anorak memory from time to time. Even part-time polish rock stars do it, when they can find their reading glasses. I'm on raptors now, that should see me to the end of the coke.

The differences between pallid harriers and female hen harriers. Mostly the underwings, if anybody asks.

Another car stops up the road. Must be the fiftieth today and I know I haven't missed one. Birders get used to doing other things while keeping their eye on the right place. A young kid gets out this latest car and waves when it drives off. He goes in one of the houses, but not the right one. It's later than I expected. Somebody must be doing overtime.

I put the field guide away and look at the clock. I need a slash, but it'd be just my luck for them to turn up the minute I'm not looking. I may have to give up and come back later.

My mobile's been lying around doing nothing. Good. Don't ring, you fucking thing. Don't even think about it. Because if you do, I'll get up and leave. Doesn't matter if it's not a tick, or even a semi-rarity, I'll get up and go for anything. Or somebody wanting to offer me a job I could do in a week's time: I'll leave immediately. So don't fucking ring. I need to stay here and see this through. It could put an end to everything once and for all.

The aussie in the brazilian shirt's come back, unlocking his bike from a bike stand across the street. Don't know if he's any good at cycling, but he's wearing the right colour jersey. Where's he been the last hour? I'm watching him cycle away when he passes a woman coming up the street and she goes into the front garden I've been watching. Fuck, this is it.

Where did she come from? I thought she'd drive here and park outside the house, there's enough spaces. But at least it's a woman. That should make it easier.

How long do I wait before walking over there? If I go right

away, she might think somebody followed her to her door, so she might not open it when I knock. If I leave it too long, somebody else might turn up, she might be going out tonight. Five minutes sounds about right.

Then suddenly she comes straight back out. She shuts the garden gate and walks this way up the street. Small and thin, mixed race. She goes into another front garden a few doors up, then back out again. She's missing out most of the houses, so she can't be putting junk mail through letterboxes. Neighbourhood watch maybe. Or collecting copies of Watchtower she left with people. She goes into the pub and it's the last I see of her.

I'm taking deep breaths. They don't work but you do them anyway. Fucking murder, all this waiting. If I had any luck, Stevie Red Bus would walk past the window about now. Come back home, angel. Don't do big things all the time, do lots of small stuff. Finish cleaning my whole house. The field guide's open at a page of winter waders, solitary sand included. Agony.

A car drives up and parks across the street. Congratulations, you're our millionth vehicle today. Somebody gets out and locks it, then he walks this way and goes into the newsagent's. The caf owner comes round from behind me and brings the blind man another tea. They're talking about cricket again. Better not use any more of his serviettes to wipe the sweat off your face.

The geezer comes out the newsagent's and walks back towards his car. Then he goes into the front garden in question. Suddenly, just like that. My pulse has been pogoing all day and it can't be arsed any more. I spend two minutes watching the little hand, and he doesn't come back out. I get up and try and do everything slow like Bish says. Pick up my rucksack, pay the bill, and stroll out, stepping over Christian's arse on the way.

I'm telling myself to stay calm, it can't take more than five minutes. But my hands are shaking on the way past the newsagent's and into his front garden. Another useless deep breath, then knock. It occurs to me there might be a chain on the door, but what can you do, you're here now. The rucksack's slipping off my shoulder and I let the strap drop into my hand.

Naturally he takes an age coming to the door. I look behind me but nobody's passing. There's a breeze out here, chilling the sweat in the crook of your elbow. Amazing some of the shit you notice.

When the door opens, I push it hard and go in and stop immediately I'm inside. I've got the door behind me now and I shut it quietly. There's a hallway and some stairs and he's taken a big step back. He's tall enough to hit the bottom of the banister with his shoulders and not the back of his neck.

Not just tall, he's a mile wider than me. If he fancies his chances, I'm fucking toast. But I doubt he'll do that. I know he recognizes me.

'Do you recognize me?'

'Yes,' he says. 'What are you doing here?'

'I don't recognize *you*. I've only seen your car, following me around.'

'If you don't recognize me, how do you know it was me in the car?'

Slightly risky reply, trying to show me how confident he is. Is he police after all, then? I tell him I took his registration number. I know there's been two of them in the car but he lives on his own.

He stands up straight to make hisself tall as he can. 'If you touch me,' he says, 'you'll be digging yourself deeper.'

'I'm not going to touch you. Who said I was going to touch you? You're twice my fucking size.'

He asks me again: what am I doing at his house?

'You're police, aren't you. If you're police, come and arrest me if you're going to. Don't follow me around with fucking cameras.'

He frowns. Then he smiles. I don't like either of them. He comes right up to me and shakes his head. Stinks of day-long sweat, but so do I probably. 'I'm not police,' he says quietly.

'What the fuck are you then?

'Why would anyone want to arrest you?'

'If you're not police, do what you've got to do. You know where I live. What are you waiting for?'

He shakes his head like he doesn't understand. Fucking cat and mouse.

'Just do it, alright? I honestly don't care. I'm ready for it, I swear to god. I want you to do it.'

'Do what?'

'I mean it. I actively want you to do it. Any method you want. Just get on with it.'

'You've lost me,' he says.

'Do it here if you want. Or at my place tomorrow. What's the point of waiting any longer?'

'Look, stop,' he says. 'What do you think we're going to do?'

'Don't play games, you can see what I'm like. Do it or fucking leave me alone.'

He starts undoing his tie. Presumably he's sweating as much

as I am, except I'm half expecting him to wrap it round his fist. 'Yes,' he says, 'we know where you live. But we're still gathering evidence. We can't do anything till then.'

'What do you mean evidence? What fucking evidence? So you *are* police.'

'Forget about the police. It's nothing to do with the police.'

'What then? Don't tell me you're some government department. I'm only a fucking cleaner.'

'That's why we're collecting evidence,' he says. 'Cleaners are prime targets. We're inland revenue.'

'What?'

'Inland revenue. The tax office.'

'What?' I'm standing here looking blank and he asks me do I want a coffee. I say 'what' for the third time in a row.

'Coffee,' he says. 'I was going to make one.'

'Coffee? I've just threatened you with fuck knows what, and you're offering me a coffee?'

'Well, I'm at a loss what to do next.'

'A fucking coffee. Haven't you got anything stronger? I need a drink.'

'Fuck a drink,' he says. 'I need a new pair of shorts. I'm shitting myself here.'

'Tell me about it.'

I smile, he grins. I'm looking at this man who I'm never going to see again and I've got this flood of disappointment, because I really thought it might all come to an end here. So I hate him almost, but there's this relief too, which feels like deep abiding love for the whole of fucking mankind. I'm the only person in the country who wants to kiss the tax man, and the tax man wants to kiss me.

He shows me into his kitchen-diner. Next I'm sitting at his kitchen table and he's got a bottle of single malt out and poured two trebles. He sits down and undoes some buttons on his shirt. Cheers, he says and we knock them back for very medicinal purposes.

'Fuck,' he says as the relief comes out of him. I say it too. We say it twice. Then he says shit, his heart rate's gone off the fucking dial.

'You should hear mine. I thought you were going to knock my fucking teeth out.'

'I thought the same about you,' he says. 'Twice your size I may be, but the look on your face. Jesus, even my knees are sweating.'

I finished my drink before he finished talking. He pours me another one and I ask him who tipped him off. Nobody, he says.

'I don't expect you to give me their name. Just tell me it was one of the people I work for and not a mate of mine.'

'Nobody tipped us off. It's a random check. We do them from time to time if you're self-employed. Anybody who might be paid in cash. How did you know where I live?'

'One of the people I clean for, he drives a minicab. I gave him your car number and got him to follow you.'

'Christ,' he says. 'Wish I had friends like that.'

'So do I. It's a business arrangement. I've got to clean his place for free till the end of the month. I'll show you the receipts.'

He smiles. 'A right fucking detective, aren't you. I'm Pavlo, since we're being so polite. I know your name.'

Pavlo, what's that: polish? Ukrainian, he says. His parents came over in the sixties. He holds his hand out and it's still shaking. I hold mine out and same thing. Cue more scotch.

I tell him he won't find anything, checking up on me. He probably knows that by now. I always put everything through the accounts. I was brought up that way.

'There's a Chauhan family,' he says. 'Your neighbours.'

'You haven't been hassling her, have you? For fucksake. She hasn't been well.'

'No no,' he says. 'We just monitored you cleaning her house.'

'I don't charge her for it. Unless you want to do me for not declaring onion bhajis.'

Another smile, another drink. 'Listen,' he says. 'What would you have done if I *had* been the police?'

'What I just did. Tell you to stop following me. Then I was going to turn on my heel and walk out. Disgruntled of Shepherd's Bush.'

'Very impressive,' he says. 'And if I wasn't police?'

'How do you mean?'

You didn't come equipped, then?'

'Equipped with what?'

'I'm not going to offer fucking suggestions, am I. You've got a rucksack. You might have a knife or something. That's why I didn't hit you.'

'I never carried a knife in my life, even when I was a kid.' I pick the rucksack up off the floor and empty it on the table. Field guide, empty ribena carton, a waterproof in case there's thundery showers after all this heat.

He picks the field guide up. 'Ah yeh,' he says, 'we know you're a birdwatcher.'

'Shit, you followed me everywhere, didn't you.'

'We thought you were going from one job to the next, but you went to that nature reserve in Lonsdale Road. Is that why you thought the police were following you?'

'What do you mean?'

'You thought maybe it was their environment people. Are you an egg collector?'

I smile inside and shake my head on the outside. 'No, I'm the opposite.'

'And what's that?'

'I used to guard a red kite nest in Wales. How long are you going to keep checking up on me?'

He shrugs. 'We've got to do this, you know. Tax evasion costs billions. Builders are the worst. I hate builders. And painters and decorators.'

'And cleaners.'

'Specially cleaners.'

'Except you already know I'm the exception. When are you going to drop it?'

'What were you going to do,' he says, 'if I wasn't the police?'

'What? How do you mean?'

'Well,' he says, 'when I told you I wasn't police, you said "do what you've got to do". You said you were ready for it. Ready for what?'

'I don't know. If you weren't police, I didn't know what you were. The kind of people who follow you around in cars. I didn't know what you wanted.'

'But whatever it was, you were ready for it? Any method I chose, you said.'

My turn to shrug. He stretches his legs under the table. 'This is a fucking first,' he says. 'Having a drink with someone who's just barged in.'

'Call the police if you want. Do it while I'm here or after I've gone, I won't stop you with what's in the rucksack.'

'Fuck the police,' he says. 'I keep my dealings with them to a minimum. But you can't just push your way in and get away with it. I'll want some compensation.'

Oh ych? What's he got in mind?

'What do you think of this place?'

'What?' I must stop saying that.

'Who do you think cleans it?'

'Nobody, by the look of it.'

'Very observant,' he says. 'I'm too busy keeping tabs on people like you. That's the deal then. You springclean it, top to bottom, and I forget you were ever here. Fair?'

'Only if I have another drink. You drive a shit bargain.'

He pours me another scotch and asks me if I want to stay for something to eat, but this is bizarre enough as it is.

'I could do with a regular cleaner,' he says. 'Say three hours a week. Just some dusting and hoovering. What's your hourly rate?'

'You know what it is. It's in my tax records.'

'Ah yeh, seven quid.' He lifts his eyebrows. 'How about six-fifty for cash?'

THE REST OF july was eerily normal for all of us, like your last summer term after exams. We even got two ticks together, a bonus when there's no migration. Britain's first audouin's gull at Dunge, and a steppe shrike in the grounds of a disused mental hospital. Quips on a postcard. Angelo Cane and Terry Chai gripped us all off, the bastards, by getting up to North Ron for a swainson's thrush while the rest of us had to stay home and work.

Jace Babb meanwhile got a local authority award for his charity work and found a dead raven for his collection, whereupon his wife lost it at last and binned the whole lot and disinfected his trophy room. They're renewing their wedding vows in october. Frostbite hitched to Norway for a male steller's eider and found love among the fjords, though the jury's out on that one.

Twitches apart, I haven't seen Bish much, partly because he went to Poland for a week's recording session. While the rest of the band were chasing the local girls, he hired a guide to take him round the old forest they've got there, looking for tengmalm's owl.

When we met up afterwards, his mind was someplace else as usual. I just hope he's not planning to do something stupid.

He didn't even stay long at the *scampagnata* for Angelo's thirtieth, a giant picnic in Richmond Park with his relatives bringing enough food over from Milan to feed the five thousand. Twenty-a-side football, half-hour bird race near Pen Ponds, and people coming up to congratulate me on going out with Stevie. Hope you're congratulating her for going out with me. Fuck that, we're trying to pinch her off you.

London must be a really dirty place, because my phone's been jammed with prospective new clients. I turned most of them down, but I had to hire somebody else in the end, one of Bish's polish mates for fridays and saturdays. I've been spending my weekends away.

Stevie packed in the bird illustrations like she said she would and gave her sketches away to Jace's wife and Terry and the rest. What she'll do from now on she hasn't said, but in any case work's been taking a back seat: she's thrown herself into finding somewhere for us to live. She went up to Suffolk to recce various places but decided against them, since when we've spent every weekend looking round different parts of the country.

Meanwhile she got her hooks into me to decorate her house with a view to selling. I'm supposed to do this at the end of a full day's work, you understand. I put my foot down. I told her: I'm the cleaner, I've already cleaned your place. You're the painter, paint.

But then she starts with the purring and the cooing, ooh baby you know I'm just a helpless female with this kind of thing. My stern resistance lasted the best part of a minute, then I ended up doing most of it with Angelo. She roped him in on the basis that tattooists know how to use paint, snared him with a flash of her emerald eyes.

I asked her why Bish left the picnic early but she said she didn't know. Must've been something important to tear him away from those logpiles of milanese salami. Come the evening and she was sitting on the grass with her back against a tree and the back of my head on her stomach and the sun going down behind Sidmouth Wood and I said listen I need to know. Why did she let me come back?

Sounds like somebody's fishing, she said. And I said yeh somebody is, but we all need to fish sometimes. Answer the question.

And she pushed her fingers through my hair towards my forehead and tucked the rest of it behind my ears and she said she let me come back because she couldn't help it, what other reason is there? Every time I looked at you, she said, when we were out birding but we weren't together any more, my stomach used to clench and my fanny went into spasm. You know the feeling.

Oh yeh.

I missed you, she said. Isn't that why you came back?

Yes, I said. I was tired of crying myself to sleep. But it's not really an answer. It's one thing to feel like that, but you don't necessarily have to act on it. I mean, she's alive and kicking and I'm the most miserable git known to man. Why would she want to be around me? I never understood it.

Because you fit your skin, she said. I agree about the miserable git bit, but you know how to just live. You don't need a vocation or ambition, or a creed, or an urge to compete, or any future plans. It's a gift.

Shit, Bus, how many lobotomies have I had? Where do you store these lists of yours?

I could feel her stomach muscles when she chuckled. You wouldn't want to live like that, Stevie. Trust me.

Trust me, I would.

There's no way you could, just by being around me.

Then fucking teach me, useless.

My turn to laugh. She said she let me come back because I was the only one who'd ever listened to her. Really listened, and wasn't scared of disagreeing with her. When people are scared of you, they agree with everything you say or they disagree with everything, because they want to show you they're not afraid. People always try to capture what they're afraid of, then mould it. She let me come back because I wanted to look after her, when nobody else realized she needed looking after. Because I could never hurt her.

Never hurt her? Stevie, I walked out on you. For no reason that made any sense.

You didn't do it to hurt me, she said. I saw your face, remember. I never saw so many tears. It was like I'd walked out on you.

Aren't you worried I'll walk out again?

Don't flatter yourself, she said. Next time I'll do the walking.

I held my hand out for my glass of wine. She slid down and reversed positions so's she could doze off. Baby. You could almost hear her heartbeat slowing down in your arms. We woke up and found Angelo had got his nieces to tie our shoelaces together.

Angelo finished stencilling temporary tattoos on their arms and brought me a glass of asti. He'd just done his annual trip to mecca, i.e. the tattoo parlours in downtown Austin, Texas. There's people there, he said, who've had six hundred hours of tattoos done on them, turning theirselves into lizards or cats. One girl asked him to insert whiskers into piercings through her cheeks.

Some of the most well-adjusted people he ever met, he said. They know exactly who they are. It's the other ones you need to wonder about. Normality on the outside, fuck knows what's happening behind it. That's right Angie, we're everywhere.

He smiled and nodded at the family scene. This is what counts, he said. Not jobs or chasing around looking at birds. I can't imagine being you and not having a big family. Come on, I'll introduce you to my cousins. If they take the piss out of birding, give them a slap. Always works for me.

One of those cousins told me it's not Angelo Cane, it's Cané with an accent. If it didn't have the accent, it'd be the Italian for 'dog'. Eek. So it's not just Bish who's disguising his foreign roots. I have the distinct feeling our Angel Dog is never going to hear the end of it.

A real day in the sun. The kind that makes you want to scream. There's a limit to how much borrowed time you can stand. Looks like it's true: if you want something speeded up, you've got to do it yourself.

BACK UPSTREAM THERE was trout, grayling, dace, chub, bull-heads, eels and minnows in the deep pools and stillwater bays. Water shrimps and even a few salmon. Some brook lampreys where the shallows had a gravel bed. Down here on the edge of the lowlands, it's mainly coarse fish: pike, perch, roach and stone loach, and a lot more bladder snails and fish leeches. Though you'll have to take my word for it.

How's that for a list. Courtesy of the Bus of course. She learned her fish from an old Observer's Book and points them out when we go birding near rivers, though they still look alike to me. She taught me the names of the common plants too, and I even remembered some of them. Like the fish, they change when you come down to the valley floor. Water crowfoot and bog stitchwort and stretches of reed grass.

When I get to the first lot of trees, I look back for a second. The rain's only just stopped and the sky's a grey wash. You won't see so much of it when you follow the riverside path along the valley floor.

It's darker down here because the trees on the bank are much closer together. There's only a few places you can look through them to the other side of the river and catch sight of the rest of the valley. It's all upland pasture with copses they planted for sheep to shelter in. Right by the far bank, there's an old tractor engine acting as a pump, taking water from the river towards the dutch barns at the foot of the hill.

But these are just glimpses really. The trees meet overhead in places, so the bank's a virtual tunnel and I'm surrounded by green. In the leaves overhead, green with white in it. In among the nettlebeds by the water's edge, green with red in it. There's a giant weeping willow, not green at all, like a fifty-foot wig. The kind of place you miss when you're away from this country. Grass you could almost eat. But gloomy, hemming you in. Probably because it's completely man-made.

Actually, nothing could look more natural. But they planted the alders and willows to stabilize the banks, and they've allowed the thistles and nettles to grow along the whole length of the bank except in special fishing bays. On the other side of the path from the river, they've planted holly bushes to reinforce the barbed wire and private fishery signs. Everything about this place says keep the fuck out.

There's not so many trout down here where the water's slow. But the place is managed for another list of fish – tench, carp, bleak, gudgeon and bream – so down the whole length of the river you can have any you want. And people do want them.

Fish are the whipping boys of the animal world. If you watch birds, say, you get a buzz out of seeing an osprey coming up out of a loch with a trout in its claws. You see the fish twisting from side to side, and instead of imagining its agony and terror or wondering how it can bend so much without snapping its spine, you're marvelling at how the raptor's talons have evolved to cope with prey that's slippery as this. A hundred gannets divebombing the tideline is exhilarating, and you enjoy showing kids a kingfisher at work.

So I never put up much of an argument when people say fish can't feel pain, and when they twist around on the line it's just a kind of primitive kneejerk. I don't disagree there's something bonding about men bringing their kids here on frosty mornings. You tell yourself you can't be expected to care about every fucking thing that moves.

Except I never really believed any of this. I've got fuck-all in common with somebody who teaches their kids how to maim things with a metal hook in the mouth. Even the MP who put up the anti-foxhunting bill, he's a match angler, the hypocrite cunt. Stevie picketed his house once, except he was on holiday at the time.

I'm keeping my binoculars under my jacket. I don't need them to see there's none of the clues I'm looking for. A moorhen's struggling back into cover between some small water lilies with uneven edges like a palette, there's a rags-and-tatters butterfly, and a bright red kitkat wrapper going downstream. A splash behind me and there's a great crested grebe shaking the water from its eyes. At last a friendly face –

The river bends again, and when you turn the latest corner you find yourself under a hanging willow, looking through at two men standing in the open near the water's edge, one carrying a shotgun broken open under his arm. The leaves and branches are still wet from this morning's rain and I pull the drawstring of my hood tighter.

The shorter one of these two, he's the reason I'm here. I've never met him face to face but I recognize him from photographs. It helps that you always see him in the same clothes: brown leather jacket over a tracksuit, pair of wellies. He owns the whole valley, John Ure Peacock, and the grouse moors on both sides of it, and he built this river. The other one, with the shotgun (I presume it's his water bailiff), he's a surprise to me, a problem – but there's no time to think about it. I walk out from under the willow just as they carry on along the bank towards me.

Before they get here, the taller one steps away from the river-bank to check part of the barbed wire fence. John Ure Peacock keeps coming. You can see those famous brown eyes a mile away. Why do him and Owen Whittle have to have the same colour eyes? Take a deep breath without letting him see you do it.

'You realize this is private land.'

'I thought it was a public footpath.'

'Oh it is,' he says. 'I'm really talking about the fishing here.'

I tell him I've only come here for the walk, and I take my ruck-sack off to show him there's no collapsible fishing rod inside. He says there's no need for that, and he smiles all over, *dripping* with charm, and says he's sorry it's just that he has to be careful. 'We've had trouble with illegal fishing, so we've become rather suspicious about anyone we don't recognize. Not many people come here just for the walk.'

'I was told it was worth a look.'

'We think so,' he says. 'Sorry if we interrupted you. Are you going as far as the lock?'

The first piece of interrogation. Without exactly looking me up and down, he makes it clear I'm not the sort he usually gets round here.

I tell him I didn't know about the lock. How far is it?

'Mile and a half,' he says. 'If you do get there, look out for the hawthorn hedges on the left. They're built on an anglo-saxon ground plan.'

He says goodbye and I have a quick look across at the other one then walk on, still trying to look oh so casual. Round the next bend, I try to forget about them and concentrate on watching the riverbanks again. Easier said than done, but I think I did alright back there. If Owen Whittle had seen me, I'd have run a mile. But here I looked back into those great bronze eyes and as far as I know I didn't give anything away. Maybe the bailiff with him made the difference: there's nothing I can do with two of them around, so I could relax and act natural. Check the river anyway, though it looks like he's learned his lesson and there won't be anything to find.

In the next small fishing bay, there's mud with some animal tracks I can't identify and the prints of a mute swan. A white butterfly hangs around the fool's parsley on the bank. The burs on the bur plants are still green and don't stick to your clothes.

I'm noticing stuff like this because there's no *evidence* to look at. I take the binoculars out and scan the water's edge on the far bank. Still nothing. For the next half a mile the only movement's the plip of a vole in the water. Good. Relief. Honey buzzards and now this. Maybe this country's getting its act together.

Dream on. The river straightens out and wanders towards the oakwood near the foot of the valley slope where the trees look like broccoli – but I find what I'm looking for close to the far bank. It won't sound very dramatic, but I've been dreading it all the same.

I looked right past it at first. It's colourless and smaller than you expect, almost hidden among the tree roots in the water. I only saw it because it's moving all the time, trapped in a sort of tiny creek lapped by the water, so it knocks against the roots like pipes. The first time I've seen a heron's bill so pale and washed out. Half open like a razorshell but with some of the skull still attached.

I knew it. Three miles of river and not a single heron standing on the bank. There used to be one every quarter of a mile along this stretch and a small colony breeding by the nearby lake. But that was before John Ure Peacock bought the rights to the river.

This far north, you'd expect to see fish-eating ducks and maybe one of the rarer grebes. Instead, for a while you had corpses everywhere. Herons, cormorants, goosanders. He even slaughtered mallards, and they don't eat fish. Shotgunned and left to float as extra food for his fish. Then one of his wardens shot at a young kid who came up to monitor all this. She lost an eye, you had prosecutions and fines and bad press, and it looked like he'd mended his ways. Except now it's obvious he just removed all trace, shooting to kill and retrieving the bodies.

So is he arrogant or just plain fucking careless, leaving one lying around like this? Maybe just unlucky. His bailiff probably winged it when it took flight, and he couldn't find it again before it died in a reedbed somewhere, lapsing into the shallows for the pike and moorhens to strip off the flesh. Its feathers are probably lining a nest somewhere.

It's not evidence enough, of course. One heron's beak. But I know it's just the start, now I'm further downstream. In the next mile I see a moorhen's skull and a goosander's wing and a piece of cormorant and half another heron. Unless there's been a flu epidemic or a shoal of fucking piranha, there's only one way this could have happened.

The cunts. No point telling them herons only take frogs and voles and sticklebacks that nobody wants. They know that. They didn't kill it to protect their fish, they did it because they could, for the crack of it. You only carry a gun if you enjoy it. I start walking back along the riverbank.

The barbed wire's new and stiff all along the river, but soon there's a hawthorn tree, and you can use its lowest branch to step up and over into the field. Once you're there, you're exposed on the hill and you have to keep an eye open when you run up the slope towards the broccoli trees at the top. The chalk soil sticks to your boots. When I get to the copse, I go in for a few yards so I'll be in shadow, then I kneel down, open the rucksack, and sit back on my heels looking through the bins.

The river's less than a hundred yards below, but the path along the bank is hidden by the hawthorns and nettles. No sign of John Ure Peacock and partner. This isn't an ideal vantage point but I had to come up here, to see if they've moved away from the river. They haven't. Check the various hillsides and there's nobody there, which lets you concentrate on the river itself.

Sure enough, the brown leather jacket and the bailiff's green waterproof start showing through the riverside trees. They're walking quite quick, so they'll probably be out of range in a minute – but I try not to hurry too much when I get the gun out the rucksack, listening in case one of John Ure Peacock's gamekeepers is up here doing his rounds.

Get the gun out the rucksack. Never thought I'd be saying that again. But I know what I'm doing this time. I'm out here because there's been too much time.

This was never in the grand plan, but then there wasn't a grand plan. I never thought any further than Owen Whittle. You shoot somebody, you get nicked, finish. I never considered what I'd do if I wasn't caught straight away. Turn myself in? Shoot every egg collector I could till I ran out of bullets? Fucking hell.

So I'm out here because it's taking them so long to come and get me. I'm trying to give them a helping hand. If they haven't got enough clues from one shooting, maybe they need a second one. Some insane arithmetic, I agree, but let's call it stress-related.

Down on the bank, the two men, they've stopped, more or less in full view with only a thin young alder in the way like a wire cage. They're looking across the river with their backs to me, the bailiff's elbow patches catching the light.

They're going to move away any second, so you need to hurry. Hold your other hand under the gun handle to stop the magazine falling out, concentrate on the back of the leather jacket and take your deep breath. You can probably have them both if you're quick.

They stand there long enough for me to have a sandwich and still do it. And my arm doesn't shake, buckle or twitch, it stays straight as a broom handle. Trouble is, it stays like that for the duration. As for the trigger finger actually doing anything to the trigger: not today. They've disappeared behind the screen of veg now. Put your arm down before something perches on it.

I unload the gun and walk out the copse and across the hill. A single buzzard's soaring in front of me, following the camber of the hill. There ought to be hen harriers up here, except the gamekeepers probably crushed this year's eggs. I put my head down and walk on.

I've reached the edge of the next copse when I hear noises off and look down. And suddenly John Ure Peacock's at the bottom of the field. He's pressing down the middle strand of barbed wire with his foot and holding the top one up for the bailiff to go through. And he's looking this way, firing his brown eyes up the hill at me. The bailiff steps through and takes his turn holding the wires apart.

They must've seen me through a gap in the riverside trees when I walked across the hill. I stand here like a lemon and wait for them. Then the bailiff snaps his shotgun shut and you can probably hear it the other side of the valley. They've got some amazing echoes round here. I turn round and dive into this next wood.

What does he want his shotgun for? There's no way they saw me waving a gun, so I'm unarmed as far as they're concerned.

What kind of threat am I posing, walking across one of their hills?

I'm younger and probably faster than they are, so I could try outrunning them. Except there's no cover after this copse. So I haven't got any choice, have I. I get down on my knees and open the rucksack. The gun handle snags on the sweatshirt inside and the bullets ping out and I'm picking them out the nettles. Even with your pulse pumping into your ears, you can hear the bailiff's footsteps coming up the hill.

Where's he going to be by the time I'm ready? Only halfway up, I hope. Or maybe so close I'll only have time to shoot from the hip. Turns out he's still a fair way down and I've got time to straighten my arm and even steady myself a bit. His green jacket's huge and his face looks so close I'm imagining I can see the individual pores.

Times like this, they tell you everything happens in slow motion. Well, fuck that, it's the opposite. The time it takes a water bailiff to run up a short hill. But the human brain: jesus. It switches to broadband. You even get to think clearly for once.

This is the time to let them do it, your computer's saying. You can't do it yourself, you're waiting for somebody to do it for you. This is the somebody. Carrying a loaded shotgun, what more could you ask. He's even smiling, the cunt, he'd *like* to do it. Show yourself when he's really close, show him the gun. He'd have to do it then. He's so close it might not even hurt.

My dad's uncle. The one who brought this luger back from the war. He had a friend out there. A latvian who survived the camps. He learned you'll do anything, he said. Doesn't matter how terrible or degrading. Just to stay alive one minute longer. It's taken me till now, with this grinning gun coming up the hill, to realize we're all latvians deep down.

I'll fire one in the air. If they hear a shot, they'll think twice about it, won't they. They'll hit the deck or turn and run. Just the noise will do it. I start twisting the silencer to get it off.

It won't move. It does about half a turn then stops. It's never been off, now I think about it. It was like that when he brought it over from Germany, and I don't remember anybody ever undoing it. I'm using my shirt to get a better grip, but the thread's fucked and it's stuck there. I'm down on one knee with my wrist going like a wrench but nothing's happening. I'm even thinking of gripping it in my teeth while I twist it with both hands –

Stop and take a deep breath. You've got time.

Never mind waiting till you see the whites of their eyes. They're so close I can hear them breathing hard as they run. No need to take aim at this range. Breathe out and don't hurry. Then bang. You can hear it smack home from here.

The bailiff stops dead. Maybe he heard the bullet when it passed and definitely when it slapped into the leather jacket, and he turns round and sees John Ure Peacock finishing his fall, knees giving way and his upper body snapping backwards like he's been hit in the spine by an axe. The bailiff looks up the slope again and now he knows the shit he's in, out in the open with forty yards of killing ground between him and a sniper he can't see. When he lifts the shotgun, I drop down with my cheek on the ground, but he's shooting blind and terrified and the pellets spatter harmlessly through the treetops above my head. Both barrels. He runs back down the hill.

I don't think he saw me too well earlier on, when I was talking to his boss. Thinking about it, I'm not sure he clocked me at all. But I can't take the risk can I, he'd understand that hisself. Stand up and follow him along the barrel of the gun.

Easy easy target, going directly away from me over ground where it's hard to swerve and sidestep. Still carrying the shotgun that's massacred who knows how many wild birds and all such big fun. Now this particular prey's firing back and he understands what it's like. Hearing the shot, seeing the one next to you go down, fleeing in huge fucking fear. *Please. I was only following orders*. Tell me about it.

Near the bottom of the hill, he's got the presence of mind to throw hisself forward and roll the last few yards, making hisself a smaller target. But there's still the barbed wire to negotiate, and he's big and slow at the end of the gun barrel when he catches his trouser leg on the bottom strand. Just for a second, he's completely still and you can imagine his gasp of terror, like a small dog.

I'm aiming higher up his torso. He's trying to kick his leg free. When that forces him into a standing position balancing on the wires, I bring the gun down and unload it again then put it back in the rucksack and sling it over my shoulder. Looking down for a moment, I see him untangle hisself and dive through the nettles and out of sight.

Then I come out the front of the wood. The sun's water-colouring the sky on the other side of the valley and I never noticed there was a wind till now. I let out a roar they probably haven't heard here since prehistoric times, from somewhere in my pit, so loud and strong it clenches your fists and shuts your eyes and bends you double so's your rucksack falls off and hangs on your forearm. When you suck the air back in, it comes hooting through your passages.

I stand up and turn round and walk away through the wood, leaving John Ure Peacock behind like a starfish on the grass. Two brown limbs, two battleship grey.

I LEFT THE cliffs to go for a walk in one of those classic oakwood valleys they specialize in round here, taking the binoculars for the pied flycatchers and what have you. The sun's not out but you don't need it unless you want the dappled effect you get in postcards.

Most types of countryside surprise you how basic their set-up is. Moorland you can imagine, but even a breckland plantation hasn't got much variety. Tall straight pines with no branches, some nettles and elder trees, that's about it.

Same with these sessile woods. Trees green with lichen, under-growth of grass and ferns, a stony stream, the end. About as ancient and natural as this country allows, satisfying shapes everywhere you look. And these welsh forests hold wood warblers and redstarts and hairstreak butterflies. If places like this don't revive you, you're already dead.

I've come back out to the bottom of the valley and onto the flat land at the coast, walking out the wood onto nothing but short grass for about half a mile to the edge of the cliffs. The sun's straight ahead and going down behind the clouds.

The peninsula's shaped like a bone here, sticking out into the irish sea, the oldest part of the Pembrokeshire coast, a place men didn't reach till the ice brought down by the great scottish glacier started retreating. This is where the first humans settled in Wales, but they're gone now. They built their hunting camps, then their sheep folds, finally their farms and their lighthouse, but the land beat them and they vanished like neanderthals. For once, and who knows how long for, the birds have won. The farm fence is a row of plucking posts for merlins. There's not even any sheep left.

We've put a rug down just off the coastal path. Food and drink and a bag with her sketchpads. She's not here just now, probably gone for a slash somewhere. I go over to the edge of the cliff and have a peek.

The rock's red down there. Purple and brown in places, marbled white, like meat that's just stopped bleeding. Except it's hard as hell, no grass or round edges. You imagine hitting it when you let yourself fall, your body freezing cold and brittle.

The whole place is like that. Granite and black serpentine. We're down to the country's skeleton here, the soft sandstone and chalk washed away. The sea's got to take what little it can, snapping off bits of the land, cracking it so's it juts and pokes and cocks. It used to be a shipwreck coast, and you can imagine the sightseers coming here to be awed.

We're here because they're the right kind of cliffs for her background drawings. So where is she? The coastal path dips down a slope on the right. Maybe she's just over the rise, take you no time to find her. Except I've just been walking for an hour. Stay here and wait.

She's put the food away in case there's gulls. I open her bag and some crumpled pieces of paper fall out. I sit crosslegged with her sketchbooks on my lap, keeping the veggie pâté away from the pages. Bins next to me just in case. Pomarine skuas have been moving up the channel.

I skip through to her speed sketches, where she gets a bird's personality in just a few lines. When illustrators do a hawfinch they usually emphasize the huge bill and fierce face, but the Bus gives you the timidity that makes it so elusive. She'll show you a robin's aggressive streak behind its little boy expression. If I was ever this good at anything, I can't imagine giving it up.

She gets the jizz right too. The different preening methods of longbilled and shortbilled waders, the flight of a big skua as opposed to a small one. There's a whole page of poms. She hasn't seen one today, has she? While I've been looking at common woodland stuff.

I have a quick scan out to sea but it's flat as jelly and there's no wind to blow anything close to shore. Sip of orange juice, wash my hands from the water bottle, and look through the other sketchbook.

This one's drawings of the clifftops round here, with shoreline and cloud formations. Then hello. Suddenly the pelicans are back.

It's all close-ups of faces and wings. A lot of faces and wings. Three pages just on one set of flight feathers. Then halfway through the book the faces and wings stop and she's drawn a complete pelican, curled up with its preposterous great beak tucked out of sight. Next page there's bird of prey in there suddenly and they're locked in a circle like they're chasing each other round and round. Then she starts leaving out the feathers and it turns into a circu-

174

lar sculpture, with the pelican's eyes shut and the raptor's beak open. Eventually there's just a circle with a slit for an eye and two slits for the beak. Then suddenly there's drawings of cliffs and fields again.

I look back through some of the pages, then I put them away and lie on my back with my eyes shut. A rook's craking as it flies over, an ooh-aar accent compared to city crows. She made the pelican look peaceful, but prey often looks like that. The adrenalin kicks in and they can't feel the death bite. Well, that's what it says here.

The sun comes out for a second and warms your face. Then it goes back in and there's a breeze on your arms. I could get used to places like this. I try and relax all of my limbs one by one, but they already are.

I don't hear her come back. First I know of it is the smell of her cocoabutter face cream and her hair curtaining my face when I get a kiss. Her kisses are like they were when we first went out, lasting for ever, sucking your top lip and making your arms go round her. Eventually she drops the sketchpad she's carrying and sits close by, propping herself on her forearm. She asks me if I've seen anything.

'Just a female pied fly. What about you?'

She's been down the side of the cliff just round the corner. There's a pair of fulmars roosting on a ledge. She flashes the drawing she's done.

'Nothing else?'

'No,' she says. 'The weather's all wrong.'

'No pom skuas for instance? So close you had time to draw them?'

'Last year's sketches, dopey. Been having a look through the work in progress, have we? What do you think?'

'You missed a bit on the wing.'

She slaps my leg and puts the sketchpad away. She has some orange juice while I lie with the back of my head on her stomach and watch the clouds following the coast, enough to send you to sleep. The sea's making its noises up ahead, the first time I ever thought of it as soothing. I doze off so long I'm woken up by the drop in temperature, even though she's put her jacket over me.

She's sitting right on the edge of the cliff, feet over the side, which looks daring, except I know the cliff goes down gradually in a series of ledges. Yawn and stretch then go over and sit next to her. The cloud cover's splitting up, the sun showing from time to time but very low over the sea.

'You've looked through all the other sketchbooks haven't you.'

'Yeh. Pelicans included. What's that for, a new field guide?'

'A new company,' she says. 'Bird tours to the Danube delta. They want a dalmatian pelican as their emblem.'

'And the raptor mixed up with it, what's that, an idea for a logo?'

'Company letterhead.'

I open the southern comfort and pour some into two glasses. She shuts one eye and looks through her glass at the sun on the horizon. I kiss her on the cheek.

'Oh yeh? What's that for?'

'I know I walked out on you last time. So I don't expect you to trust me yet. But if you're not going to tell me the truth, don't tell me anything. Or else tell better lies.'

'Right.'

She knows as well as I do: the pelican's a symbol of sacrifice, every birder knows that. The medieval old bollocks about feeding its young with its own blood. So she's gone back to her old graduation theme.

'Yeh,' she says. 'I'm doing the real work again.'

'Why didn't you want to tell me?'

'Because you know what I'm like,' she says. She has a sip, then a proper glug. 'When I do the real work, I don't do anything else. There's no room for anybody. I thought if you knew I'd gone back to it, you'd piss off again.'

'Well I do know. And I'm not going anywhere.'

'You say that now.'

'When else can I say it?'

She smiles and holds her glass out for a refill. 'I don't need statements of intent,' she says. 'I need you to understand. If I go back to the work, I won't be with you the way I am now. That's something I learned from you: I'm on my own with this.'

A gang of jackdaws nip across the cliff front on the other side of the bay. They land on the cliff face and get chased off by a kestrel I didn't see hiding there. 'I'm glad you're doing the real work again, Steve.'

'No you're not,' she says. 'You won't be able to handle it. You'll want me all to yourself.'

'Pardon me for wanting what anybody would want. But I've got a choice, haven't I. Find somebody I can have to myself. Or Stevie Red Bus as she is. No contest.'

'Don't start melting me with words, it's not fair.'

'Yes it is. If I don't, you'll panic. You'll be the one that pisses off. Don't do this, Bus. I'm too fucking vulnerable.'

She puts an arm round my waist and I kiss her forehead through her hair. The water's calm down there, so you can see the greens and dark blues where the sea bed goes up and down.

'I can't stop you feeling vulnerable' she says. 'How can I when I'm wrapped up in fucking pelicans.'

'It'll be easier than you think. I'm pretty low maintenance.'

'I know,' she says softly. 'You always were.' She huddles closer and I can feel her breath through my shirt. She pulls herself up level and kisses me the way she does, like if she took her mouth away for a second we'd be apart for ever, breathing through her nose on my cheek. Just to make sure, I put my arms round her and lock my fingers together.

She pulls away in the end, but only a fraction. Her mouth's touching mine when she talks. It's getting late, she says. Up we get.

'Right.'

We stay there another half-hour, alternately snogging and staring, probably matching each other's facial expressions. Another thirty years of this and we'll start looking like each other. In the end we pack the blanket away, leaving the pitta bread for the gulls, and she uses my arm like a rope ladder on the walk back.

The village we're in is three miles away and the path takes you down towards the harbour wall. Ten feet thick with a gap for boats and a pool of safewater behind. Iron rings in the stonework. Two hundred years old.

It's really quiet now, just the water gushing out a pipe under the road into the pool behind the sea wall. It does that all day and night. The granite hills don't absorb the rain, and it washes straight through and out to the sea. You can hear it from the place we're staying, the only sound usually, and you wonder if one day, for one fucking second, it might ever stop.

'Let's stay here a minute,' she says. 'We can watch the sun go down. It sinks really fast around here.'

So we lean on the iron rail and the sun's a classic red ball and you can actually see it moving, going over the edge. The island offshore is a bird sanctuary, and the gulls are streaming towards it overhead, without a sound for once in their lives, thin black ticks on a sky that goes completely red once the sun's gone.

'It's dead dull. I like the night, but this is just dull.'

'I think so too,' she says. 'I only stopped because I thought you might want to.' She's smiling, and I get the sense of loss I felt when she first got under my skin.

'We can't live in places like this, Stevie. And no more of these weekends. If your work's going to take over, you might as well do it at home.'

'Agreed,' she says. 'But let's stay till monday, is that alright?'

'Shit yeh, we've paid for it.'

She puts her arms round my neck, but she never holds you, Stevie, she puts them round you so's you'll hold *her*. The insides of her forearms slide along your neck, leaving her ribs and waist open, and your arms go round her instinctively.

Fine by me. I like this arrangement. I never needed anybody to hold me. They did, when I was a kid, but I was always one of nature's huggers, not a huggee. Snog time again, tasting the salt left by the wind on her mouth. On the way back, the wind's come up so it's muffling the sea. Flash of light from the caravan site when somebody opens a door and lets their dog in.

Sometimes it's so quiet it wakes you up. You keep forgetting there's hardly any sound in the country, and it's *totally* dark at night. You'd give anything for a lamp-post outside the window, head-lights flashing, some decent traffic noises. You can't lie there too long.

Specially as Miss Red Bus isn't taking up most of the bed for once. Wait a second in case she's in the bathroom, then get up and get dressed. I don't want to put a light on, so I trip over a bin bag when I go in the kitchen for a glass of water.

She's not in the house, so I go outside, where it's so dark you have to feel with your feet as you walk. I zip my jacket up and go out the garden gate onto the coastal path.

Left or right? Left probably, away from the village. There's a breeze in your face this direction, and you feel like it's waking you up. There's a car brumming in the distance.

This is our last night here. Yesterday she sent me out birding all morning while she stayed indoors with her sketchpads. But she stopped at lunchtime and we had the afternoon together. Tea in a hotel overlooking the bay, tour round an old church with toothaching gargoyles. Come sunset we're paddling in the sea with our trousers rolled up and she's yelping like a little girl every time a wave comes in. Somebody even arranged for the sun to go down behind her off a red and black mackerel sky.

You can see traces of that sky now, even in the dark. The

coastal path runs parallel with the road at one point, and a car comes up behind me and blasts the clifftop with light, leaving everything even darker when it's gone.

Then your eyes readjust and you can see the curves of the coastline against the sky – and just her head and shoulders where she's sitting down, on the lip of the escarpment itself. Sitting with her knees up to her chin, not legs over the side.

She's an incorrigible drama queen, the Bus. I think her and Bish must be brother and sister sometimes. She came out here to be on her own, but not for long. I had to wake up sometime, and obviously I'd come looking for her, and find her here in a dramatic setting, sheer drop in the dead of night. No full moon, but you can't have everything.

But the fact that she's attention seeking is precisely why you give it. I walk past her and stand on the edge of the cliff.

She heard me before she saw me. I've carried the bin liner here from the kitchen and it's crunkling in the breeze. When I get to the edge of the cliff, I start undoing it. Oh fucking hell, she says.

It's packed tight like a kitbag but very light because it's only full of crumpled-up pages from her sketchpads. I turn it upside-down and empty it over the cliff. You can't see the bits of paper in the dark, but you can hear some of them bouncing crisply on the rocks. Most of them reach the sea presumably, where they start turning to slush.

I give the bin liner a good noisy shake and flatten it into a neat square, then I put it on the grass next to her and use it to sit on. She says fucking hell again, but she isn't going to give me a hard time. Hundreds of pelicans went over the side, and they'll take some explaining.

I get a bottle of water out my jacket and she has a sip. I have a yawn. There's a ship on the horizon, signalling somewhere.

'Do you know who Cassandra is?'

'One of your publishers?'

'No,' she says. 'It's me.'

She puts the water bottle down and leans forward to pull her socks up. 'When they brought the trojan horse in,' she says, 'Cassandra told them it was full of greeks. They didn't believe her. They brought it inside the city walls and the greeks came out in the middle of the night and massacred them. The gods gave Cassandra the gift of prophecy, but they withheld the power to make people believe her. That's me.'

'This is your work you're talking about.'

'Yeh,' she says. 'I can't persuade people I can do it. And they're right. That sackful of drawings was a single morning's output, proof that I still can't cut it. You haven't got anything to drink, have you? Not the water.'

It just so happens. I hand her the quarter-bottle of brandy we bought yesterday. She has a drink and gives it back. I tell her Cassandra was right, wasn't she. She was the only one who was. The fact people didn't believe her doesn't change that. 'Maybe your time hasn't come or something.'

'Meaning what? They might look at my work differently when I'm gone? The analogy doesn't stretch that far. Cassandra knew she was right, that was her curse. I don't know I'm right. I need other people to decide for me. And if they say I'm not good enough,

I haven't got anything of my own to fall back on. So I've been a ghost in my own town since I left art school.'

'And it's no good me and Bish saying you're any good.'

'Exactly,' she says. 'You don't count. It's an elitist thing. There's people who know and people who don't. Which is how it should be. And the people who know, know I'm not good enough.'

'If you say so. Except I remember the things you did at art school. That broken glass sculpture.'

'The one you said made you cry.'

'What do you mean, *said* it made me cry. It made me cry. It made Bish shut up for once. It was top of the class that year. So somebody else must've thought you were good enough. Somebody who knew.'

'Alright I was a star pupil,' she says. 'But that's all I am still. Imagine being labelled promising all your life. Nearly a good artist. Give me that bottle back.'

'When I've finished.'

'That's what I hate about Bish,' she says. 'He does have talent, and he wastes it playing in pubs. Meanwhile I haven't got any to waste. Fucking session work. He's better than that.'

'What else can you do with a mouth organ?'

'Why does it have to be a mouth organ? It could be a guitar or a piano. He can play anything he wants, the bastard. You know how long it took him to learn the mouth organ? Twenty minutes. In between burger kings. He only plays it because he doesn't have to work at it.'

'He used to work at it. Till his run-in with the police. You know all this, Stevie.'

'Alright,' she says quietly. 'I'm just saying I'd like a fraction of his talent. I've told him so.'

I have another drink then I give her the bottle, and I was right to hang on to it: she nearly finishes it in one go. The dawn's on its way up. I can see her as well as hear her.

She sits up straight and pulls her hair off her face with both hands. 'I don't know why I'm singling Bish out,' she says. 'I resent everybody. People with talent that gets recognized, people who know they've got no talent and can get on with their lives. I've always hated you. The way you can just live.'

This isn't my cue to say anything. I button my jacket up because the breeze is freshening.

'So I've ended up in solitary fucking confinement,' she says. 'I go birding and go on demos, I spend time with you. But I'm always frantic to get back, to be on my own with work I can't do.'

'And it stops you being close to anybody. I know.'

'I would be close,' she says. 'If I could do the work. Or so I keep telling myself. One good piece and I'll be alright. When you do good work, you get rid of something, you can function with people. You and me could travel and have a world list. I wouldn't laugh at your jokes unless they were funny. One good piece and I can start living.'

I tell her I feel like Bish used to feel. I want to wave a magic wand. 'You know I can't fix this for you, Stevie – so why did you let me back in? Just to have my arms round you? I can't believe that's enough any more.'

'I've missed them,' she says. 'When you're holding me, I don't think I'm a bad artist, I think I'm a good lover, who deserves to be held.'

'Except you don't want me to hold you all the time.'

'That's the lobotomy I need,' she says. 'The one Bish has had. He'd give up the music if he found somebody to hold. Meanwhile I can't tear myself away from something I'm no good at.'

I have a swig of the brandy and give her the last bit. She twists the top back on like she's wringing its neck.

'The worst thing,' she says, 'is the fear. I'm coming to the conclusion the only good artists are young ones and very old ones. When you're young you're so fucking stupid you don't know how to be scared, and when you're old you're probably past caring. In between, you're always, always afraid. Jesus. To keep going back to it when you know it's beating you.'

There's bird silhouettes against the sky but naturally you don't try identifying them at a moment like this. It's only gulls.

'That's what I fell for, Stevie. Not your shy retiring personality or the red hair. Your courage.'

'Oh fuck. You prat. Can you see me crying in this light?'

'I can hear you a bit.'

'So why are you sitting a mile away?'

I move over and my arm comes out like a batwing and I get my fingers caught when I brush her hair off her face. Her hands are cold through my shirt and she's shivering like a whippet. 'I need some more of that water,' she says. 'To wipe my eyes.'

'And your nose.'

She laughs. More of a snort than a laugh, which proves my

point. The one thing I didn't bring out here was any tissues. She burrows in and she won't be cold for long.

'Phew christ,' she says. 'What a trio we turned out to be. We ought to go into business, start our own retirement home. A cleaner, a painter and decorator, and somebody to lead the singsong. We'd make a fucking fortune.'

My laughing sets her snorting off again. I tell her I can't look after her any more can I, and she says no that's right. 'I wish you could,' she says, 'but you said it: we have to fix things ourselves in the end.'

Relief when she says that. When I have to leave her, she won't be hurt so much. 'What happens now? Do you want me to go?'

'No,' she says. 'I want you to stay and we'll do our best. But we can't be the be-all and end-all. I know that now.'

'Understood.'

'Can you stay on those terms? They're not what you came back for.'

'Where else am I going to go?'

She holds me tight round the middle and leans up into me and kisses me. Her tongue's really hot and her tears are cold now they've dried. Angel, she says. You've come back and I'm not there any more.

I tell her it's alright and I hold her best I can. The wind means it by now, and I tell her it's time we went back in, but she says fuck that, she wants the fresh air.

'The fresh air is why you're shivering to death. We can do this inside.'

'Another ten minutes,' she says. 'I've got two tops on.'

186

'Bed, Bus.'

'Yes, boss.'

She gets up and pulls me to my feet, then she finds a handkerchief and blows her nose loud enough to warn local shipping. 'Hey, fucking hell,' she says. 'All that paper down there. You polluting show-off. You could've recycled it.'

'You're just jealous. If you'd done it, you'd call it a temporary installation.'

'Ah yeh, but I'm allowed to. I'm the Stevie formerly known as artist.'


She went to sleep with her cheek on my heartbeat. Two hours later I'm not so much holding her as leaving an arm round her. There's no point trying to match my breathing to hers: she takes two breaths to my one and I'd end up hyperventilating. I'm so wide awake I can't imagine ever falling asleep, like christmas eve when you're a kid. I should've brought some of the pills Bish gave me.

She still melts every time you touch her, but it's not enough for her any more. From now on, the best you can do is help her sleep. You and a quarter-bottle of brandy.

Meanwhile I'm so fucking wired I can't shut my eyes, and I'm holding her responsible. I lay there earlier, listening to her talking about Owen Whittle at long last. It all came out. Her mixed feelings when she heard. The fascination, the visualizing. What it takes to lie in wait in a wood like that, keeping the intention even though you waver. The fear you'd have.

I imagined putting the gun to her head then. Then turning it on me. Best thing for both of us. But there again I used to imagine it when we first went out. Somebody you care about, lying there trusting you, and bang, just because you could. Best not to go there.

When she was about to doze off, I asked her what the bird of prey was, in her pelican drawings, and she said goshawk.

Oh?

That was a sacrifice too, she said. If you shoot somebody, you know you'll get caught. My cousins made sacrifices for me, Owen Whittle's killer did it for goshawk eggs. A rich seam for any artist, yeh? Even one who always fucks it up.

She held me very tight suddenly, and cried, and said sorry again. I came back and she's not there for me, all because an egg thief got killed. Angel forgive me.

She rolls over in her sleep now and lies flat on her stomach with her face turned to one side and facing me. She's breathing through her mouth and some of her hair's stuck in it. I draw it out slowly and pull the duvet down off her shoulders because she gets hot at night.

At the other end of the country, John Ure Peacock's probably still lying on his back. Be a while before he can move his limbs, according to hospital staff. But he opened his eyes yesterday, after nine days in a coma, and they say he's breathing more regular.

I'm staring straight ahead. It's a cloudy morning thank god, so the daylight's not blasting in and depressing you because you're still awake. The window's open, which explains why my shoulders are shivering. It's an onshore wind, bringing those poms within binocular range. If Bish was here, he'd be daydreaming of a south polar skua, but that's a fantasy too far.

SHEPHERD'S BUSH TUBE isn't much to look at, I suppose. The overland station, Hammersmith and City line. They gave it a touch of blue paint a while back, but it's still basically two wooden sheds and whitewashed breezeblocks. If Slough or Basingstoke had an underground system, it'd look like this. A corrugated iron roof, for fucksake. They've put chicken wire on the underside to stop the pigeons nesting.

Still, it's the first station I ever knew, a gateway to everything. Up to Paddington or King's Cross and therefore the rest of the country, or south to Hammersmith and the river, the reservoirs with all the new birds you might see. So it's still my magic old place, even when there's a defective train at Royal Oak and I'm late.

I would've got here earlier except I had a job in North Pole Road. It didn't take long, the flat's so small you can hoover it all from the same powerpoint. But I couldn't see a bus when I came out, so I walked down Bloemfontein Road past the bolted-up shops. Two streets called Bloemfontein, another called South Africa

Road, pubs called the Springbok and the General Smuts – in an area that's half black. Nice one, somebody.

It's gone midnight, sky black as pepsi, and there's only an old black woman on the other platform. You see them every day, London's army of black workers, going out to clean an office block or packing pitta bread. Some of them are illegal, and their employers wait two weeks before telling them to bring in the national insurance number they know they haven't got, getting a fortnight's unpaid work out of them. I did it myself once, supplementing my giro, three days before I sussed it, and I know nothing's changed. God's own country.

The woman on the other platform might be leaving for the night shift. She's still sitting there when the electric tickling comes in along the track and I get on the last train out.

It's only two stops then I'm on the towpath, with Hammersmith Bridge looking its best at this time of night, olive-green and lit up. When I get to the pub, I see Bish was right about the late licence: they're charging admission and there's a queue outside.

Birders hate paying entrance fees. We'll spend five hundred quid on a flight to Shetland, plus taxis and accommodation – then moan about forking out two pound fifty to get into a bird reserve. Fucking Skye toll bridge.

The pub's packed so's you can't move. I down a double southern comfort in one and nurse a bottle of holsten because it's vegan and easy to hold. How's the band going to fit on a stage that's fifteen foot by ten?

At least I timed it right: the support band's just finished. There's so many people you have to keep your arms in and somebody's always butting into you. Easy, slim, I've got a luger in the attic. You're beginning to wonder why you ever go to things like this – then the drummer appears, no stool to sit on, and stands there hammering out the first rhythm with just one stick, and you remember why.

I've known the guitarist since we were kids. He does session work at the Riverside and his lead breaks go straight through you. Meanwhile the drummer's fills mess with your heartbeat. So when I say you hardly notice them all night, it means something. All eyes are on the Bish.

Stage presence? Well he fills half of it without moving, so yeh. He seems to be dressed for maximum sweat. Black biker jacket, black polo, shades, face like rain on butter. I mean it: one of the great sights of London at night.

And that sound. That fucking sound he must've sold his soul for. He's got a voice like a corncrake (not a compliment) so they don't let him do backing vocals. But anyway the lyrics are just interludes between bursts of that amazing blues harp, howling like sex in dracula's castle or the funeral of your first born. If butterflies make you believe in a god, this makes you dead certain god just died and the devil was last seen dancing on the grave.

God dear he's a bitch tonight, absolutely cooking the place, hooting out old blues standards followed by irish famine songs about burying dead kids in sand dunes, makes you want to shoot anything with an english accent. The drummer's doing his Velvet Underground impersonation, bat bat bat bat bat bat bat bat, the bodies are jumping, and when Bish catches my eye he doesn't show he knows me let alone he's pleased I'm here. And I don't give the slightest fuck. You could die tonight and feel privileged.

And when it's finished, three encores later, I could pull anybody I wanted, male or female, just because the bouncer knows I'm a mate of Bish's and lets me go backstage. The place is still going like a heart muscle, the walls are sweating onto the floor, and my ears are still flinching from his last solo, like an ermine with its tongue stuck on the ice.

Same night, exterior. I'm sitting on the sea wall, looking back in. It's dark but you can make out the general layout of the saltmarsh, the electricity pylons showing against the sky and Bish getting stuff out the car.

The waders are just starting up, the redshanks first as usual then a curlew calling out its name. You look around but it's hard to pinpoint waders even in better light. I've stood around at Barn Elms trying to locate the bird that's going pee-pee-pee only to find out it's a car alarm in Rocks Lane.

This was one of our favourite places when we started out. We didn't know Stevie then or anybody else with a car, and we hadn't seen too many species, so it was always a thrill getting out to the Thames estuary, train from Victoria and a long walk. We had our first laplands here, so close you could see the tigerstripe tertials with your naked eye, a really fantastic british bird. Our first snow buntings and bartails, thinking we were the bollocks in our classic birders' uniform, jeans and trainers and BHS anoraks, which made you sweat like horses in summer and soaked up the rain like a bathmat. Suffering for your birds was the thing.

And how. If we weren't being drenched to the skin, we had

our heads down in a force nine sandstorm looking for shorelarks. You kept your mouth shut tight but the sand came in through your nose. We've seen shitloads of shorelarks since, including two in London, but it was still worth getting sandblasted that first time.

Nobody else came here much, so we had to find everything ourselves. Ortolans and yellowbrowed warblers, a red-spotted bluethroat with a chest like an archery target. We'd check every wader in a flock of thousands and scan the waves for shear-waters and rare grebes, slogging around in drizzle or fog or clammy heat, all day sometimes without seeing a thing. Doing bird, Bish called it. Not a care in the world except whether we had enough to buy a drink as well as the tube fare back.

Bish comes back from the car and sits next to me on the wall. 'How's the Bus? How's that going?'

'Fine. Moving house is doing her good.'

'Or getting back with you,' he says. 'Fucking false modesty.'

'Yeh it's going well so far.'

'So far? What a pessimistic cunt, even when we were kids. Just as well I'm chuffed enough for both of us. Are you listening? I'm really pleased for you, you dismal toss.'

'I know.'

'Good,' he says. 'I've told Stevie I'm pleased too.'

'Look, let's stop this. I don't want half an hour's suspense. Spill it. What have you done?'

'Drink,' he says. 'You won't take pills so you'll have to take drink. I've just done a gig and I need to come down.'

'Yeh yeh. Fucking tell me.'

'Shut up and neck this.' He's brought some cans of holsten and half a bottle of southern comfort for me, chinking when he puts them down on the concrete. Jamesons and guinness for him because he's gone irish in his drinking after twitching a yellow warbler at Cape Clear.

'What makes you think I've done anything?'

'Piss off. Bringing us here to the old place, all this booze. The equivalent of sitting me down with a stiff drink before you break the news. Drama queen as usual.'

'Everybody's a drama queen to you –'

'Anyway I saw you on stage. I don't know, like a weight's off your mind.'

He sits down next to me and starts butting his heels on the wall. It's not a cold night, but he's got his hooded parka on after all the sweating he's done. He's brought a miniature ghetto-blaster which he keeps turned down low, a Feelgood harmonica solo. There's four samosas in a greaseproof bag, two lamb two veg.

'Your drummer asked me if you were on steroids.'

'That emaciated cunt. I hope you put him straight.'

'I said it was human growth hormone, not steroids.'

'Thanks a fucking heap. Why are my eating habits so important nowadays?'

He drinks half the guinness in one go, wipes his mouth and gives his first samosa a sideways look, then asks me if I really think he's put on weight. 'And don't take the piss like everybody else, tell the truth.'

'I'm a bit concerned about you.'

'I weigh the same as I did a year ago. Honest, to the fucking ounce.'

'Yeh but what's the muscle-fat ratio? You don't look quite good, Bish. We're worried.'

He makes a joke about putting on bodyweight before migration, whatever that means. Then he says the light's getting better, we could start looking through the gulls on the nearest pool.

'How many gull flocks have you checked in your life? About.'

'Hundreds,' he says. 'Fuck knows.'

'A million birds, give or take. How many rare gulls have you found?'

'Four glaucous, five iceland, that slender-billed they wouldn't let me have at Cliffe. Why?'

'Sounds a good return to me.'

He looks across in the half dark and sees I'm not taking the piss. He pushes the hood of his parka right back and rubs his hair with both hands then leaves it down instead of tying it back. 'What did you think of the gig tonight?'

'Best I ever heard you play. Humbling, if you want to know.'

'Yeh,' he says quietly and has another swig of his guinness. 'Yeh, wasn't it.'

'Stevie says when she used to do good work, she got rid of something. Is it like that with you?'

'You think that's what happened tonight, do you? I got rid of something?'

'You'd have to ask her. It was just a gig to me.'

'I never get rid of anything that way,' he says. 'I never do enough good work. Anyway you only get rid of something till the next time. Second gull on the left, it might be a caspian.'

Coming from anybody else, this would be bollocks of the highest order. You can hardly see the fucking things, and you can only safely tell caspian from herring gull by the tongue and the underside of one particular feather (I kid you not). But if anybody can do it just by structure, in shit light, it's Bish. There's times he can do no wrong.

We drove all night once for a baillon's crake at Stithians, but it was gone when we got there. There were no other good birds in the area, so we thought we'd go and sit on the beach at Kynance Cove. On the way, Bish said he'd seen the weather maps and there was a giant anticyclone over the Med, which meant something good was likely to drop in, like a bee-eater or a woodchat shrike. Hoots of derision at this – but then lo and behold the first bird we see on the peninsula is a stunning male woodchat, which was a new bird for Stevie and me, perching in full view on a fivebar gate while we're bowing down in front of the Bish giving him the allah.

He likes that memory and relives another one, a bird race three years back, when four teams broke the record for most species in a day, us included, and we would've had the number one if we hadn't heard there was a whiskered tern on one of the Walthamstow reservoirs.

To get to it would use up time we didn't have, but we went anyway, because we had Jace Babb in the car and he hadn't seen one before and we wanted him to have it on his list. Not him, he was furious, Bish had to hold him down in the back seat. He was shouting how he wanted to win the race not see the fucking bird, he could get one any day. Sod that, we said, you're having it, your list's as short as your dick. Stevie could hardly drive straight for laughing.

We went all the way to north London and back, saw the tern, and lost the national title to a bunch of shooting mag editors in a merc. At ten o'clock we're driving down country roads with me and Jace leaning out the back with torches, flashing for owls.

'Christ,' says Bish. 'Remember when we wasted half an hour in that Happy Eater? I thought Jace was going to kill me at long last.'

His chuckle's so big his tits bounce. I can't see them in this light, but I've got my memories.

'Notice how we keep talking about the past recently?'

'Yeh I know.'

'From my point of view,' he says, 'it's because I'm finished here. I'm leaving. That's what tonight's all about.'

'That could mean anything. Leaving? Leaving what? Fucking pregnant pause.'

'What do you mean, it could mean anything? I could be saying I'm leaving this sea wall to go for a slash, could I? Tosser. Leaving the country, what else could I mean. Farewell gig. I've got a flight back to Poland next week. I wanted to come here for a last look at the place. With you, you miserable fucking misery.'

I look at him but he's not looking at me. I stare at the southern comfort as you do. 'What do you mean, *back* to Poland? You never fucking lived there.'

'I've just been out there,' he says. 'Looking at flats. Greg's already there. He offered me a job and I took it. He sold that polish caf and went home.'

'And that's it, is it? I knew you'd done something. I thought it might be more drastic than this.'

'What do you mean, more drastic? Your best mate supposedly, leaving for good. That's not big enough news for you?'

'Yeh.' I say it quietly. 'It's big enough news. A fucking horror story.' He finishes his glass and I pour him another one. Quite a long silence before I ask him what the job offer is and he says running a nature reserve. Greg bought it with what he made from the caf. 'Bish Nowak, warden on a nature reserve, imagine that.'

'I can, that's the problem. It's just what you need, specially as it's away from here. Fuck.'

'I agree: fuck. I've never even felt polish, that's the stupid thing. Deliberately didn't learn the language, as you know.'

It was only warm out here because we were hot after his gig. Time to put a jacket on and over-indulge in alcohol. There's some patchy cloud, dirty pink on the underside from the town lights on the right, but some stars too. 'Fucking hell, Bish.'

'I know.'

'You're really going.'

'I should've gone years ago', he says. 'We both know that.'

'Fucking hell. I can't believe there's nothing to keep you here.'

'There's everything to keep me here, what are you talking about. You and the Bus and my british list. But you know how I feel about this country now.'

'Anyway,' he says, 'it's time the poles went back to Poland. They only left because it's got no natural borders. No alps or channel, so it's easy to invade and partition. And when the poles emigrate, they stay emigrated. Where do italians and jamaicans hold their wedding receptions? The local polish or ukrainian club, there's one in every town. Built by people who know they're never going back.'

'I've denied that part of me long enough,' he says. 'Letting people call me Bish just because Zbishek's a bit of a mouthful. Let them fucking learn it.'

He throws a stone out towards the creek. Must be all mud out there, because you can't hear it land. I ask him if he's leaving because he's been chased out in any way. Have the police been talking to him? About the shootings.

'No,' he says. 'I can account for my whereabouts. Anyway, they leave me alone nowadays. They know I'm harmless.'

'What about the people Owen Whittle was borrowing from? Do you know if they've been down here?'

'No, that never materialized, did it. Probably just Frostbite's reporter winding him up. Stevie says she's given up drawing birds. Is that right? She's really gone back to the other work?'

'Yeh.'

'Even though she thinks she's shit at it?'

'Well, it's weird. This latest thing she's doing, she says she can make it work. And she's stopped taking those pills you give her.'

'This thing of hers,' he says, 'has it got anything to do with music?'

'No idea. What makes you say that?'

'She's been talking to a sound engineer at a studio we use. He's an acoustics expert more than anything. I wondered if she was using music this time.'

'If she was, she'd have consulted you, wouldn't she?'

'The balls on that woman,' he says. 'I don't know how she does it, working on her own all the time. If I did that, I'd be just a busker. I wouldn't play a note if I couldn't do it with other people.'

Talking of which, I ask him if he's told his band he's leaving.

'Ah well,' he says. 'No group of men stay together very long. They'll get on without me. And there's bound to be bands over there that need a mouth organ. They play some terrible shit in eastern Europe, but maybe I can do something about that.'

He has another sip and says 'Fuck me, what am I saying? Playing mouth organ in the backwoods of Europe. Stevie's right: I'm always running away. Me with my cowardice and her with her fear. You're lucky you haven't got any talent.'

'So I'm told.'

'Tell her I'll buy this latest thing of hers, whatever it is. We'll put it up in reception at the nature reserve. Are you going to stay with her or piss off again?'

'It's not down to me this time.'

He puts his hair behind his ears and has another long drink, sucking a vacuum out the can, loud enough to set the redshanks off. I've seen him sit here in the dark playing his mouth organ one note at a time, imitating curlews so well they were answering him. He can't do it now because the harmonica's full of spit. He'll let me have it as a goodbye present if I want. Christ no, leave me it in his will.

He knew about me and Stevie, didn't he. First time around.

'Oh yeh,' he says.

'So why pretend you didn't?'

'Well,' he says, 'we thought you were keeping it a secret.'

'We? So everybody knew? And nobody said anything. You tossers.'

'That's because you're confusing us with people who gave a shit. Nobody's interested in anybody. People are only close to people in bed, far as I can see.'

'That's not why you're leaving, is it? Because of Stevie?'

'Don't be a cunt,' he says. 'Anyway, Grace is going back too. She's already there, buying stuff for the flat.'

'Who?'

'Grace. Grazyna. Don't know if you know her. She worked in Greg's caf. Blonde, speaks quite good english.'

'The one with the white hair? Not that one?'

'Isn't that what I just said?'

'You're going back to Poland with her? We're talking about the same girl, are we? White hair, face like an ice angel?'

'Straight blonde hair in a fringe, yeh. Ears are a bit big for an ice angel.'

'How the fucking hell did you manage that? The best looking girl in the world. How the fucking bloody hell?'

'Bit gobsmacked, are we?'

'Bit fucking heartbroken. That hair of hers.'

'You thought she might be up for it, did you? Interesting.'

'Never mind interesting. That's where you disappeared to, was it? Not doing some soul searching on your own. You were shacked up for the whole of last month with the most stunning woman in the world. There's no fucking justice.'

'Well,' he says, 'I had to go over there and do a recce.'

'Yeh, I bet. Not that nature reserve and its fucking birdlife.

You were doing a recce on her perfect white body while I was here wondering about the state you were in.'

'How do you know it's perfect?'

'Oh please. With a face like that. Yeh go on, laugh.'

'It's alright,' he says. 'It shows you care.'

'You must've sold your soul for this. Christ, now you're look-ing bashful. What a horrible sight that is.'

'Amazing, isn't it. And she hasn't even heard me play. She's something, isn't she. I knew I was in trouble first night.'

'First night? I knew it first time I saw her.'

'I asked her out a bit late,' he says. 'She only had one night left before her visa ran out. Anyway, miracles never cease, we're in bed before it's dark. Except we're not safe, right? So she's going down on me at the end, and when it comes to it I start pulling out –'

'As you do.'

'Except she won't let me. She said it was the only way she could take a part of me back to Poland.'

'Dear christ.'

'Well that finished me,' he says. 'I'd have followed her anywhere after that. With her and the job offer, there's no way I could stay here. If I ever get rid of anything, it'll be through her.'

He probably can't see me smiling in this light. Jealous and pleased as piss, so relieved he's going to be alright.

'People in Poland are as big as me,' he says. 'And that's just the girls. I'll lose some weight when I get there. Either that or feed Grace up a couple of sizes. She's been teaching me ten words a day in polish. Barn owl.'

There is too, beating over the reeds at the back of the first field, I should've noticed it myself. Ghostly white's the usual description, and that's fair enough in the dark like this. That stiff-winged flight you never get tired of. It sweeps up into a hawthorn bush and sits there looking out. It can see us better than we can see it, but we're too far away to be a threat.

'Look at that,' says Bish. 'Who'd believe those ugly chicks could grow into something like that. Like miniature dodos when they're young. Look at this fat sod, must've been a vole summer round here.'

The owl's not moving anything except its head, that famous face like the bas relief of a crusader in a helmet but with a beak like a clitoris. Why are they white if they come out at night? We watch it till it flies off, then Bish says 'Tell Stevie this is why I've never done more with the music. I'd give it all up to find one new species for Britain.'

'Or Poland.'

'That too.'

'Bish Nowak's polish list. I can't see it somehow.'

'Nor can I yet,' he says. 'But I'm young enough to start one. Aquatic warblers, great snipe displaying, all those continental owls. They're saying it might be the new Lesbos. The Bialowieza forest, the Biebrza marshes, best peatbogs in Europe. Might start finding my own birds again.'

'They hunt wolves in that forest.'

'It's good for woodpeckers and tengmalm's,' he says. 'Old growth national park.'

'They cordon it off with red netting and drive the wolves towards it.'

'I know –'

'The wolves won't cross it for some reason. Then everybody comes in and shoots them at close range.'

'I'm not saying it's the fucking garden of eden. But I might have a chance to change it a bit.'

'You could still do that here.'

'Don't say things like that, you know I can't. Greg asked me if my arsehole had fallen out completely and I said in this country yeh.'

'He used those words, did he? Arsehole fallen out.'

'Yeh, why wouldn't he? He's lived here, he knows the phrases. I told him this country beat me but I might be alright over there. He said that was good enough for him.'

I sit and drink for a minute, then I mention his magic wand. The big thing he's always wanted to do, change the world in one go – that's running a poxy nature reserve, is it?

'By my standards now, yeh it's a big thing. This is my last chance to unfuck everything.'

'What's it got, this place? Reedbeds, wader scrapes?'

'Don't start making conversation, for fucksake. Time's too short. You'll see it one day. You and Bus can come and visit.'

'I think I need another drink.'

'I'll get it,' he says. 'After I've pissed this one out.'

There's the slightest hint of dawn by now, so the sea's just beginning to shine and the estuary's like it used to be when we started. You can make out some of the waders now, their silhouettes anyway, tucking into all that protein on the mudflats. There's going to be one of our slow northern hemisphere dawns, a petrol-blue sky nobody else has got.

We used to say we loved this kind of place, birds or no birds. Most people hate it, how flat and barren it is, but that was part of the crack for us, not just the mud and saltmarsh and smell of seaweed but the big sky and the fact nobody else liked it, so we had it to ourselves.

Except it wasn't true. Without the birds, you wouldn't spend five minutes in places like this, they're as desolate as everybody says, pylons and power stations and nothing to stop the wind cutting through you, the smell of seaweed mixed with sulphur and sewage. Only reason you come here is because a few snipe might fly out the saltings or a greenshank jump up piping from a creek. You might get brent geese in the snow or a family of bewick's swans on the river.

That's what made us up get up before the milk, arriving here at first light when the fields were covered in those threads money spiders string out, or we'd stay till dusk when the finch flocks were coming back to roost by the lights of the refinery. Places like this make you realize what the great british countryside is like without birdsong.

I want to tell him to stay. Don't run away to Poland, I need you here in the time I've got left. But I'm too pleased for him. Airpunchingly grinning in the dark happy. I don't care about the whole planet like Stevie, but I want people round me to be alright. Anyway there's nothing I can say to change his mind, now he's been rescued by an ice angel. And he's right, this country beat him.

People generally take the piss out of Bish nowadays. He's always preaching about environmental abuse and doing nothing about it. But they didn't know him a few years back. You hardly ever saw him in those days, he was always out on some direct action or other. A weekend's sabbing, a fortnight up a tree. The jokes about him blocking underground tunnels have all been made, mostly by him.

Then he stopped. He came back from an action and never did another one, took him a month to tell me what happened. All this time I've never helped him get over it, but then nobody could've.

He was into the second week of a protest about the development of the old Crystal Palace, a place where some weird shit was going on. The police were stopping people for hooting their car horns in support, and Bromley council took a pensioner to court for bringing the demonstrators a bread and butter pudding (true story).

The eviction started early one morning. The usual drill, cherrypickers going in to pull people down and dismantle the tree houses. Bish and everybody else down below locked theirselves onto concrete slabs and got ready to sit it out. There's two hundred police and bailiffs forming a cordon. He hears an officer telling them to keep their legs together so's the locals won't see what's about to happen. They even get the construction firm to use their earthmovers as screens.

There's always an under-sheriff at these things, never the sheriff. One of the protesters starts telling him they're not doing any damage, so this is a civil matter, so on and so on. Not so, says under-sheriff, you're obstructing a lawful activity. Bish used to know it word for word . . . in accordance with section S44 . . . terrorism act 2000 . . . following reasons.

Nobody bothers with the reasons very much, the usual procedure is they go in and start dragging people out while the sheriff's still reading it. At that stage Bish isn't worried. He knows the routine by heart, and it always takes an age for the police to take people away, they need two or three to every protester. What they'd like is those electric batons we sell to the saudis, but you can't do that here yet.

Except that day they didn't need them. Suddenly Bish hears somebody near him screaming – then two police are telling him to let go or face reasonable force. It's usually taken more than reasonable force to make Bish let go of anything, so he just asks them their police numbers, which they never wear on these occasions – then one of them gets his fingers in behind him, in the back of his neck, and finds the pressure points. New standard technique, home office approved.

The pain feels like he's broken a bone in the hinge of his jaw and he goes deaf in one ear, the police sound miles away though they're shouting in his face. While this is going on, one of them's twisting his wrist and somebody starts kneeling on his calf to make him fall on his knees, then they kneel on his thigh muscles. When they bend his wrist back again, they twist his elbow too, and then he screams and has to let go. Five hours later in the police cell, his wrist's swollen and there's shooting pains in his arm. You're amazed every time you hear him play the blues harp, because they left him partially deaf in one ear. He got a caution and Stevie wrote three letters to the home office.

They broke the Bish that day, he's never been the same since. He didn't just stop the protests, the spark went out of him in everything. Now he eats too much and can't get through a day without pills, and the nearest he gets to physical danger is having glass bottles in the bathroom.

All because of his size, he says. Sixteen stone even then and strong with it, the confidence it gives you when you're not necessarily confident about anything else. And yet they could manoeuvre him off that concrete in twenty seconds, knowing how humiliating it was. Come on, big fella. Let go now, big man. Sixteen stone and they'd fucked him up the arse and pissed him in the mouth. By law.

So now when he hears about crack dealers laughing when they shoot an unarmed police in Clapham, he laughs too. The police in Poland might be even worse for all he knows, but until they do something like that to him they'll be angels in comparison. He saw a policewoman in a wheelchair once, outside Westminster Abbey, and she misunderstood and smiled when he stood in front of her and started clapping.

'Hey,' I ask him when he gets back with more cans. 'All this birding. Have we been wasting our time?'

'Who gives a shit?'

'I think I do now.'

'No you don't,' he says. 'If it wasn't birding it'd be something equally fucking pointless. We all need the drug.'

'That's the Bus talking. The human condition is to stay stoned out your mind.'

'Never mind the Bus,' he says, 'there's nutters everywhere.

Angelo's cousin in Italy, she's a nurse. They brought this sixteen-year-old kid in, he had a lethal dose of propane and butane in his body, sprayed hisself with two cans of deodorant every day, obsessed with his own BO.'

'Two cans a day? Bang goes the ozone layer.'

We start giggling like kids, and I'm already pretending he'll be back in six weeks, bored stiff and missing the marmite. He bites into a slice of pork pie with a boiled egg in it and says 'Human growth hormone ay? That's what Janis Joplin got hooked on. Maybe I should give it a try.'

The light's slightly better, just enough to start scanning with our bins. We're not expecting to see anything special, but right now the birds are just a background for a nostalgia session, blowing our own trumpets a bit. We really did get very good at this.

Bish would pick out a first-winter arctic tern in a flock of commons by the translucent triangle on the trailing edge of the upperwing – but anybody can do that. Finding a baird's sandpiper in a flock of five hundred dunlin because it was the only wader that wouldn't wade – now that was showing off. And that was me.

'Fuck this place,' he says. 'I fucking hate it.'

'Yeh, I know. Because you love it.'

'Exactly. My own fucking country. And it turns round and bites me.'

'You can always come back.'

'Except I can't, can I. I'm always going to feel like this about it. Jesus, look at me. I'm not even angry, just beaten. You heard them at the solitary sand. I'm all mouth.'

'Since when did you listen to them? Lamebrains like that. Jace Babb, for fucksake.'

'They're just saying what everybody thinks, you and Bus included. Big only in body.'

'Not for a minute, no –'

'Admit it,' he says. 'It was only a bit of physical grief. I should've recovered. What sort of cunt crawls into a corner after the first setback in his life?'

'The sort of cunt who never thought his own country could do that to him and go unpunished. The sort who stood in the front line when all the other cunts sat at home. Cunts like me. What they did to you, Bish, it would've beaten anybody.'

'Thanks but bollocks. It didn't beat everybody else on that protest. They went straight on to the next one.'

'Then either they're fucking superhuman or they cared more than you did. You didn't care enough to take any more pain. We've all been there.'

He accepts that as a get-out clause and pulls me over by my jacket, leaning me against his shoulder. I look like a ventriloquist's dummy probably, but it's the right place to be. There's a boat in the creek. It's dark but you can't stop fishermen fishing.

'You didn't care about Owen Whittle, did you. Or John Ure Peacock. I thought you were joking.'

'No,' he says, 'I didn't care. The initial shock, then fuck it. I didn't even know they switched his life support off till Terry Chai rang me. You?'

'I read it in the paper.'

'No, what do you think about the whole thing? Owen Whittle

and the Peacock. If you were going to talk about it, you'd do it in your own time, I thought. Is this your own time?'

'No, it doesn't matter now. You're leaving the country and I can't stop you. Owen Whittle and the Peacock can fuck off.'

'My sentiments exactly.'

'I still can't believe it.'

'Poland's only three hours away,' he says. 'You can practically twitch it –'

'I can't believe it. You and that white-haired girl. It's just not natural.'

'Yeh who'd have thought it,' he says. 'Big fat Bish getting a girl like that. Talk about luck.'

'I bet she does. She's got a bargain.'

His smile's one of the best things you'll see. He unhands me and turns the tape over in the ghettoblaster, *Spanish Bombs* by the Clash, and asks me if I'd swop her for Stevie.

'If she was seriously interested? If she wasn't going back to Poland?'

'Yeh.'

'Not in a million years.'

He chuckles into the neck of his latest guinness. The dawn's coming up like blotting paper.

'Me and Grace,' he says. 'Putting my arms round her and every-thing's alright. It can't be that simple. I mean, I can do that.'

'Time to face up to it, Bish. The power we've got.'

The marsh is shit to look at. Almost literally, like it's made of lumps of it. But when it's the last time you'll be seeing it together, you don't care about that. You look at the winding streams and dykes in it, so thin it's like they've been put there with one of Stevie's silver pencils, cutting through the bottle-greens and shades of brown, more colours than you ever thought it had. There's cress growing by some of the banks, yellow as rape except it belongs here.

'Fuck this place,' he says. 'It's only a country.'

'Exactly.'

'The three great joys in life, you can take them anywhere. All food, most birds, and Joe Strummer pronouncing *corazon*.'

ONCE I FINISHED what I came here to do, I went out on the balcony to have a look. Eight floors up in central London you're high enough to see the whole town. I used to see it when I was a kid, looking down from our towerblock on White City Estate – but you get a different view up here.

You can see Cambridge Circus, which is the best circus in the world, specially at night like this. Any road leading off it goes somewhere good. Angelucci's and the Centrale like in the songs, bookshops for your bird books, Stevie's school of art. Charing Cross Road traffic versus Shaftesbury Avenue traffic, pedestrians taking their chances between the dodgems.

I've helped myself to a second glass of water and I'm drinking it out of her best wineglass. She won't mind. Plenty of ice. The sun's gone down in the time I've been here, and the lights look weak under this in-between sky. There's two street pigeons looking down from a gutter, giving a big mac carton the evil eye.

The balcony's as big as a bedsit. The railing on its own probably cost more than all my furniture at home. This is how the other half live when they make their money from selling peregrines' eggs abroad.

You can see Vauxhall Bridge from here, if you stand on your toes, and lean over the edge, and use your imagination. Best bridge in the world, day or night – but only when you're on it, so you don't have to look at it. Dirty red and flat. The view is what you go there for, specially with all the lights on. The great London riverfront. Boats and roosting gulls like the coast, except you tell the time by Big Ben here.

Do you like it? Bish said once.

What are you on about? We were born here.

Yeh but do you *like* it. It's not a fucking interrogation. Yes or no.

Alright, yeh, as it happens. I love it. The river, bright lights big city. You know I do.

*Huge* city, he said. That's what's so good. It's only our home town like anybody else's, except ours is the biggest fucking city this country's ever had. What a massive great buzz that gives you.

I thought that's what I said –

I even love the fact there's no good buildings, he said. All concrete blocks after it was bombed in the war. But then I never understood why towns should have to be pretty. I've been to Paris and that's pretty. Intact, anyway. But only because they surrendered.

They haven't got Cleo's Needle in Paris.

You never told me you liked that. Always thought it was a bit nothing myself.

No, the benches near it. Those metal camels on the ends. Fucking horrible.

He looks like a big kid when he smiles. We can do better than that, he said and led the way down onto Albert Embankment then stood looking at one of the lamp-posts on the parapet, the ones with two giant black metal fishes coiled round the base facing away from each other.

There, he said. Remember these? Nothing like them anywhere in the world. Gorgeous. Ugliest fucking things you ever saw.

I told him to put his finger in.

What? Fuck off.

I always think they're going to bite your hand off.

He touched the first one's tongue and said he used to try and imagine who the sculptor was. Somebody racking his brain a hundred years ago, needing a masterpiece, then coming up with these, eureka, a pair of black bug-eyed fish like something out of Stingray, mass-produced from here to the estuary. Hope they gave him a fucking knighthood.

We used to have barbecues down there, next to Millbank Tower when there was still some waste ground left. Bonfire made out of genuine Thames driftwood, Bish letting hisself be persuaded to play the mouth harp he'd brought along specially.

We stripped off to go in the river once, it seems a good idea when you're out of your skull. The three of us in line, water still warm even at midnight. We'd have let the current take us all the way to the Thames Barrier if Stevie hadn't seen sense. We were too stoned to swim back against the tide so we ran nude along the Embankment from Lambeth, me and her taking it in turns to hide behind Bish, laughing like witches.

He'd be gobsmacked now, seeing me out here on the balcony

of this flat owned by one of the big egg dealers. Eight floors up with the lights on you and the whole city looking up. I could've had anything I wanted out the drinks cabinet, but ice and water rules. I take it inside, shut the french windows and pull the curtains.

I've left just the one light on in the sitting room. I finish the water and go in the kitchen and rinse the glass out and wipe it with a dishcloth and put it away. I walk through to the dining room, sucking the last ice cube.

It's the biggest room in the house. When you press the light switch, lights come on over the framed paintings. There's a dozen of them round the walls, all originals and all birds. A regency still life with dead pheasants, a surrealist picture of a woman flying with a white dove, and what looks like an original Audubon. You could pay an army of cleaners with what's on these walls.

There's a particularly ugly bunch of ducks swimming about in marshland. The colours are the worst. Something as common as a mallard, and they even fuck up the green on the head. It's always a horrible vivid dulux or the colour on a dead bird. Thousands of years and we still can't get it right, so why keep doing it? This obsession with capturing everything. No wonder Stevie does installations instead.

Talking of her, there's nothing but bird books in the bookcases, some of them with Stevie's illustrations inside. Anywhere you can put an ornament, there's a bird ornament. Being rich doesn't mean you have to give up being naff.

This is Phoebe Pink's place. She bought the flat and her house in Suffolk and whatever the fuck else she owns with the proceeds from exporting wild birds' eggs. Birds of prey mostly, with a

sideline in capercaillie and rednecked phalaropes from her oper-
ations in Scotland. She started when she was fifteen, selling wagtail
eggs to local collectors in Epping, then worked her way up to
peregrine chicks at twenty grand each for the middle east market.
Wasn't long before she had other people doing the dirty deeds
for her, two of them are inside for hitting a warden with their
jeep in Speyside. There's been fines too, but they're chickenfeed
to somebody like Phoebe Pink. I should have gone after her at
the start.

My pulse was going like a bass when she opened the door, and
I'm standing there with sweat patches appearing as we speak –
but she probably put it down to the weather. Assuming she even
noticed. All she saw was a cleaner like they all do, tugging a
cleaner's forelock.

You'd think she might be watching her back a bit, after Owen
Whittle and Co. But she let me walk behind her when she gave
me the grand tour. She talked me through the bird paintings without asking if I was interested. She took the piss when I said no to
a scotch, just tapwater with a bit of ice.

I've left her in her study. Seemed appropriate. It's where she
spent most of today, she said. The one room she didn't let me into.
The rare bird stamps are in there, the first edition bird books. Like
some victorian wife with her collection of what the butler saw.

I never understand people like her. They care about birds so
much even birders think they're mad. She was even named after
a bird. So what makes her threaten their fucking survival the way
she does? I could've asked her, I suppose.

I go back out to the sitting room and open the rucksack. The

photos on the mantelpiece are crooked and I straighten them.
There's no birds in here, they're pictures of her husband who left
her and the daughter who died. The flat's spotless. Run your finger
along the mantelpiece. Cleaned by somebody who knows what
they're doing.

I get a cloth out the rucksack and wipe the photo frames, then
the door handles in here and the one to the dining room. Then I
put the cloth away again, do the rucksack up, and shut the door
quietly on my way out. The lift's one of those old edwardian jobs
with two wire doors, and normally they're a laugh, but I don't
want to wait so I walk down. Nobody comes out the other flats
and the courtyard's empty outside. Put your collar up because it
looks like rain.

The sky's a mix of black clouds and pale blue by now, with a
gaggle of blackheaded gulls flapping across it. Wherever you are
in this country, inland as well as at the coast, you can set your
watch by gulls flying in to roost. I go out through the security
gate into the little alleyway outside. Turn left and there's a police
van suddenly, blocking the way out.

It wasn't there when I got here. Black windows, enough room
for a whole swat team or a cruftload of alsatians. I go down the
alley in the opposite direction, and there's two police walking
towards me.

One male one female, jackets three sizes too big, like they've
got bulletproof vests under there. Truncheons and radios and you
know what my heartbeat's doing. The female one shows me a smile.

'Evening,' she says. 'Do you live in there?'

'No, just visiting.'

'I see. Would you mind showing us what's in your rucksack.' Somebody winds a window down in the van.

'It's only a rucksack. What do you think I've got in it?'

'We'd just like a look,' she says.

'That means I've got to show you, I suppose?'

'It's just a safety precaution.'

'You're concerned for my safety, are you?'

'Could we just look inside? It won't take a minute, then we can all get on.'

The security gate shuts automatically, so you can't get back into the courtyard, and the sides of the alleyway are the sheer walls of houses. I take the rucksack off my shoulder and start opening it. 'No it's OK,' she says, 'we'll do that.'

I'd rather they didn't, my gear's in there and it's tricky to get out, I don't want it spilling everywhere. She says don't worry they'll be careful.

'It's a real mess in there. I'll get it.'

'It's OK,' she says, 'we're used to this. Anything you want to tell us before we open it?'

She must have a ring on her finger, you can hear metal touching metal when she puts her hand in. She tries getting stuff out but it gets stuck and she has to start again and pull the drawstring open all the way. Then she takes a steel scraper out, with a triangular blade on the end, and hands it to her mate. A tin of metal polish and an old toothbrush. She doesn't bother with the j-cloths and what have you.

'What's this?' She takes the scraper off him. 'Been doing some DIY, have we?'

'No, some cleaning. I'm a cleaner.'

'What do you clean with something like this?'

'It's for going round the bathroom tiles. Can I have it back?'

'Whose place have you been cleaning?' her mate asks, just when I was wondering if he knew how to speak. I ask him do I really have to answer all this, and he says there's a prevention of terrorism act, so yes.

'And you're expecting some terrorism round here?'

The female plod hands me my can of polish. 'If you could just tell us where you've been working,' she says.

'Phoebe Pink's. Number fifty-three, on the eighth floor.'

'And you signed in with security before going up?'

'You can check my signature in the book.'

'Is Mrs Pink there now?'

'Why don't you call her and find out?'

She gets her radio out and makes enquiries. Somebody gives her Phoebe Pink's number and she rings it. I'm not listening to her, I'm watching her partner, who's giving me the look. You can tell the ones who only joined the police for their own protection. She puts the radio away.

'Mrs Pink says you've done a good job,' she says. 'Very thorough.'

'Can I have my scraper back? They cost money.'

'It still looks like a weapon to me. We'll give you a receipt.'

'I know your boss. I clean his house at weekends.'

She smiles and her mate tries to look even grimmer. She gives me the scraper and starts walking towards the police van. The other one asks me how I started working for Phoebe Pink.

'Word of mouth.'

'Do you know how she makes her money?'

'You tell me.'

'Selling the eggs of endangered birds,' he says. 'And here we are, protecting her. A known criminal.'

'So this isn't a terrorist alert.'

'An egg collector got shot a while back. And a big landowner. They think the likes of Mrs Pink might be next. You can but hope.'

'Not your favourite person, then.'

He nods towards his partner. 'Me and her,' he says, 'we worked in environment liaison. Some of the wardens on grouse moors use hen harrier chicks as footballs. The Phoebe Pinks of this world want shooting. Have a good evening.'

She's left me to put everything back in the rucksack. I start walking the opposite direction from them and somebody in the van uses a camera on me, you can hear the motordrive from the other end of the alley. Nothing personal.

Cambridge Circus is good and heaving. Nip up the street next to the theatre and you're in the heart of Soho. Sit outside with your holsten and the petrol fumes. Except not tonight, I'm shattered. Join the crowd getting into Leicester Square tube.

I'm not like Stevie, I like being a ghost in my own town. No tax people on your case, your secrets safe with you. Nobody knowing what went on tonight. Specially as it's something you didn't do.

Phoebe Pink got my name from somebody I work for. Her previous cleaner went back to Slovenia for a funeral. I couldn't believe it when she said her name on the phone. Fucking fate, what else could it be.

Except it's too late and she's lucky. Whatever made me do what I did, I got rid of it one way or another. So I left the luger at home and just went to clean her flat. Which means another generation of our peregrine chicks are going to be spending their lives with hoods over their faces in Saudi fucking Arabia. Sorry, guys, I just haven't got it in me any more. For what it's worth, I won't be cleaning her flat a second time. Shame, because she's a good tipper.

Just as well that female police left me my scraper. I'm going to be needing it now I've started taking my work home. Me and Stevie bought a place together.

We sold the places our mums left us and found a terrace house this side of Hammersmith. Edge of Brackenbury Village, going upmarket in our old age.

The place is habitable enough, and when I'm through with it it'll be the cleanest house in London – but it needs work: we're turning the whole of the top floor into a studio for her. I say 'we're', but that doesn't include either of us. People assume if you're a cleaner you're virtually a qualified plumber and plasterer, I've had clients ask me to lay a patio. But I'm shit at DIY. I can't polyfilla a sill properly or sand a floor without corrugating it. When I say I haven't got a talent for anything, it's not false modesty. We're getting somebody in next week.

The house is dark when I get back, but I know she's in. The light's always on in the studio.

I empty the rucksack and put everything away. There's some

post: building society statement and a month's money from an old lad who still uses postal orders. I make myself a sandwich and eat it in the kitchen. Glass of tapwater, no ice.

The door's half open in the room she's working in for now. Normally she'd hear me coming upstairs but I'm in my socks. I'm bringing her a glass of scotch and I have a sip on the way up.

She's got the anglepoise on and it's the only light in the room, bleaching the paper she's drawing on. At the end of the table, there's a bowl with a spoon in it and a glass of water, half empty. She's probably been in here for hours: its warmer than downstairs and smells of sticky rice and farts.

The light's on the other side of her, so her face is mostly in shadow. Call the bowl and glass a kind of still life, then she's like one of those renaissance portraits I used to think were amazing, just like photos, till she told me that's exactly what they were, all done with mirrors, a camera obscura. They couldn't paint any better than us, she said. They just knew how to cheat better.

She's working with a set-square and a protractor, so it looks like another installation. She's put her hair up, with a big red butterfly clip at the back. An ancient old sweatshirt, cut low so's you get the full length of her neck. Her neck's the best part of her probably, beating off competition from her belly, eyes, tits and upper back. But what softens your heart isn't that, it's watching her rolling her sleeves up again.

You can see it in the speed she's working. She was like that with her graduation show, finishing it in a hurry because she knew she'd got it right. Her tongue's sticking out in concentration and her face is alright again.

223

I could claim a part in that. I could present evidence that she wants me there more than ever. She won't sleep unless I hold her with both arms now, she says she works best when she knows I'm downstairs in the house, and the lovemaking's gone off the scale, ejaculating so much she wets the bed, like her body's wringing itself out.

But take a good look. What she's doing right now, this has got nothing to do with me, and I'm finding it hard just watching her. My fault for making assumptions.

I had this idea. In the time I've got left, her and Bish were going to be there for me, that was their role in life from now on. They weren't going to have concerns of their own, they'd be serene and solicitous and take the piss in ways that kept me smiling. No change, in other words. Instead they're both in places I can't follow, and I've got a new reason for missing her.

I asked her how it was going, and she said fine, it's nearly done.

Is it going to make me cry?

It's making *me* cry, she said. Best thing I've ever done. By the way, when it's finished, it's just me and you.

What does that mean? We're not the be-all and end-all, remember. Your words not mine.

I know, I know, she said. She kissed me to shut me up, but I was pissed off with her. What am I, a fucking yoyo? Playing with people's feelings. You can't change just like that.

You did, she said. You came back.

That did shut me up and this time she kissed me for different reasons and took me to bed. That always knocks the hard edges off of you, and I'm holding her gently when I tell her I don't believe her. Just being with me wasn't going to be enough any more. She'd want to go straight on to the next piece.

No no, she said. This is the last one for me. Be prepared: you're going to get my undivided attention. And she made me hold her harder and kept her face so deep in my neck we're talking minor bruising.

She's moving the set-square around now and I'm looking for clues – because I don't know if I buy this sudden transformation of hers. One minute she can't do the work to save her life, the next she's bossing it. That's what artists do, is it? In the middle of their despair, they can suddenly go bang, eureka, best thing they've ever done? If so, we'd all like the recipe. I doubt she's told me everything, I just hope she's alright.

She puts the palms of her hands on the back of her head, leans back against them and yawns. Her neck looks strong as a stag's from the back and like a madonna's from the side. According to her, a good piece of work should challenge and comfort you at the same time, and I'll go along with that. I go back downstairs and take the drink out onto the balcony over the back garden. Sit and listen to the indian dentist putting her kid to bed next door.

It's dark but not quite. The light pollution that keeps birds singing all night. A robin's started up, a feeble song for a perky bird like this, starts bold then peters out. What do you do, red robbo, sleep all day? Or exhaust yourself singing twenty-four seven and get too tired to have sex? In the countryside, they probably breed better because they sleep better.

She's upstairs taking on the whole huge subject of sacrifice, meanwhile I'm dwelling on insomniac robins. But we all need the robins, specially when things are closing in.

John Ure Peacock's water bailiff couldn't identify the killer, he said. Either he didn't get a good look or he thinks I might go back up there for him. But the same gun was used both times of course, so they can forget about Owen Whittle owing people money. And since the only link between him and John Ure Peacock was bird crimes, they're looking in the right direction at last. Hence police protection for the likes of Phoebe Pink. My borrowed time's nearly up.

Meanwhile, halfway across the country, three of the four goshawk eggs hatched in Owen Whittle's wood. Two of them pecked their weaker sibling to death and pushed the corpse out the nest. They were national celebrities by then, and the local ringers came and put metal rings on their legs – so when they fledged and moved to another wood fifty miles away, they were easy to identify once one of them was found shot dead and the other one was killed by a car while it was feeding on a female pheasant by the side of the road. Frostbite sent me the newspaper cuttings.

The dentist's light goes out, then another one in somebody else's house. A blue tit's singing now, and the robin answers back. We'd all swop places with birds and animals sometimes, I doubt time ever drags for them. Still, you wouldn't wish it on them. Not when we make scotch as bad as this.

THE DIY ISN'T going to do itself, so I called Jace Babb in, who's got his own business and specializes in loft conversions. Mad as a loon as I say, but that includes having a work ethic bordering on the pathological. Him and his brothers have been working round the clock, or at least till we throw them out in the early hours, finishing things off to Stevie's designs while Jace listens out for urban owls.

I can't take this all day every day, so any chance to escape I'll grab it. Today it's the familiar drive to north Norfolk, listening to Terry Chai all the way, which is a right fucking burden when you've been up since five.

Terry Chai used to be the best bird artist in southeast Asia, which is saying something. He's won awards and his work on eurasian warblers is seminal. He's spent half his life in Britain but had his permanent home in Hong Kong till the chinese takeover. Now he's got a big place in Kingston and never goes short of work, yet he's always on about lack of funds, which gets on your tits when you see what his originals sell for. There's plenty who'd change places, Stevie for one.

What he hasn't got is a Stevie in his life. When he's not moaning about money he's bemoaning his chronic lack of legover. To hear him talk, you'd think he'd never had it off in his life, which might even be true now I think about it. Something about a five-year courtship with a girl whose parents matter to his parents. Nice girl, he tells me with a face like doom. Nice nice nice.

Just as well there's birds to take his mind off it. I've never seen anybody so enthusiastic about them, even the common ones. 'Look for the bird's eye, yeh. No need to be a painter. Everybody look for the bird's eye first, instinctive.' We're going up to Norfolk just because he admires whooper swans, there's no commission in it.

We do the coastal reserves first, dropping into Titchwell for the autumn buntings but not bothering with Cley because he objects to paying the entrance fee. 'Everywhere you go, pay up pay up. Fuk sek this country.'

He does some weird and wonderful things with the english language, Terry Chai. He knows the words and grammar, but he likes to talk quick, because that's the chinese way and because he wants to come across as fluent. So he eats his words all the time. His favourite throwaway phrases are 'sort of' and 'you know', but he puts them together so they come out as 'sof-yu-no' or even just 'sofyu'. He uses the word 'illustration' a lot, turning it into 'stretcher', and even that's just the best translation I can manage. The original's unpronounceable.

So a typical Terry Chai conversation might go: 'Then they want to use same stretcher second time sofyu, but they don't want to pay twice, and they fob me sofyu no, they say it's good publicity for me, like I should be fucking grateful. Rip off everywhere yeh, fuk sek worse than back home.'

He can't even say his own name too well. Why would chinese parents give their kid a name like Terence? Mind you, it's nothing compared to what I do with chinese, which always gives his sisters a laugh.

The whooper swans, having come down from Iceland for the winter, are in a field south of Cromer. Terry Chai's freezing his arse off sitting on the bonnet of his car to draw them. Like Stevie, go birding with him and you're guaranteed some time with the birds, plus the odd lesson in looking. 'See how the birds are slimmer in silhouette, the light eats the edges sofyu.'

He draws like he talks, fast and a bit approximate. But it's meticulous too, he doesn't miss any important details – and the end product's really good as well as idiosyncratic. What I resent is the way Stevie and him can sketch for an hour in this weather with no gloves on, whereas me I can't feel my fingers as usual. Come on Tel, you can draw these things from memory. Fuk sek.

He keeps taking his glasses off to wipe them when his breath steams them up. Real bottle-bottom specs, his whole race is blind as moles according to him. His optician can't see his own eye charts.

You can see for miles out here. Much as I hate the place, at least being flat it gives you a horizon, which you don't get in town. And you can feel the shape of your nostrils when the air's clean as this. There's a line of brent geese so far away they're just stitches on a sky that couldn't be any bluer if it tried.

'Hey, long face.'

'Yes, Tel.'

'The police talk to you yet?'

'The police? No. What about?'

'Owen Whittle and the one with three names.'

'Why would they ask me?'

'They asked Frostbite. Hitch-hiker like him, could go anywhere in the country. Hard to account for his movements.'

'They actually interviewed Frostbite? About the shootings?'

'What did I just say? Same with you, yeh. Cleaner, self-employed, same thing. If you need an alibi, not easy.'

'They'll be after you first, Terry Chai. Self-employed illustrator, loves birds.'

'Let them come,' he says. 'I got two alibis. Have they talked to Stevie yet? Matter of time they go to Poland to interview Bish.'

I put my bins up on a mixed flock of finches flying across the field. Mostly linnets. It's nearly winter, so you check for a twite's pink arse among them. Get back in the car soon, I'm shivering now.

'Why would they be talking to us, Terry? Last I heard, they were looking into debts.'

'Oh yeh, you think that's likely? Small egg collector with beard, and filthy rich man?'

'John Ure Peacock lost money in the foot-and-mouth. He had to close half his land.'

'You think him and Owen Whittle borrowed money from the same people? They lived different ends of the country. Police don't believe it, baby.'

'Yeh but why would they pick on somebody like Frostbite?

Alright he's a birder and they think a birder's involved. But he lives miles away from the shootings. He's hardly the nearest fucking suspect.'

'Maybe they already talked to closer people. Anyway, naturally they talk to him. London birders, we're the elite group, they ask us first. Who's the number one suspect?'

'How the fuck would I know? Jace Babb's wife.'

'Yeh, you laugh. I laugh too. But the net's closing in. Zoom. You see.'

'And you're happy with that, are you? Pass us that twix.'

'Not happy not sad,' he says. 'Owen Whittle and the other one, to me just hands in the water. You put your hand in the water, yeh. You take your hand out, you leave ripples. Ripples stop, water back to normal. Nobody remembers your hand was there.'

'Don't tell me: old chinese proverb.'

'Old chinese sports show. Repeat: name your number one suspect.'

'Somebody who thought they had nothing to live for.'

He takes a bite out his piece of the twix, looks through his bins, and sketches the swans, all with just two hands. For memory's sake, he says. When you look at drawings, you can feel the cold air of the day you did them.

Memories. Bish and his photos of the birds he's seen. My mum and dad died before they were old, and memories were already all they had. 'Are you just a hand in the water, Tel?'

'Whole human race, baby.'

'Your bird pictures. Don't you think they'll leave a ripple when you've gone?'

He takes his glasses off and cleans them with a lens cloth from his telescope case. 'You think we don't know the truth, yeh.'

'What's that?'

'You only get in touch because fat polish fucker gone. Oh yeh, you get in touch with people now. But you need ten of us to make up for one Bish.'

'Not ten, twenty.'

'Hey listen to this. Fucking good.'

He's turned the CD player up in the car, rewinding it to play the guitar part at the start of *Should I Stay Or Should I Go*, over and over.

'Very nice, Tel. What's the occasion exactly?'

'Honour of Bish, yeh. He showed me. Sounds like great reed warbler, listen. Crik crik crik.'

Mad? I probably am. I agree with him.

Maybe I could tell him it was me. Why not. Tell him what I've done. He's not as close to me as some people, be less traumatic all round. He'd drive off and leave me here probably, in case my rucksack's loaded – but he'd have to listen first. I want to stay around now, Terry, not stop at five hundred. I want the roses round the door – just when I can't have them for long. Somebody's playing a wicked trick, yeh.

He's sketching again, leaning on the car door. I smile when he swears in both languages in the same sentence. We'll have to get you laid soon, bird illustrator man. You don't belong with us long faces.

They're called whooper swans because they whoop, except this lot are imitating mute swans, stuffing their faces with loose spuds and anything that isn't actual mud. If you're going to be covered in feathers, they might as well all be white. Camouflage you as well as keep you snug in snow. If you're the god of birds and you came down on earth, this is how you might look. I get the thermos and hipflask out and put some scotch in our coffee.

At the end of the day we go for an indian, and Terry Chai gives me some of his sketches to get Stevie's opinion, he defers to her even though his bird drawings are just as good. Trade all his talent, he keeps telling me, to be able to do one of her pieces. Better still, for one night with her. Don't fucking leave her this time. We know where you live.

'Yes, Terry.'

'Stevie Red Hair Oxford,' he says. 'God yeh. Marry and have six kids, all paint like angels. You leave best kind of ripples that way. Alternative marry you and have team of cleaners.'

IT'S BEEN A long day and I fell asleep in the middle of it. I was up at six to get the tube across London and pick up a commission in darkest Kentish Town. It's all recommendations in this job, and I know a birder who knows an office manager who sacked his cleaning firm. I told him I'm not a firm, there's just me and my can of mister muscle. Take the job anyway, he said. Do two days a week. Thanks, but it's just not a long-term proposition.

I got home and went straight out again to do four jobs back to back. No lunch break and nostrils black with dust from a pensioner's attic. Putting in the hours even when they're running out.

I had a kip in the afternoon but it wasn't enough and I've been yawning like a monkey for the last hour, so I turn the lights off downstairs and go up and sit on the balcony for five minutes. You never get enough air in this job. I put my feet up on the railing and have a beer. The stars are out and you can see the rooftops and back gardens. Who needs a horizon?

The light goes off in her studio. She's finishing quite early tonight. Our robin's singing again.

We got a letter from Bish this morning. Photos of hisself and Grace and a pratincole that landed on the wader scrape they're putting in. Designed to make us jealous. I like the grin on his face.

The robin's stopped and you can hear a police siren heading north towards the Bush. Stevie comes out onto the balcony and puts her arms round my neck from behind. 'Fancy a nightcap?'

'I don't exactly need one. I'm falling asleep out here.'

'Have one anyway,' she says. 'To celebrate.'

'You've finished it, then? Good.'

'Nearly,' she says. 'There's nothing more I can do up there.'

'When can I see it?'

'When it's in place.'

'Christ, I'll have to wait months.'

She pulls up another chair, takes my beer off me and has a sip, then puts her head on my arm. 'What's that star?'

'No idea. They all look like the plough to me.'

But she's only asking so's she can show off. She takes me through the main ones you can see from here, her finger waving through them. Learning the stars is just a case of joining the dots, she says. You can draw a line from beta to alpha in the plough to reach the pole star. That one's orion's belt, fifty thousand times brighter than the sun. From there you can find aldebaran and the seven sisters, which look blue through binoculars. Me, I didn't even know the plough was part of the great bear, which looks about as much like a bear as I do.

She tells me this is the best time of year for seeing perseus and andromeda. 'He rescued her from a sea monster, you know.'

'Christ, Steve, I thought *I* was an anorak.'

'Well, stars are easier than birds. No juvenile plumage.'

I smile and she sits up. She used to watch the stars when she was a kid, she says. A little girl under her duvet with the window open, surrounded by soft toys, imagining the floor was miles below her and the bed was a spaceship in the night.

I tell her with me it was watching scary films. All the lights would be off and we'd be in sleeping bags, me and my mate who was staying over, with just our heads sticking out. The soft toys were too scared to show their faces.

'And you couldn't sit on the floor of course.'

'No, no way, always on the sofa. You had to be off the ground to be safe.'

'Same here.' Her bed was always in transit, never heading for a particular place. 'You're right,' she says, 'what a fucking anorak I've become. Does everything end up like this? I got interested in stars because the universe was immense, birds for their bright colours. Now everything's a list and all I want to do is identify things.'

'Everybody does that. Man needs to name the animals.'

'I suppose.'

'And do cave paintings of them.'

'Hm. All that room up there,' she says. 'The second nearest star is a quarter of a million times further away than the sun. Ninety-three million miles multiplied by two hundred and fifty thousand. Figures you can't grasp.'

'You can prove there's life up there, apparently. They reckon it's a mathematical certainty. Not just other planets but a world identical to this one.'

'Do you believe that?'

'No. There's just us in billions of empty square miles.'

'I agree,' she says. 'Takes a greater feat of the imagination to believe we're completely alone. Stuck here like billions of fridge magnets, going round and round, a thousand miles an hour, always on the same course.'

'So we all go mad.'

'Oh yeh,' she says. 'Mad in the way children are mad. Kids don't have any real say, so we paint pictures and play mouth organs and turn our beds into flying saucers. Making up worlds we can have some control over. All manic and clinically fucked.'

'You can't talk like that, Steve. It's alright for me, I'm a philistine git.'

'So am I. I told you: I'm an ex-artist.'

'An ex-artist and you've just done your best ever work?'

'Yeh well,' she says. 'I'm going to beat the bastards at their own game.'

She's gets hold of my hand and I ask her what's this for.

'I don't need a reason, it's mine. I think about your hands every day. Best part of your body.'

'Wish they were good at something except cleaning.'

'That's what gives them their texture. I can feel the calluses even when you're not there.'

'Horny hands.'

She kisses my knuckles and puts a finger in her mouth. Pack that in or neither of us is going to get any sleep.

She's soft tonight and a bit dreamy, like she's just stopped crying, except there's no evidence of that. Like a warm night after rain. Probably just knackered. She asks me if I'm going to Barn Elms tomorrow.

'I might do. Why?'

She wishes she'd gone there more often this year. She misses it. The normality of your own patch. Be good to go back there when she's finished her piece.

'If you go tomorrow,' she says, 'can you get me that photographer's phone number out the logbook. Bish wants me to send him some prints.'

'Come with me and get it yourself. I'll buy you lunch. Celebrate finishing your work.'

'Maybe,' she says.

'Tell me about it. What's it look like?'

'No, you're too tired.'

'For a blow-by-blow description maybe. Just tell me if you're happy with it. And don't say happy's not the right word.'

'It's going to slay the fucking lot of them,' she says. 'Punters and critics alike. Even the ones who hate it will be bowled over.'

'Listen to her. Where's all your fear now?'

She puts her cheek back on my shoulder. 'Listen,' she says. 'I want to cut down on the birding. Not go on any more twitches. What do you think?'

'Oh yeh? You finish a piece of work and that makes you want to end it all? The thing that keeps us sane.'

She smiles. 'I want to do a year zero,' she says. 'Scrap the lists and just watch birds for their own sake. Get back some of the early innocence.'

'You can't get it back. Birders without a list. Try saying it out loud.'

'You're right, it's a stupid idea. We'll stay alive as long as possible and have the biggest lists in the country.'

'Shouldn't be too hard. People live longer nowadays.'

'We'll be one of those old couples with bins,' she says. 'Except we've been twitchers, we'll have a past. You'll get young birders being condescending, explaining common birds to us – then we'll pull a switchblade on them by telling them how we drove all night for grey-tailed tattler and rufous turtle. We'll keep a thermos in the car.'

'Can't wait.'

'I'm serious.'

'So am I.'

Her arm goes round my waist and squeezes. She holds me really tight but I can't do that in case I crush her. Settle for one arm round her shoulders and the other stroking her hair, brushing her ears with your fingers the way she likes. She's taking very deep breaths like she's asleep. Maybe Bish is right and this is the best anybody can do. So shouldn't it feel better than this?

She moves away when my latest yawn comes up. 'Yeh,' she says, 'me too. What time are you going to Barn Elms?'

'Not too early. I need to sleep in.'

'You're right, maybe I should come along. If I hang around with you I'm likely to see something, the kind of year you've had.'

'I haven't seen much there.'

'Yes you have,' she says. 'Male sparrowhawk, for instance. Allegedly.'

'Allegedly? I'm going to string a sparrowhawk, am I? It came down for a drink outside the main hide.'

'I haven't seen a male for years and you get one on the deck. In blazing technicolour, you lucky tart. You've had that kind of year with raptors. I haven't seen a merlin all year and your notebook's got one in february.'

'You've been busy –'

'Merlin. Goshawk. Marsh harrier in London. We used to see all our raptors together and now I'm being left out. Did you know we've ticked five together? I was counting them the other day.'

'Have we?'

'Five bird-of-prey lifers,' she says. 'And we found four of them ourselves. You can't buy memories like that. We ought to have that nightcap now.'

She gets up and disappears behind me. There's no lights on in the backs of the houses. The city that always sleeps. A family of sparrowhawks hunt in these back gardens, but if you ever see one it's an event, and even then it's invariably a grey female. That male I saw from the hide was a real bonus. Blue back, orange chest, out in the open for once.

Five raptors as lifers together. I didn't know it was that many. I remember gyrfalcon and monty's harrier, but not the other three. Oh wait, red-footed falcon at Rainham. Not rough-leg buzzard, that was me and Bish. Monty's was a tick, gyrfalcon was a tick, redfoot too. What else? She can't be right. Monty's. Gyrfalcon. Redfoot. Tick. Tick. Tick.

Tock.

My borrowed time just ran out.

I won't need to check my notebook. I know every word I wrote. On one page, in early spring, the only goshawk I've seen all year. Date, location and weather.

I didn't exactly write 'Probable goshawk in flight, shot Owen Whittle dead'. But it's a date and place branded on both our memories. I told her I was at Barn Elms at the time. The habit, the fucking mania, of writing everything down.

How long's she known? Since we moved in together or months ago? Christ in hell.

She couldn't resist the theatrics could she, even with this. One day she's direct and straightforward when she's telling me about her work, next minute she reverts to type. She couldn't just come out and announce she knows what I've done, she had to drop it in the conversation and let me work it out for myself. Part of her charm, so they tell me.

When she comes back out, she's brought the southern comfort and two glasses, and I knock the first one back in one. She asks me what's going through my mind, now I know she knows.

'Embarrassment.'

'Ah.'

'The other things'll follow in a minute. But right now I just feel like a kid who should've owned up.'

'I see.'

'Never mind "I see". And "ah". And "oh really". Like a fucking counsellor. A minute ago you're holding my hand, now you're sitting at the other end of the world.'

'Which only adds to your embarrassment.'

'Exactly. Just when I want to crawl into your womb. Don't smile, you look like my fucking teacher.'

'It's only a smile. It doesn't mean I'm laughing at you.'

She's brought her feet up and sits with them under her on the chair, sausaging her leg muscles, one of her best poses in my opinion. And every detail that's attractive about her makes you feel lonelier.

Now she knows, what's she going to do about it?

'I've already done it,' she says. 'I bought this house with you.'

Oh jesus. Oh fuck, I never expected that. The dam we've all got behind our eyes just collapses and I can't believe one human being can mass-produce so many tears so suddenly. Pouring down your face and burning your eyes and dripping off your nose, they really do all that and your shoulders really do judder and the underside of your tongue starts aching. She comes over at long fucking last but it's going to take more than that.

'Angel,' she says. 'It's alright.' But I get the word bollocks out in between sobs. It's only alright if you call the police coming round any minute alright.

She puts about three fingertips on my mouth. She's shushing me, so I shush.

'We're on a balcony,' she says. 'The neighbours might all be asleep, but there again. Anything you say may be overheard and used.'

I laugh, which comes out as a real mess. 'Might as well shout it from the rooftops, Steve. There's no point hiding any more.'

'Drink this,' she says. 'No, drink it. Now let's go in, I'm getting cold out here.'

She pushes me through the door and locks it behind us. She has to undress me more or less, before we get into bed. Hurry up, she says, so's she can put her arms round me. But fuck that, I do the holding in this house. And I need to wash my face first, my eyes are really stinging. Blow your nose, she says. Drive me mad with all that sniffing.

She's lying with her head on my chest, holding me hard again like she's trying to pin me to the bed. Her shoulder's cold while my face is burning. She cools it best she can by dipping her fingers in the glass of water on the bedside table. Now have another drink, she says. It'll get you to sleep quicker.

She props herself up so's I can see her, and she says can she ask me something.

'Go ahead. I haven't got much left to hide.'

'What did you do with the gun?'

'I've still got it. It's in the utility room with my dad's stuff.'

'What, the suitcase I carried up? Oh wow. Has it got a silencer? They didn't hear you in Owen Whittle's wood, so you must've had a silencer.'

'Yeh yeh, it's got a silencer.'

'Oh wow.'

'I shot two people, Stevie. I didn't mean to shoot the second one, but the first one was deliberate. You can't stay with me any more.'

'I don't think I can, no. But then I knew you hadn't come back for long.'

'So why let me in again? If it's just temporary and shit.'

'Because you needed it,' she says. 'You didn't want to face it alone. And because I had you back for a while.'

Oh jesus. I pull her back down and the tears are back, just a film across the lens this time. She starts crying too, I can feel her shaking very slightly as she sobs. She kisses me then dries my eyes with her fingers and tells me she wants to drink a toast.

'Christ, Bus, you pick your fucking moments.'

'To the three of us,' she says. 'The big times.'

Memories again. The time we drove down to Cornwall for a scops owl and the horn on the hire car packed in. Bish refused to slow down, grandprixing down those narrow country lanes, and she's warning oncoming traffic by sticking her head out the side window and making beep-beep noises at the top of her voice. The time Bish got Frostbite to smoke a reefer made out of dried capercaillie shit then gave him his last fifty quid for a waterproof. Or when he disappeared during a twitch up on Teesside and Stevie found him chilling out by sitting in a wind farm listening to the vum vum vum.

She's filling my glass up again. Except I can't get a taste for it tonight. Last request: make some love instead.

'Fine by me,' she says. 'Any anaesthetic that's going.'

'You and your drug metaphors, Bus.'

'Let's see if I can tickle your tastebuds a bit.'

She puts her glass down, and her mouth's slow and soft again and makes me push at it. Her tongue just edges onto her lower lip and I'm sucking it in, southern and comfort. You can feel the pulse under her cheek and you know her pussy's going to be clamping round your hand like one snake swallowing another and when she comes she'll be quick about it. She knows I'm on the point of crashing out.

Effect of the booze obviously – except I've hardly had any. She's pouring small shots and I'm taking small sips, but I'm getting pissed faster than usual. Probably the emotion of it all.

She's really gentle when she goes down on me. Looking over her hair I can see out the window, and there's gulls again, coming in from the reservoirs, just silhouettes over the rooftops. Blackbacked gulls on a hooded crow of a night.

Afterwards we do our pair-bonding thing of talking with our mouths touching, and she starts telling me how good her latest piece of work is. Maybe her best ever.

So that's why she's so laid back tonight.

'Am I?'

'Like you can relax now.'

'You spotted that.'

'It's really good is it, this latest piece?'

'You know me,' she says. 'I'm terrified it's shit. But it's going to have an impact.'

She gets me to lie with my head on her chest so's she can hold me for a change. I tell her my eyes are crossed, I can see two of her.

'Your ultimate fantasy,' she says. 'Go to sleep, you're knack-ered.'

'No, I'm alright.'

'You can't stop yawning.'

'Just bored, that's all.'

'Oh yeh? Then why are you laughing?'

'Because you are. It tickles when you chuckle. No, stop it, I need to go to sleep.'

'You need another drink.'

She's been saying that all night. And I've drunk every drink she's given me. So I'm laughing but not because it tickles. If she tickled me I wouldn't feel a thing. Her body could be cold as ice for all I know. I know she's touching the whole length of me but I can't feel it.

I'm laughing because I know what she's done. I know why the booze is knocking me out and why it tastes like this. It tastes familiar, so I should've guessed earlier.

It happened a couple of times before. Try some of that, Bish would say. He'd never tell me what it was, it's always a cocktail of something long and pharmaceutical and I'd never remember the names. Then you'd crash very fast, a really big dark rush.

Weeee, you'd say. Got any more? But he never would. Take slightly too much and it could be fatal, he said. And I'm not being dramatic.

So why did he do it?

Because it could be fatal.

She must've found the ones he gave me recently, in the drawer where I put them. I don't remember telling her about them but I didn't lock it either. There was a month's supply even by Bish's standards.

I'm grinning because she's been so sneaky about it, and because it's exactly the right thing to do. She eases me off and hands me the next glass of hemlock.

'Are you having some?'

'I've had enough,' she says. 'This is your round.'

'Go on, then.'

'Just a drop this time.'

'No, it's fine. Much as you want.'

'Sure you know what you're doing?'

'Never been more certain.'

'You'd better be,' she says. 'After this glass, there's no going back.'

'I'm surrounded by drama queens. Give it here, life's too short.'

'The police might never get here,' she says – but she knows that's bollocks. And there's no way I'm ever going to go with them. Prisons are like cemeteries. No good birds. A friend of Bish's did three years in Wandsworth and Leeds for dealing. Best he ever saw was a grey wag. Nice adult male, but christ. Even us latvians can only take so much.

She's had enough role reversal for one night. She spoons into me as usual and gets me to hold her tight. 'You're a dark horse,' she says. 'Have I told you that? Spooky dark horse in the night.'

'Look who's talking.'

'Well, I told you. This is the best work I've ever done.'

'What does that mean?'

'What's happening with us now,' she says. 'It's part of my latest piece.'

A beat while I take this in, then my biggest grin ever. This is what she's been working on? Oh wow.

'It's the last work I'm ever going to do.'

'I've never been called that before. Coo fucking hell, I'm flattered. Just don't make me look like a pelican.'

I'm sending signals to my arms to hold her tighter. Whether

they ever do it, only she can tell. She always knew, didn't she, she'd have to help me with this. Yes, she says, she knew. Most people can't do it on their own.

She turns round and kisses me again, hard so's I can feel it, that glorious great wide mouth of hers for the last time, fingers on my face, wrapping herself over me. I can feel her thigh between mine.

'You came back,' she says, 'But I wasn't really here.'

'You've said. It's alright –'

'But you never came back completely, did you? Not all of you.'

It's an effort to shake my head. I'm crying again.

'I haven't got you and I can't do the work,' she says. 'So this is my attempt to combine the two. I thought this way at least I could do something for you.'

'Ssh, I know.'

She's got her face right up against mine because she knows I can't see too well. Her eyes are green as green. I thought John Ure Peacock had eyes. These are eyes. Months and months I looked into them and they looked into mine and all four lied by omission because they had to. Her two are looking at my two without blinking and her voice drops right down and she says: 'Forgive me?'

'What?'

'Please.'

Forgive her? Is she crazy. It's what I always wanted.

'Be serious. I need to know. If you don't forgive me, I can't go through with this.'

I put on what I hope's a serious face and I tell her this is the best thing anybody can ever do for you. She can say that's bollocks, but not till I'm asleep.

'No I agree,' she says. 'Life's for those who really want to live it.'

'Christ, Stevie, why does everybody leave you in the end?'

'Tell me about it.'

I'm crying again, or at least that's what I must be doing. I can't feel anything on my cheeks, but my vision's blurred and my eyes are hot, so therefore. 'What do I look like, Steve?'

'What are you talking about?'

'This is the last time you're going to see me. I don't want to look like shit.'

'Don't talk crap. You always look like shit.'

She tucks herself deeper into me and her mouth must be right up against my ear because her voice is coming from inside my head. 'You never looked more beautiful,' she says. 'Like an angel. I've waited a long time to see you look peaceful.'

I'm going to believe she's crying again by now. It's time to let my eyelids go down, and when they do it's like I'm going deaf and my pulse is slowing down beat by beat by beat.

'Oh shit, before I forget. Can you hear me? Somebody ought to write a note, tell people it was me, I'm the culprit. Get me a pen.'

'Lie still,' she says. 'I did it yesterday. It's on the computer.'

Fuck, she's thought of everything. She's the dark horse round here.

'Not as dark as you,' she says. 'My god. You're black. You're a dark horse and its rider and I shouldn't be lying here letting you hold me like this. Woo, you're scary.'

'Safest place you can be.'

'Dark horse. Coal black. I can feel your breath on my neck. Stay there but move something, my tit's going to sleep.'

Me, I can't feel my limbs, saving the best sensation till last. My blood's heating up and thickening, bulging the veins like hammocks no doubt.

And look at me now. I was never going to make much of my life, but I ended up a work of art. I make sure her hair's in my face at the end.

I still don't know one star from the next, even after her crash course, but I recognize the moon, with that turquoise light you always get with moonclouds. Alright, moon? We're speeding through space together, though you'd never know it by looking at us. You're a real man-in-the-moon moon tonight. Chin and everything.

SO THIS IS purgatory then.

Another boat trip for another bird on the latest godforsaken rock. Even the crossing's taking an eternity.

The other passengers, they're mostly at the front of the ferry for the view, but I'm right at the back, watching for seabirds attracted by fish churned up by the propeller. Nothing but herring gulls so far, but we're barely out of West Loch Tarbert and the open sea's still to come. You can see it up ahead between the headlands, and it looks flat from here, so at least the sea's calm thank god, nothing like the last time I was on it, when we swore we'd never get on a boat again. It's taken me four years to find the courage.

It was the worst almighty pelagic trip of all time, the memory's still so strong it's like a video we keep playing back. An epic, a legendary horror story. I'm not sure we ever really recovered. Even a sea as flat as this makes me go up and down just looking at it.

It was the annual chartered boat out of Penzance, five in the morning and three hundred on board. Most of us were after wilson's petrel, the most common seabird in the world but a real fuckinghell in british waters. Bish needed cory's shearwater too, having missed one on a previous seawatch by sheltering behind a rock to light a spliff. We got the wilson's, plus thirty cory's, an adult sabine's in full summer plumage, great shearwaters and all four species of skua, every star seabird you could ask for.

But oh fuck did we pay for them. Me and the Bus usually survived on water, but I was sick before we were out the harbour, and I wasn't the first, somebody already had their head down the pan when I went below. Stevie took two seasick pills before we set off and brought them up in the first twenty minutes.

None of us could understand why we were so ill at the time. The boat's flat-bottomed admittedly, to get into the shallow harbours on Scilly, which makes it less stable at sea – but we'd been on it before without getting ill, and the sea wasn't rough, just a medium swell. Turns out they'd dipped on wilson's the year before, so this time they set off faster to have more time at the feeding grounds. On the way back, they took it much slower and everybody recovered.

But before then I was sick, on and off, from five in the morning to three in the afternoon. I was stretched out across three seats downstairs and didn't get up for the first two hours except to puke, and even when I finally crawled up on deck I had sickbags in both pockets. Somehow I saw three tick species, including a med shearwater right under the boat, but hated every one of them for living at sea. Frostbite and me sat in the back with a sickbag in one hand and our bins in the other, puking so much our stomach muscles ached the whole weekend.

Everything made you puke. The smell of the sea, the smell of the pasties from the bar, the smell of the blood and fish guts they were ladling over the side to attract the birds, the smell of the puke.

You'd come up on deck and wonder why nobody else up there was being sick. They were, of course, but over the side, the antisocial tossers, heaving where they stood so's they wouldn't have to give up their prime viewing spots. I'm holding on to the handrail at one point when it feels sticky. I look down and the side of the ship's spattered with technicolour and I'm swearing and wiping my hand and asking Stevie if she's responsible and she says of course she fucking is, did I think the boat puked on itself.

After the fourth or fifth puke, you'd be bringing up nothing except what looked like spit, but it's not like being sick after a night out. Your body can stabilize then, but the boat never stopped going up and down, so you just kept on retching. With eight hours still to go before we got back, I lay down intending to sleep through it, telling myself I wouldn't get up unless there was a little shearwater, which is just about worth dying a slow death for. Then when I'm half asleep the tannoy announces the first wilson's of the day, the last thing I want to hear, and I'm staggering up the steps with six other zombies, trying to catch a glimpse between people's shoulders.

God christ it was terrible. Ten hours. Some of us were seriously contemplating clubbing together and giving the pilot five hundred quid to take us back without seeing a single bird. Either that or throw us overboard.

Bish was just about the only one who didn't puke, that armourplated gut of his. And it wasn't even a close thing. He spent the day sitting on the upper deck knocking back cans of guinness to wash down the pasties and an entire tub of sauerkraut his granny sent him from Poland, which must've come by road and taken a month to arrive if the smell was anything to go by. Oh jesus. It was the closest he ever came to being lynched, and the whole boat would've turned a blind eye. What's he doing at sea in the first place, said Jace, I didn't know his country had a fucking coastline. You ignorant twat, where did you think the Solidarity shipyards were? The what shipyards?

On the way back, a willow warbler landed on the boat. Just about the most ordinary looking migrant we get, but we all moved to the back to get our bins on it. The ultimate twitch. When Land's End appeared, it flew off towards the mainland, struggling on those tiny wings, round of applause from everybody on board. Go on, my son. Go on, my daughter, for all I know. You can't tell the sexes apart with warblers. Or pelicans.

When we got back on dry land, Stevie and me thought we'd better eat something, our stomachs being totally empty. We're trawling round Penzance at night looking for something she could eat, and we find a place that does veggie kebabs, the last thing you'd expect out there in the sticks. We're walking home with pitta bread stuffed with shredded cabbage and carrot smothered with humous, looking like what we'd just puked up. Delicious too.

Big day. Anybody who was on that boat talks about it like we've all been in the trenches together. When you look back on it, you don't remember the horrors of puking but the sight of Bish on that top deck like an admiral on the poop, still undamaged by things, muscles bulging under his shirt. Stevie with her hair pony-tailed against the wind, the look on her face when the sab's gull hovered in the wind just off the bow. And two dutch birders with a camera gun the length of their arm, saying please don't mention it when you were sick on their shoes.

Nothing like that today, it's a millpond even when we veer left past the first island and set off towards Islay. So flat I even brave one of the ship's pork pies. Soon as I unwrap it, two herring gulls appear on the guardrail at the back, head on one side like butter wouldn't melt.

People tend to love-hate gulls. The way they glide when they fly, some mystery they're supposed to have, but also the fact they're fucking dustbins. They eat *everything*. Fag ends, sweet wrappers, each other's kids. They've got no shame either. They'll line up when you're trying to have a pie in peace – and beg, in something that's half yell half gulp. I've always had a lot of time for them personally. For being great survivors and that heh-heh-heh in their eye.

I toss two bits of pork pie on the deck and they drop down for it. Mostly pastry but some meat too, good and pink, and a nice bit of jelly.

We're out on the open sea by now, and the birds have already improved. Eider and gannets and flocks of scoter like rows of black dots. You're facing into the sun at the back of the boat, so the coast of Kintyre looks like polished bronze in the glare. There's some waterfalls coming down the cliffs, and the high land behind them is rolling hills not peaks.

Stevie would've liked this view. It stays there as you sail away from it, so she'd have plenty of time to draw it. The land's made up of blocks of colour, the way she showed me.

I didn't wake up till lunchtime, mother and father of a headache but quite glad to skip work. I wanted to go back to sleep but I was really cold all of a sudden, teeth chattering so much they made my neck ache. She was cold too, even her hair. You never realize how cold hair is, the heat from your head and neck keeps it so warm. People who keep their granny's long hair in boxes, it gives you the creeps because it's so chilly. Then I realized I was cold because she was. And when I moved her arm it kept falling back. And she wasn't making a sound. So then I get one arm under her so's I can hold her with both of them, pulling her against me to keep the small of her back warm with my belly, like if I could just get some heat back into her she'd be alright. If I rocked her she'd move and that was better than this terrible fucking stillness.

She'd messed herself in the night and there was some bleeding, it was on my legs – but I would've held her all day probably, and never taken my face out her hair, if the police hadn't rung the doorbell at one o'clock.

Stevie sent them. She typed an email the night before and set the timer for that morning. They only sent two of them round, they knew there wouldn't be any trouble: the email told them they'd find her like she was. I let them in with tears down my face and her blood and shit on my legs and they were apologetic almost. One of them made me a coffee.

Meanwhile the other one goes straight up to the utility room and finds the gun. I thought she'd shopped me, but then they tell me her email said it was her who shot Owen Whittle and John

Ure Peacock, and the gun's got her fingerprints on it. And I stood and stared at them.

Obviously she gave me a dose that was just strong enough to knock me out. Then she got the gun out my dad's old suitcase and wiped my prints off it, held it in her hand with her finger round the trigger, then put it back. She typed the email, took the rest of the pills and came back to bed, wrapping my arm round her. I had to unpick her fingers to get my hand out of hers when I woke up.

The police didn't keep me long, considering. They didn't have any trouble believing her email, not with her background. I got the questions you'd expect, but I don't think they were specially interested. They'd already got a body. Plus she'd written in her will that she'd done it, in case they thought I'd typed the email and given us the pills. She always was thorough.

Bish came back for the funeral and cried the whole time he was here. I can't remember him eating anything either, though that wasn't just grief: he'd lost weight since he left, that gaunt look people get when they lose it too quick. Meanwhile Grace had put it on like he thought she would. 'Stone and a half, the fat cow.'

'That's still six stone less than you, Bish.' I asked him how it was going, him and her, and he said the usual ups and downs. The spark settled down after the first mad rush, you can't expect that to last for ever. Anyway it'll be alright after the baby.

Glad to see that going back to his roots hasn't changed the Bish. He'd been here two days before telling me his partner was pregnant. Congratulations, for fucksake. Yeh, he said, it'll be good. Christenings and funerals, ay?

At the service, he read out something he'd written, about how the demons that made her do what she did were gone now and he refused to remember her that way. I could never have read it, and he only got through it because he'd read it out aloud to hisself till it was just words. In the church, he held out till the last line, how he hoped she wasn't too scared at the end and he was glad I was there to hold her. Afterwards everybody's hugging him because he cried, and he's telling me how weird it is. He misses Stevie so much he wakes Grace up by crying in his sleep, but when he read his lines out he was on stage, so it was a good gig, how terrible is that. There's other things to think about, Bish. Go home and get ready for your kid.

At the wake, I collared Jace Babb, the greatest anorak of our time. I dragged him outside when it got dark and got him to show me perseus and andromeda in the stars. They're easy once he pointed them out.

Why them specially?

She rescued him from a sea monster, Jace.

Other way round, I think you'll find.

Whatever.

I keep putting the bins up on anything that flies over the sea, but it's all common. Islay's come into view up ahead, looking flatter than I expected. And they're obviously not short of mud up here.

The way I planned it once upon a time, this boat trip was going to be my last. Like the prow of a longship or shading my eyes like columbus. I know the place from books. Peatbogs and lochans and rough lowland pasture. There'll be low-flying eagles, and choughs so close you can see the different shades of red on their bills and legs. Give me a chance to see their black claws for the first time.

And the target bird. One last lifer, or so I thought. The first grey geese have already started arriving from the arctic, bringing in the snow goose that's been with them the past few years. Make the last tick an easy one, a bird the colour of an ivory gull in a field of greenland whitefronts. Single white non-breeder. The world needs more of us.

Once I'd seen it, I was going to load the family gun for my personal use, or find the highest cliff on Islay, assuming they've got one. Flying with the herring gulls one minute, food for them the next, good bit of recycling. Embarrassing, I know.

It's not the last lifer, it's number four-four-seven, as anonymous as they come, the one before four-four-eight. Closing in on Stevie's total on my way to five hundred and beyond.

After the funeral, I thought I wouldn't see Bish again for ages, but he was back in a month. Soon as Stevie's last piece of work went up in Tate Modern.

I had to get a special pass, tell them how I knew her. I wouldn't have got in otherwise. They'd never seen crowds like it. The whole of the plaza in front was packed all day and you had to book a week in advance.

Half the crowd seemed to be people with placards, objecting to them showing her work after she'd killed two people. Relatives of the dead men, plus a country alliance rent-a-crowd and dozens of security. Some of Stevie's relatives didn't come to the funeral.

It's still not clear if they showed her work just for the

controversy. Even the people who know, as she called them, they were split. So she wasn't Cassandra to all of them, which is as much as she expected, I think. But even the unbelievers bought weekly passes. She was right: it slayed them all.

She measured it to fit the Turbine Hall, which is the size of a rock venue. Other artists filled it before, but nobody filled it with noise too. She called it The Pelican and they made you stand well back to look at it.

She designed it in two identical parts separated from each other. Each one was a huge metal cone forty-two feet high, half the height of the hall, fixed to a metal stump that secured it to the ground. They were joined to their stumps by a hinge, so's they could rotate like windmills.

As the hinges turned, one of the cones would swing round vertically and come down, very slowly, from the ceiling. When it reached the floor, its own weight opened its tip and released a small amount of red liquid. This liquid dripped into a slot in the tip of the other structure.

The liquid didn't weigh much, just exactly enough to tip the other cone downwards. As it tipped, a metal flap came across and shut, enclosing the liquid inside it. And the counterweight at its rear end set this second cone on its circular journey, down towards the ground then slowly back up to the ceiling. It was balanced different from the other cone, so once it got to the top, instead of coming down slowly it teetered for a second then just fell to the ground, just dropped like a dead weight from eighty-five feet up, and hammered like a giant beak into the nose of the first cone.

The speed it came down, and the noise it made – you'd see

people staying there to watch it twenty times, and flinching every time. When the second cone smashed into the first, the first cone began its own slow climb back up to the ceiling. On the way, it nudged the other structure and made it open a small slot which dripped the red liquid back into the original cone, though you couldn't see this from ground level. They explained it in the blurb on the wall.

The two cones went round and round for ever, depending on each other for their motion. One was giving and the other one was taking then assaulting its donor, so they looked different even when they were exactly the same.

Then very slowly they began to change shape as the pounding from one cone disfigured the other one. They were made of tungsten, so this took days and you couldn't see it happening with any given blow. While it was being beaten up, the donor cone grew a face. A twisted mouth and crushed cheeks and eyes squinting in pain. And the face changed from day to day and became other faces. She'd had it made in such a way that even when its beak was flattened and twisted it could still deliver its red liquid.

The other cone grew a facial expression too, as the tip of its beak was slowly flattened by all the blows it was delivering. A kind of sneer, or something like irritation, or disgust at what it was doing, you had to decide for yourself.

The sight of this terrible beak smashing down onto the thing that had just given it its own blood, then the donor beak getting back up, slowly and painfully, to do the same thing all over again. The drip of red. The noises designed for her by Bish's sound engineer: that crash followed by an echo that sounded like a scream that never quite died away, then the groan of the battered cone as it struggled back up to the ceiling. Jesus god.

I went there five days in a row, three of them with Bish, watching those beaks go full circle. Her work led to what I did led to her work. I mixed with those wall-to-wall crowds, listening to any reactions I could overhear. I bought the book and read the reviews. Stevie didn't leave any notes, so speculation abounded. The pelican equals her sacrificing herself for the birds (ho hum), or feeding the monster (her own art) that turned on her. One of the metal beaks was male, the other one female, their endless cycle her take on all relationships. Well, obviously.

Killing yourself for your art is spectacularly embarrassing, they decided, and who am I to disagree. But killing yourself for your art when only one other person knows the real reason – well now. Some complicated questions about the nature of fame. We all leave ripples, some are more visible than others.

Though some of her relatives didn't come to the funeral, the church was still packed. I knew people liked Stevie, but I thought I knew who they were. All the birders were there, and even the police sent somebody. But there were so many people I didn't know, and I hadn't expected not to know people. We all think the person we're with hasn't got a life outside of us.

In her will, she split the money from the exhibition and her share from the sale of our place. Half to Bish's nature reserve in Poland, half to the two cousins who brought her up. I got to meet them at last and they said they didn't condone what she'd done but in a way they'd been half-expecting something like this. When Stevie's parents were gone, the way she saw it her life was over.

She got a second chance when her cousins brought her up, but she could never shake the feeling she was living on borrowed time.

I asked them about the sacrifices they made for her, and they shook their heads. They kept telling her, they said. She'd given *them* a second chance, not the other way round. What a gift she was to a childless couple. But they couldn't convince her she wasn't some kind of charity case. When your mum dies and your dad walks out and you're only eight years old, it's easy to believe you deserve it. A father who didn't sacrifice himself for his child: they asked me did I see that in her work, since I knew her better than anybody.

I didn't know he walked out. I thought he died.

He did, they said. In New Zealand, when she was sixteen. Please don't judge her too harshly

Bish broke down again when he heard about the money. She left him the giant pelican piece too and he shipped it over for the nature reserve, though they set it up so's it wouldn't move. He used these extra funds to buy some adjoining land for the reserve, which they called *Czerwone Autokar*, which is polish for Red Bus. Red Coach actually, but he thought *Czerwone Autobus* was a tad pan-european. They've had pelicans on the floodplains there. Both species.

At the airport he said sod her email, he'll never believe she shot Owen Whittle. You can't do your art any more, so you kill an egg collector then top yourself. Fucking likely that is. And he hugged me like he wanted to crush me and went back to Poland and I don't know when I'll see him again.

I didn't see anybody or go birding or do any work for three

months. I let most of my clients go and had to rebuild the business from scratch. Once I sold the place, I moved back into something smaller and nearer where I was born. Yesterday morning I was hoovering an asian textile shop up in Willesden. I don't know how I cope with the excitement.

I don't exactly live life to the full, do I. I don't live every moment like it's my last. But only mad people and kids try and do that, they can only survive in a world they invent for theirselves. Whereas me who thought I was bored with life, all I was doing was recognizing it for what it is, in my humble opinion. If you think about death all the time, maybe it's because you want to stay alive so much. Three people died while I was discovering that, but I can still live with myself. Stevie couldn't.

Me and her, we should've had each other's lives. If I'd had the slightest scrap of talent, I might've been an artist. I live an artist's life. But there wasn't any talent, so I'm a char and a murderer. Go fucking figure.

So I'll just live, then. Anonymous in my own town in a world that's coming round to my way of thinking, building whole houses for single people, birth rate down, divorce rate up. This is purgatory. Me still alive while a woman like that is dead. Somebody up there likes a laugh.

Bish needn't have worried, I don't think. I doubt she was scared at the end. I just hope she didn't dream. I'm not having them any more. I dreamed about her every night for sixteen days (I counted). I'd wake up sweating because I was convinced we'd just been running for the cab rank in the rain at Queensgate or raiding the bootleg stalls outside Dingwalls.

I'm not having the dreams any more, and one day I'll stop seeing her face. Not how she looked the last night but her face when I ended it the first time, somebody else walking out on her. I saw it in the crushed face of her last installation. The damage we can all do. You don't need a gun. The only way I can deal with it is by believing the pelican piece worked and she got rid of something at the end.

When this boat was pulling out, I found one of her hairs on my jacket (how corny is that) and flicked it out to sea. I'm still finding them around the house. Even the way I clean it.

A flock of manx shearwaters dash past, skimming the waves at speed. The way they can stabilize theirselves in the air just by shifting a wingtip slightly, like lifting their pinkie.

Some of the petrels are no bigger than starlings yet they spend most of their lives on giant oceans. These manxies bank so steeply sometimes, one wing brushing the surface, the other pointing vertically up ('shearing' the waves), it makes them look like flying crosses according to the books – but comparing them to something else doesn't do them justice. Seabirds says it all. Birds of the sea, at home in elements we can't live in.

Forget trying to capture them and just observe. The air force based one of their tracking systems on the locking device in a peregrine's eyesight, and they copied its nostrils in the design of jet planes. It reaches 190 mph in its dives and survives G forces that knock human pilots unconscious. Birds and us, we're pretty equal. They can fly, we invented the automatic pistol.

So I'll never believe I wasted my life watching them. Anything I ever learned, I learned through birding. Geography and rock formations and how to read a weather map. Biology, latin, species classification and a bigger vocabulary. Palearctic, leucistic, decurved, skein, the proper use of endemic. I met my best friend and my best lover and saw all the world I wanted to see. If it wasn't for birding I wouldn't have had a life.

My eyes keep welling up. Fucking salt spray gets everywhere. Wipe it away and you can see Islay's getting close. If the snow goose is on this side of the island I could probably see it from here – but let's wait. You don't want your first view of a lifer to be a white dot in the distance. Drive past every field if need be and get it with the naked eye.

Manxies overtake ferry boats very fast. There's a single sooty shearwater at the back. Then suddenly nothing except the flat sea, so it's easy to spot the single tiny bird flapping past in the oppo-site direction, battling into the breeze towards the shore. A meadow pipit, common as they come, five inches of streaks and desperate flight, like they're having trouble staying airborne. Hey, mad mipit. Why migrate a thousand miles when the habitat's the same as where you came from?

Fuck off and die, you flightless cunt. We'll be here long after you've gone.

Woh. Save your breath for flying if I was you. Wings the size of bayleaves and the coast's still two miles away.


GO ON, MY SON.